Keeper of the Gate

The Three Sisters MacBeith
Book One

Laura Strickland

ARE YOU SIGNED UP FOR DRAGONBLADE'S BLOG?

You'll get the latest news and information on exclusive giveaways, exclusive excerpts, coming releases, sales, free books, cover reveals and more.

Check out our complete list of authors, too!

No spam, no junk. That's a promise!

Sign Up Here

www.dragonbladepublishing.com

Dearest Reader;

Thank you for your support of a small press. At Dragonblade Publishing, we strive to bring you the highest quality Historical Romance from some of the best authors in the business. Without your support, there is no 'us', so we sincerely hope you adore these stories and find some new favorite authors along the way.

Happy Reading!

CEO, Dragonblade Publishing

Chapter One

Northwest Scotland
May, 1620

M OIRA MacBEITH EYED the man who sprawled on the stone floor of the armory, where swords, shields, and a litter of broken weapons had been kicked aside hastily to make room for him. A big man with a loose-limbed, raw-boned build, he somehow seemed even larger than usual here in this cramped space.

He did not look dead. In fact, with a draught of air sweeping across from the doorway, causing the torches to dance, his features appeared to move as if he might speak to those who stood above him.

Moira knew better. Her father, Iain MacBeith, would never speak to her again. His beloved voice, so often raised in a shout, an enthusiastic command, or in irresistible laughter, would nevermore come to her ears.

How could she accept it? Da had always been there, a kind of northern star in her life, a constant strength and reassurance. He had survived many a battle against their neighbors and foes, the MacLeods, had come through many a skirmish, and endured many a wound.

No man, though, however strong, could have survived the

slash Da had taken during the skirmish just past. Indeed, had not Moira, fighting close beside him, herself seen him take the blow and pushed him out of the way? A mighty swing it had been, inflicted by a tall MacLeod clansman's sword. It had skittered off Da's shield and taken him at the side of the neck.

He had not gone down at once, not even when she'd nudged him back behind her, and behind their war chief, Alasdair, who had also been fighting at his chief's side. Moira had not realized at once how dire the wound was that Da had taken. She doubted their enemies had realized it either.

Not till after the battle turned and the MacLeods withdrew did Moira find Da kneeling in the rough turf, one of their youngest men, Calan, at his side.

Da had met Moira's eyes in a wide-eyed stare and gasped, "Daughter!" Only that one word, no more.

They'd carried him home, the group of them, hoping— hoping. But before they reached the keep, Moira knew the truth. She knew because the terrible wound at the side of Da's neck stopped bleeding.

And she guessed what he'd tried to tell her.

She'd had him carried here by those most loyal to him. Those who had been fighting close by and her two sisters, Rhian and Saerla. Saerla had been a part—like herself—of the fight. Rhian had come running.

Now silence filled the armory, not a sound except for that of the leaping torch flames. Rhian fell to her knees beside Da and reached out with her gentle hands to touch him softly. A butterfly touch at the gaping wound at his neck. A smoothing of the wild mane of gray hair away from his face with the tenderness she might offer a child.

Emotion clogged Moira's throat, near choking her. On its heels came blinding anger that any MacLeod sword should have gotten close enough to their chief to do such damage, and an almost paralyzing need to deny. Stark terror. What would she do now? What would she do without him?

Saerla joined Rhian on her knees at Da's side. Aye, she had been there, a part of the small group of five fighting near Da when he was struck; that included Alasdair and Calan, who had helped bring him home. Only these five knew the truth. Och, aye, the whole group of MacBeith warriors was aware their chief had been injured. Only these five knew he—

"I canna believe it," Saerla whispered. "He canna be dead."

Saerla had the right of it; he could not be. Not Iain MacBeith, who had led his besieged clan with strength and wisdom for so many years. Who had sheltered them, provided for them, and defended them through every danger and ill wind. Through every attack by their enemies.

Moira's mind stuttered and stumbled over it. He could not be dead, or their safety, their entire way of life, would crumble. One man stood between clan MacBeith and ruination.

And he lay here sprawled on the floor.

She exchanged a look with Alasdair MacBeith, the giant of a man who had been Da's second-in-command. He was the one who had lent most of the strength to carry Da home. Now she saw in his dark eyes the same desperation that sped up the beat of her own heart and wracked her mind.

A warrior to the bone and a good tactician, Alasdair was. Did his thoughts match her own? Did he fear that as soon as the MacLeods, led by that sharp-blade of a young buck, Rory, found out Iain MacBeith was dead, all restraints would fall away? The fight they'd carried for generations could well be lost. Only one answer for it—

Clan MacLeod could not be allowed to find out that Iain MacBeith was dead.

She drew a great breath that shook her body. For five years, ever since the death of her brother, Arran, in a skirmish not unlike this one, she had strapped on her weapons and fought beside her father. She and her youngest sister, Saerla. Even Rhian had been known to wield a sword from time to time when the fight came to their own walls.

In hard combat, no one took the time to wonder if Moira was a man or a woman. Leather armor padded her frame. She kept her bright red hair confined out of her way. She became no more than a blade, another arm in defense of what she loved.

And she did love this place fiercely. Just as fiercely as she loved the man who lay stretched upon the floor.

Rhian wept over him, shedding salt tears that he could not feel strike his face. Saerla—she had laid aside her sword and her shield, and appeared to be praying. Seeking the magic that came so easily to her? But Da had slipped beyond any magic she might summon.

Loudly and clearly, Moira said, "No one can know."

They all stared at her, their faces varying reflections of grief. Och aye, Iain MacBeith had been well-loved.

Only Alasdair, his dark eyes burning, seemed to catch Moira's meaning. The others merely looked askance.

She said, hushed now, "We cannot let the MacLeods know Da is dead. That means we canna tell the rest of our clan."

"Not tell our people?" Saerla bounded to her feet. Tears burned in her fey blue eyes, but did not spill over. "But they have to know. This will change everything."

"Aye, sister. We canna tell *because* this will change everything. Respect for Da—and old Camraith MacLeod always had that—is all that has stayed Rory MacLeod's hand." She spoke the name, Rory, as if it tasted bitter in her mouth, which, in truth, it did. "Och, aye, we have endured skirmishes, raids. We've had our cattle stolen. But what have the MacLeods wanted since first they came here, time out of mind? Our land."

There had, aye, been a mutual respect and an odd sort of bond between Da and the patriarch of the MacLeod clan, Camraith MacLeod. But Camraith had died last winter—not in battle but, it was said, in his bed. Now Camraith's son, Rory MacLeod, was at the head of the clan, and a fierce man he was.

Rory held Iain MacBeith in respect because his own father had. But if he learned Da lived no more—

Saerla seemed to glean that truth in the mysterious, almost instinctive way she had. "We canna tell," she whispered, and the words sounded like a spell in the enclosed space. "We canna let anyone know he does not still lead us."

"But," protested young Calan, who stood liberally splashed with Da's blood, and who looked shaken to the core, "everyone on the field saw Chief Iain take that wound."

"They may have, aye," Alasdair said in his deep voice. "And they saw us help him away. They will no' ken he is gone from this world."

Rhian looked up from her place kneeling at Da's side, her face streaked with tears. "We will never be able to keep it from our folk. And"—she gestured wildly—"what of his body?"

"If we say he lies wounded in his chamber and wants none but ourselves to tend him, our folk will respect it. Rhian—that will mainly be a job for you."

Their mother had died of a fever, left them even before Arran had been killed. Since then, Da had been mostly on his own in their chamber, only servants to see.

"Aye." Rhian too climbed to her feet. "That will do for but a short time. Eventually, those who serve us will begin to wonder."

"I need only a time." Moira bit her lip and exchanged another look with Alasdair. "Just long enough to convince Rory MacLeod we sisters are a force to be reckoned with in our own right. To convince him he would be mad to attack us full force—whether Da is here, or no."

"I see." Rhian frowned in distress. "I see that, but why can we not tell our folk the truth? They adore—adored him." Two more tears trickled down her cheeks. "They need a chance to mourn."

Aye, they all did, but were not likely to have it. "Sister, all it would take is a slip from one pair of lips—"

That turned her indignant. "I trust our people. I trust them, every one!"

"As do I, but such a secret might be given away without intention. By a captive, perhaps, taken in the next raid."

"She is right," Alasdair declared. "For the time being, no one can know the chief is dead."

They all gazed again at the man stretched out on the floor. Arms flung wide, he seemed to entreat them. If his lips could in truth move, he would ask of them only one thing.

Defend our home.

She whispered, "Only we five can know. We must swear it."

She eyed each of them in turn—Alasdair first because he already agreed with her.

"Aye," he said hoarsely, his grief stark in his eyes.

"Aye," said young Calan, more slowly, tears now tracing a path down his blood-spattered face.

Next, Saerla. The youngest of the three sisters, she might appear misty and oft-times lost in dreams, but she, like Moira, had trained beneath Da's and Alasdair's tutelage. When needed, she could fight like any warrior.

She turned her gaze on the man lying at their feet. A half sob escaped her before her eyes returned to Moira and steadied. "Aye."

Moira nodded and turned to Rhian. Rhian, the keeper of their hearth, she who had mothered them all since Ma died. As fierce in her way as the rest of them, she could well stick on this.

And then what?

Moira had a sudden, blinding vision of Rory MacLeod, black hair and tartan plaid flying, a naked blade in his hand, breaking through the gate of the keep. All restraints gone, bringing blood and death and loss beyond imagining.

"Sister?" she beseeched.

Rhian's fingers clenched. She bowed her head and her dark red hair tumbled over her face. They all possessed the same wild, red hair, the daughters of Iain MacBeith—just like his before it went gray.

"Sister, it is a dangerous course you set, and beset with pitfalls."

"I ken that fine."

"What of our father's earthly remains?"

"We will care for him. You will. I propose we disguise Calan as Father, and let everyone see you and I leading him to his chamber. Alasdair and Saerla can take his body up to the holy place above the loch, and lay him to rest."

Loch Bronach, that was. The loch of sorrows. A ring of stones stood there on the height. It seemed a fitting place for the Chief MacBeith.

"Just for a time, Rhian," she urged. "Until we can find our feet. Until we can convince Rory MacLeod he still has worthy foes here, standing strong. Otherwise—otherwise, I fear he will destroy us."

Rhian drew herself up. Keeper of the hearth she might be, but the spirit that dwelt within her burned as brightly in defense of MacBeith as any other.

"We cannot let that happen. He would not want it," she breathed. "If believing Da is alive will stay the worst of Rory MacLeod's ire, then aye, 'tis what we must do."

She fell to her knees once more beside her father. Quickly, she unpinned the brooch that held fast to the fabric of his bloodied plaid before kissing his brow. The flickering torchlight made it look as if Da's features moved, his deeply-carved mouth quirking in a faint smile.

Rhian got to her feet, and went to Calan. She drew his plaid up higher on his shoulders and pinned it with the broad brooch Da had worn so long. She raised the young man's hood to cover his hair and part of his face.

Saerla, having watched this, bent to kiss her father. When Moira's turn came, she took Da's sword from Alasdair and folded her father's blood-soaked hands around it, upon his breast.

"For MacBeith, Da," she whispered, and kissed his cold forehead. "For you. I promise your daughters will not fail."

Chapter Two

"**F**IONA WILL HAVE to be told." Rhian stepped out from Da's chamber and drew the door shut behind her. "I do not see how we can keep such a secret from her."

Moira blinked. So far, her determination, her shock, and her anger had kept her upright. Now that they'd implemented her plan, far more drastic reactions set in. She became aware of weariness, bone deep, from the fight. Bruises, scrapes, and at least one wound still oozing blood.

"In truth, sister, I forgot about Fiona."

A matron of the clan, and made a widow by clan warfare, Fiona had stepped in to do much around the keep, including, so Moira suspected, sometimes sharing Da's bed.

"Surely we can trust her."

Moira would like to think so, yet everything within her cried *nay*. "The more people who know," she nodded at Calan who, having played at being Da, stepped past them once more in his own guise, "the more risk we take."

Rhian bit her lip. "If she believes Da is badly wounded, we will never keep her out."

"Just for the time." Moira touched her sister's arm. "You stay here. Tell her, if she comes, Da does not wish anyone seeing him in such a weakened state. We three will care for him."

Rhian's jaw grew tight, but she nodded.

Moira turned to Calan. "You'd best go get your wounds tended."

He stammered, "Aye. But first—first I will go back and help Alasdair and Mistress Saerla tend to the chief. I want to do that."

"Very well, lad." Da's burial must be completed while it was yet dark, and the more hands the better.

"And you?" Rhian eyed Moira.

"I must go see to the prisoners."

She hurried off, defying the heaviness that dragged at her, pushing the sorrow—deep, dark sorrow that near paralyzed her heart—away for now. She must focus on the defense of this place, protect what she loved at all cost.

It was what Da would have done. What he would want now.

Yet, as her boots struck the stones of the passageway, her mind set up a litany in time with them. *He canna be gone. He canna—*

She burst into the forecourt where most of their warriors, far too many of them wounded, had gathered.

They all swung toward her. Faces old and young, all of them well-known.

"How fares the chief?"

"Aye, how is Himself?"

The calls came clear on the night air, and caught at Moira's heart. Caught at her throat too, so she could barely speak. These were tough, sometimes bloodthirsty men. But the love they offered their chief fairly shone.

Och, how would they ever go on without him? She could not imagine it.

"He has taken a blow to the head that fair scrambled his wits, along with a few other minor wounds." *Blood, flowing down his neck, splashing across the hands of Calan, who held him upright.*

She had to blink hard to dispel the image and focus on the concerned faces of the men.

"Rhian is looking after him."

"Ah well," said one of them. "That's all right then."

Rhian's gentle hands had bandaged and soothed the wounds of more than one of these men, who usually refused to admit to hurt or pain.

Briskly, Moira turned to Bean, the tall, dour warrior who often helped Alasdair. "What of the prisoners?"

"Prisoner," he corrected grimly. He'd been hit in the mouth during the battle and now wiped his still-trickling lip on his sleeve. "One o' them has perished and is bound nowhere but his grave."

"Where is the other?"

"We have him back i' the cattle shed, under guard."

"Take me. The rest o' ye—" Moira paused and looked at the group of them, noting their various injuries. "Ye fought well. *We* fought well this night." 'Twas what Da always told them. "MacLeod will no' be eager to come calling again."

Defending their home—the determination to do just that—ran deep among these men, a force that almost visibly united them. They nodded and murmured. Moira turned to Bean. "Let us go."

A wind—the same that had flickered the torches in the armory—chased their heels as they went. The settlement here was old and well dug in. Moira wondered if the very stones knew their chief was dead.

Aye, she could hide it from the folk, but not from the land itself. A fancy? Nay, her sister Saerla would say it was so. Moira sometimes thought Saerla as fey as the wee folk.

A fairy with a sword, and a bloody one at that.

Torches appeared out of the darkness ahead of them. A handful of men stood guard beneath the wall that sheltered the stock pens. They had put the prisoner in one of the rough enclosures used for beasts during raids. It would do until Moira decided what to do with him.

A captive might prove a most useful thing.

She stepped up and eyed the guards who, like everyone else, looked the worse for their evening's activities.

"What have you done wi' the dead prisoner?"

Bean jerked his head. "Threw him out back, so we did."

Her lips twisted. Even a MacLeod deserved better treatment. "We will gi' him a decent burial come first light."

She passed through the gate of the pen, leaving Bean behind with the guards. The man inside sprang to his feet.

He looked overly-large in the small confines of the pen, a tall man with considerable bulk of muscle. A tangle of brown hair, well-streaked with blood, hung over half his face. A beard covered his jaw, so she could see little enough of him. They had bound his hands behind him so he could do little to uncover his eyes when he looked at Moira. A hard, level brown stare that burned with intensity.

One of Moira's brows jerked upward. No fear in him, at least none she could see. You had to hand it to these MacLeod bastards, for gall.

She placed her hand on the hilt of the sword she still wore. The captive's gaze followed the movement before returning to her face.

Taking a wide-legged stance, she growled, "What is your name?"

"MacLeod."

Insolence filled the response and Moira's lips tightened. Her first reaction came in a desire to strike him in the face. She knew he was an accursed MacLeod, did she not? His plaid declared it, and the blood on his hands.

If he would not answer her any better than that, how could she establish whether he might be of value to Rory MacLeod, who now headed that troublesome clan? Och aye, all Rory's men were doubtless of value to him, but her fingers fair itched for a captive of particular importance. She longed to strike back at Rory. For revenge.

This man looked the right age to be a contemporary of Rory's. Who could tell?

She drew her sword and, in a swift movement, one that made

her tired muscles scream, swung it against the captive's neck, just the place where Da had been struck.

He did not have time to step back. Given the confines of the pen, he had not much room to retreat. But his eyes went wide and his throat worked as he swallowed convulsively.

"Insolence, is it?" Moira growled. "You offer me insolence? My blade, MacLeod, has had a demanding evening. It's acquired a few knicks lent by MacLeod bone and is filthy with MacLeod blood, but 'tis still sharp enough to take off your head."

His gaze on hers did not waver. He did not speak.

Slowly, slowly, she leaned forward till she spoke directly into his face. "Tell me, if you wish to keep on drawing breath. What do you mean to Rory MacLeod?"

Chapter Three

H E WAS GOING to die. With the kiss of cold metal at the side of his neck, and the warrior's angry face glaring into his own, Farlan MacLeod felt certain of it. He drew a deep breath, believing it might well be his last.

Who was this warrior who faced him? He dimly remembered seeing the fellow in the midst of the battle—this fierce battle that had started out as nothing more than a raid, but had so swiftly gotten out of hand. Fighting near to the Chief MacBeith himself, this man had been.

Not a big man, he was agile and quick, and handled the blade now threatening Farlan's life as if it were an extension of his arm. A face liberally splashed with dirt and mud, a head of red hair tightly braided—well, many of the MacBeiths were red. All Farlan could see was a pair of blue eyes that held absolutely no mercy.

Whoever he might be, he wanted Farlan's death. Or mayhap a hostage, a valuable captive he could use against Rory. Despite Farlan's conviction that he was about to die, he experienced a rush of loyalty. If he had to choose between betraying Rory and death, he knew what he must choose.

Rory MacLeod was not just his chief, but his best friend.

A hulking man entered the pen behind his questioner. He, Farlan recognized. Alasdair MacBeith, Chief Iain MacBeith's war chief and first man. He stood at least a head taller than his companion. A huge man, Alasdair, and likewise covered in blood. A nightmare, he was, on two feet.

"Answer me." The blade quivered against Farlan's flesh. "Answer me or die."

"My laird," Alasdair rumbled. "No need to wet your blade. I ken fine who he is."

My laird? But Iain MacBeith's son and heir, Arran, was dead. Who else would Alasdair address this way?

Alasdair's burning dark eyes met Farlan's. "One Farlan Mac-Leod. Close to Rory, are ye no'? Seems we have a fine prize on our hands."

"Aye?" The blade lowered and Farlan's stomach did a slow roll. He did not want to die, nay. But captivity could be much worse and detrimental to his clan.

He hoped, now that they had snatched him, Rory would just let him die. Knowing his friend, though, he doubted it.

Alasdair touched the shorter man on the shoulder, turning him so he might speak in his ear. Farlan caught his breath, realization hitting him in the gut like a hard blow. Something about the way his questioner turned, a certain grace in the movement, a delicacy in the profile there presented—

Why had he failed to see? Why had he failed to see that he was actually a *she*?

One of MacBeith's daughters, she must be. Aye, surely so. Word had it Iain possessed three, and that they sometimes joined him on the battlefield. A hard thing to credit, that the fierce warrior he'd seen fighting beside MacBeith was, in truth, a woman.

She turned back to him, her discussion with Alasdair done. She looked, if possible, still angrier, her gaze cooled to ice.

"My man tells me you are the one who delivered the blow to our chief this night, the one that took him out of the battle."

"Aye." Why try to deny it? They'd been fighting far too close for denials. Alasdair had seen. "Is he dead?"

She tensed. "Why should ye think so?"

It had been a canny blow, that was why, and had taken the old man in a dangerous place, staggered him so he'd fallen back. And he himself did not stand here questioning Farlan now.

It meant he must be either dead, or sorely wounded.

But this woman, this mysterious female with the blood spatter on her face, the long scratch still oozing blood on her cheek, and the hard eyes would not admit it.

"You be his daughter, aye?"

She froze, and a flush of heat stained her skin. She narrowed her eyes still further at him, and the sword twitched in her hand.

Alasdair took a step forward to loom over Farlan. "Sit ye down and shut your gob," he ordered, "unless ye wish to die."

Farlan did not. He took a step back and lowered himself to the filthy floor. Beasts had been quartered here, and recently. He only hoped none of his wounds took poisoning from the dirt. Mayhap he was fated to die either way.

He thought about that. Was he ready to leave this world, having lived only twenty-six summers? Och, nay. But he did not see how he was to get out of this.

"Your chief," Alasdair thundered, "has stolen our cattle and slain three o' our men."

"As ye have slain ours," Farlan retorted.

Alasdair slanted a look at the woman. "This one does no' ken when to keep his mouth shut."

She tossed her head, looking regal as a lioness. "Mayhap he needs to lose his tongue."

"Aye, but then he will no' be able to tell us all Rory Mac-Leod's secrets when we apply the blade. Or the irons."

Farlan drew a breath. It was to be torture then. Had he the balls for that?

Naught worse on the face of the world than a man who bleated and wept when a red-hot iron met his flesh. He and Rory had often sat and talked about it—in a distant sort of way, that was.

No distance here.

The woman gave a hard nod. "Let him stew for a time. Perhaps he will tell us anon what Rory MacLeod may be willing to trade for him."

They went out, the woman having cast Farlan one more look of disdain mixed with such hatred it felt like a blow. The gate slammed shut and Farlan was alone in the dark, the filth, and the cold.

Not a good position in which to find oneself, and not just from his own perspective. He would be less of a danger to Rory had the MacBeiths killed him outright.

But that woman—who was she? Had to be one of MacBeith's daughters, aye. He tried and failed to remember their names, the three sisters MacBeith. Likely, he'd never known their names, them being just women. Insignificant.

Only, this one was not.

What kind of woman donned armor, strapped on a sword, and went to battle? A strong one, that was what. Having lost his son, had old MacBeith enlisted his daughter to take his place?

Was old MacBeith dead?

The mysterious woman had not answered that question, in truth, and Farlan had his suspicions. He squeezed his eyes shut and relived that moment on the field—the bright noise and danger of it. Rory and he caught in that knot of warriors, which included Chief MacBeith. Alasdair fighting like a wild man. Two others battling hard, one of whom must have been this woman.

MacBeith had swung for Rory—Farlan remembered that. Rory had raised his sword just in time to parry the blow. Farlan had stepped forward and struck back, a hard sweeping blow that stuttered off MacBeith's shield and met flesh.

The old man had staggered back, with the others closing in to defend him. Had Iain gone down? Farlan did not think so.

It had perhaps been but a glancing blow then. Though—nay, Farlan did not think that either.

Who could survive such a strike?

If Iain MacBeith was dead—why, it would change everything.

The entire balance of the glen would shift and alter.

Iain MacBeith and Rory's father, Camraith, had been contemporaries who had contested for this land since they were young men. A mutual respect had existed between them that prevented outright warfare.

Rory had often argued with his father over it. He believed if they brought the whole might of clan MacLeod down upon the MacBeiths, laid siege to their stronghold, starved and burned them out, they would ultimately vanquish them.

Chief Camraith had always said, "Ye do no' do that, son, to a worthy enemy."

It must have taken root in Rory's mind, because even after his father's death last winter, he'd not done more than raid for cattle. Perhaps he still heard his da's voice in his head.

But if Iain MacBeith was dead—

That meant the old tacit pact between the two chiefs would be torn asunder. Rory would no longer have to stay his hand.

Clan MacBeith was tenacious, aye. They had held on here a long time, but Farlan believed, as did Rory, that clan MacLeod had greater might.

If the young woman with the gory blade believed that also, she might well be playing at a deception. A right dangerous one.

Chapter Four

"ARE YOU CERTAIN?" Moira peered up into Alasdair's face. She could not see him well in the dim light, but she could feel him, his anger burbling up just like her own. "He—that man back there—is the one who struck the blow?" The blow that killed her da.

"Aye. And I know he is close to Rory."

"His war chief?"

"Nay, that is an older man who also served his father. But I ha' seen this one in other battles, close always at Rory's side."

A friend, mayhap. Or a cousin. Someone Rory MacLeod held in high regard.

She stopped walking, her feet dragging to a halt, and Alasdair half turned back to look at her. She needed to think, but weariness pulled at her, muscle and bone, and her wits struggled against terrifying grief. She could not afford to make any mistakes, or it might cost MacBeith everything.

She reached out and clutched Alasdair's arm. "Do you think we can make use o' him? As a weapon, I mean."

Alasdair appeared to contemplate it. Here in the dark beyond the cattle pen, they were as close to alone as they were likely to get.

"Aye. And we need every weapon to hand."

"You are sure you ha' seen that man—Farlan MacLeod—near

to Rory?"

"Aye, on more than one occasion, and ha' seen them defend one another."

"Any clansman will defend his chief."

Alasdair shrugged.

"I need him to be of value." Moira glanced back at the pen.

"I will station guards, Moira, and make certain he has no chance o' escape."

"Aye. But I was no' thinking o' that. We should send a healer to him and be sure he does no' perish before time."

Alasdair grunted. "After the healer has seen to all our men. And yoursel'."

"I am well enough."

Alasdair put a surprisingly gentle finger to her cheek. It came away wet with fresh blood. "Ye are no' and will take a scar there, if ye are not careful."

"Aye, so." Moira sighed. "But get those guards in place."

"I will. And then I am bound back up on the rise to see if Saerla is all right." His face twisted. "After we buried Himself there, she refused to come down."

"You see to the guard. I will go."

Alasdair hesitated. Moira could almost feel him deciding whether he should argue it farther, insist that she tend her wounds first. He shrugged. "As ye will."

They made to part, but at the last instant she asked him, not without an edge of desperation, "Will Calan hold his tongue?"

"Och, aye. The lad is sound."

"Even when the clansfolk begin asking questions? Or if he gets a skin full?"

"He will hold his tongue."

Alasdair plodded off then. Moira heard him calling for guards in the deep growl few ever disobeyed.

She wondered whether they'd done the right thing. If denying the Chief MacBeith was dead could work, and for how long. The certainty she'd felt while standing over Da's body in the armory had evaporated.

But och, if she could choose any one ally to have at her side, it would be Alasdair.

⋙⋘

THE TREK UP to the height above Glen Bronach drained the last of Moira's strength. A steep pull it was, and no mistake. As a girl, she'd often marveled at how the ancients had managed to transport the great stones up here, the ones forming the circle that dominated the height. Some of them had long since fallen and lay in the tall grass like sleeping giants. But the form of what had once been here could not be mistaken.

A place of magic, or so Saerla insisted. One she now apparently refused to leave.

Moira saw her sister at once when she reached the high place, kneeling beside what must be Da's grave. Others were buried here before him, looking out over the beloved glen.

In daylight, the view was magnificent. Now, despite the bloodshed below and the rawness of their grief, there was a measure of peace. The mountains slept like great drowsy beasts, and a uniform gray color washed the land. Only far to the east did a line of gold show the coming of the new day.

A day without Da. Och, how would Moira face it?

Saerla still wore her padded leather armor and sword, along with a quantity of her father's blood. She knelt beside the gash in the earth that showed the new grave. Later—later when they could, they would build a cairn. For now, Saerla and Alasdair had just replaced the turf, causing a surprisingly small amount of damage.

It was as if the earth had opened its breast to take Iain Mac-Beith in, near its heart, and closed back up again.

Saerla never looked up when Moira joined her. She'd assumed an attitude of—well, Moira supposed it was prayer.

"Saerla, sister, be ye well?" A foolish question. To be sure, Saerla was not well, and she did not bother to answer. Nor did she look up.

Moira fell to her knees on the opposite side of the slit that had received Da's earthly form. If she believed in anything—*if*—he no longer inhabited that form and no doubt hovered somewhere close by. Could he see them, even though they could no longer see him?

Of one thing Moira felt certain. He would not leave this place he loved so well.

"Sister," she said again.

Still no reply, and alarm spiked through Moira. Saerla was fey, everyone knew that, and the fey often teetered between soundness of mind and something else. After losing Mother, after losing Arran, and so many others close to them, would this be the thing to break her?

She reached across the grave and touched Saerla's arm. Saerla did tip up her head then. The rising sun filled her face. A bonny face it was, her blue eyes wide and customarily dreamy.

"I keep listening for him. Not his voice—och, I ken fine I will never hear that again. But for *him*. His spirit."

Moira did not know what to say. A woman who dealt with realities, with survival, she left such fancy to her youngest sister.

"Come awa' now," she murmured gently after a moment. "You need your hurts tended."

Saerla ignored that. "I ha' been asking whether this is the right thing to do—pretending he is still alive. Deceiving our people."

"I believe it is, for the now. By doing so, we deceive Rory MacLeod. Listen to me. We have a prisoner, one who may be important to MacLeod. We may use this, and him, to gain the time we need to find our feet."

"Can we find our feet? Can we, wi'out him?"

"We must. I will not see MacBeith lands left vulnerable, Saerla. I will not."

Saerla focused on Moira for the first time. "You ha' a warrior's heart. Like Arran. Like *him*."

"I was no' alone back there, wielding a sword. You it was, sister, who stood beside me."

"I would die for this place," Saerla said simply. "You, though, are the one wi' the flaming sword."

Would it be enough? Moira knelt there gazing at the ground that had received her father and wondered. Without Iain MacBeith, could they stand against Clan MacLeod? Superior in numbers the MacLeods might well be, and now led by a man rumored to be driven by ambition. Could even a flaming sword be enough?

"Come, sister. You ha' spoken your prayers. And if you linger here, folk will begin to wonder." Moira got to her feet and weariness swamped her. She swayed where she stood.

Saerla rose also and looked about. The gray mist that filled the glen had begun to lighten, and here on the height radiance caught the stones and turned them golden. A new day began, whether Moira wanted it or no.

"Do you know, Alasdair carried him most the way up here when my strength gave out. Slung Da over his shoulders like an ailing calf. And he wept all the while."

Moira felt that in her gut. "'Tis a loss we all share, even as we share love for this land."

"Aye, but how will we ever disguise such grief while pretending he yet lives?"

"I do no' ken." With an edge of desperation now, Moira begged, "Come awa' out o' this, Saerla. Come let Rhian tend your hurts."

"I will if you will."

"Fair enough."

Arm in arm, they helped one another down off the brae.

Chapter Five

A HEALER CAME at mid-day, a woman who looked enough like the warrior lass Farlan had seen last night to be her sister. She had the same broad forehead and oval face, though perhaps a bit less stark with it. She wore her dark red hair loosely bundled at the back of her head rather than tightly braided.

The greatest difference, so Farlan decided, might be one of expression. The woman last night had kept her emotions tightly shuttered. This one had a softer look about her mouth, though he perceived little enough compassion in her eyes, at least not for him.

A guard followed her in, a big strapping fellow with a fearsome snarl. "Get up," he ordered Farlan.

Farlan's wounds had stiffened overnight. Chilled to the bone, he stumbled up, and his stomach turned within him. He desperately wanted a drink. Even water would do.

He'd slept little and had watched the sun come up, setting the air in the shed to dancing. He wondered what was happening at home right now. Rory would have figured out he was either captive or dead. What would he do about it?

He knew his best friend—none better—the quick temper schooled to disciplined thinking. Rory's first impulse would be revenge, and a desire to get him back, if he could. He would not be foolish about it, though. Once, perhaps, aye, but now with the old chief gone the weight of leadership had settled on Rory's shoulders.

Broad shoulders they were, and capable of carrying that weight. But Farlan figured he could not expect rescue swiftly, if at all.

That meant surrendering to the indignity when, the guard having untied his hands, the woman ordered him to strip down.

Searching him for wounds she was, and her dispassionate glance argued no other interest. What she found, she treated—the long gash to his sword arm, and the wound to his shoulder that he'd taken from the over large war chief after he'd struck old MacBeith.

He said nothing during the treatment, emitting only a grunt or two when the young woman prodded at him. She had a quick and skillful touch, but her expression at every moment showed how she despised him.

Just like the woman last night. At least they did not intend to let him die of his wounds.

When she finished, she glanced around the pen and said to the guard, "He canna' stay here."

"Why not? 'Tis better than the cur deserves," the man spat. "Him, a MacLeod."

"He will take poisoning in his wounds. Moira wants him whole."

Moira? Was that the warrior lass's name? Curiosity consumed him.

The guard, evidently a man of few words, growled, "Where, then?"

"Let me ask her. Meanwhile, he'll ha' to be fed. You can leave his hands free for that. Then bind him again."

A woman giving orders to the guard? Aye, and the man obeyed with a nod, as if it were commonplace.

They had to be MacBeith's daughters, acting in his stead while he was laid low.

Or dead.

Farlan could not quite leave go of that thought. He'd felt his blade connect. Tough as old leather Iain MacBeith might be, but could he survive such a strike?

"Now," he heard the woman say to the guard as she left the pen, "I maun awa' to my father. I do no' like to be long absent from him."

So, she might well be MacBeith's daughter and he might well still be alive.

She swept out, moving like a queen, and followed by the guard. Farlan went to the door of his cage and seized the bars in both hands. Meant to pen beasts, they did not fit tight and he could see out. Two guards stood firm with their backs to him. Other folk hurried by. He could hear still more than he could see—voices, calls, bustle. Someone hollering what must be a child's name.

Had he any hope of escape? Slowly and carefully, he made his way around the pen, avoiding the piles of shit left behind by the last inhabitants. Roughly-built the structure might be, but he would not be able to break out of it, not without attracting the attention of everyone nearby. A dirk at the throat would likely be his only result.

What then? Would they send his body back to Rory as a message? Since they'd seen him fighting alongside his chief in the battle, they might well figure Farlan was close to Rory. Alive, he made a hostage. Dead, he would be a taunt.

Food arrived not long after, delivered by yet another surly warrior who fair threw it at him. Stale oatcakes and sour ale, and not much of either. Farlan did not care, being famished by then. He devoured it all.

Then he went back to listening. His life might well depend on anything he learned. The guards spoke little, and eventually started up a game of draughts to pass their time.

Farlan, having no such diversion, paced and contemplated his situation. First, his physical condition. The slice to his arm hurt like the very devil, but would heal. The wound to his shoulder worried him far more.

Despite the healer's competent bandaging, he could feel it still oozing blood. The blade had caught him in passing, shredded his plaid and torn the flesh beneath.

He'd seen men take poisoning in such wounds, in much cleaner surroundings than these. He'd seen them die.

Ah well then, that would solve Rory's problem for him, would it not? Keep him from taking stupid risks to get Farlan back. Keep the MacBeiths, for that matter, from torturing him to learn Rory's plans. Indeed, a good friend would up and die to save all that trouble.

His lips curled on a twist of dark humor, but the worry remained. He went back to pacing till his strength began to flag then he found the cleanest place in the pen to sit, and waited.

Late in the afternoon, she came. Farlan knew it was late in the afternoon because the sun had arced overhead and begun once more to descend. A chill tinged the air.

He almost did not recognize her; she looked so different. No armor this time, and the only weapon a dirk at her side, strapped on over a dun-colored gown.

The color did naught for her, save to pick out her freckles. Farlan decided she needed little help from her clothing. Clad as a woman, she fair took his breath away.

She'd removed the braids from her hair and wore it mostly unbound. A riot of curls it was that flamed in the dying sunlight. He had never seen the like.

The brown wool of her dress clung to a form both strong and slender, outlining a pair of high, firm breasts and a supple waist. Farlan had to imagine the rest.

His weary wits, though, seemed well up to the task.

The jagged cut still marked her cheek. It had been cleaned and had scabbed over, but appeared an abomination against her milky skin. Would it leave a scar?

However differently she might be clad, he could not mistake her eyes. Like two war shields they were, bright with anger and defensiveness. Her hatred of him preceded her into the pen.

How could such bonny blue eyes deliver so much of a threat?

"Bring him," she said to the guards who followed her. And nothing more.

Chapter Six

MOIRA HAD SPENT much of the afternoon in her father's chamber with Rhian, trying to discipline her grief. She'd not felt the like before and did not know what to do with her pain.

She'd wept, of course, upon the death of her mother. Sona MacBeith had been a woman who in many ways combined Moira's brand of fearlessness with Rhian's compassion. Gentle strength, as Moira thought of it, and in many ways, it had held together both family and clan.

And aye, she'd wept—sobbed, in fact—at the death of her older brother, Arran. Bright as a drawn sword he had been and as dangerous, yet with a big laugh that echoed Da's.

But this felt different. If Ma had been their heart and Arran their strength, Da had been their life, the shield that defended them. Always there, his wisdom and humor steady as every sunrise.

Now she sat beside his bed, empty except for the bolsters that played at being him, and pretended to keep a sad vigil. She and Rhian both did, Rhian making certain those beyond these walls saw her carrying in bandaging and other supplies.

Rhian, with her skills, was needed elsewhere from time to time, and in fact, at one point, went out to tend a group of their men. Moira was left fielding the many callers who appeared at the door in varying states of alarm, fear, or concern for their chief, including Fiona.

Fiona arrived early, just as Moira had expected, and fairly demanded to be let in. When Moira refused, saying her da had requested only his daughters see him in his current state—implying he'd become disfigured in some way—Fiona exploded.

"I care little for how the man looks. Mercy, lass, let me in."

There would be a terrible reckoning in this when the truth finally came out, that Iain MacBeith was dead. Anger and dreadful grief. Those like Fiona who loved Da best would feel cheated out of their chance to mourn.

She could not think about that now, just as she could not reveal her own pain. She must carry on in Da's stead as if he instructed her from his bed. Terrifying as that prospect might be.

An abyss had opened beneath her feet. One misstep and she would fall.

Thank God for Alasdair who was in on the secret and made a fine tactician. She was able to step out of Da's room several times that day while Rhian was present, and confer with him.

"We ha' put it about that the chief is gravely injured," he told her in hushed tones outside the chamber door, "but holding his own. I canna' go three steps wi'out someone stopping me to ask how he fares."

"Aye."

Alasdair glanced at the door of Da's chamber. "I scarce ken what to do wi' my own grief."

That made her look at him more closely. So, she was not the only one who struggled to disguise her pain.

"Alasdair," she whispered, "ha' we done the right thing?"

"Och, aye. Should the truth be known, Rory MacLeod would be mustering his men at this moment to come and destroy us."

It had been Alasdair who suggested they should interrogate the prisoner. Apply a wee bit of pressure and persuasion, as he put it. Show how they meant to go on.

Moira could not think clearly enough by then to make a

sound decision. She'd had no sleep, and exhaustion pulled at her. Her wits moved beneath a thick, heavy blanket.

"Where?" she asked.

He'd answered immediately, "In your father's hall."

So she found herself leading the way there with Farlan Mac-Leod at her back, flanked by two guards. All along the way, folk stared. Some detained her long enough to ask, "Himself—how is he?"

"Well enough," she answered them all. "Ye ken fine the strength o' our chief."

Some they passed spat in the direction of the prisoner. Some hurled curses.

When Moira glanced back at him, she saw he came with his head high. The guards had once more bound his hands and he held them in front of him proudly. He did not look left or right.

The hall, a fine and lofty meeting place that smelled of pine logs and wood smoke, stood empty except for Alasdair. The war chief, heavily armed, awaited them looking large and dangerous.

He had stationed himself beside the fire wherein, as Moira could see, rested several irons. Heating.

If she could see that, so could the prisoner.

Da had hated the use of torture. Aye, he was not above letting an enemy's wounds go untreated for a time, or bargaining over his welfare. But the application of pain? He'd always said they were above that.

And yet—these were extraordinary circumstances. Da was gone. Did he guide them yet?

"Stand there," she ordered Farlan MacLeod. "You," she added to the guards, "wait outside."

She turned and faced MacLeod, took her first good look at him.

She'd had an impression earlier, and no mistake. Now she studied details. He stood a good height, though naught to Alasdair's. And he could not be considered aught but a good-looking man despite the battering he'd taken in the fight.

Brown hair, neither dark nor light, had started out confined in a tail at the back of his neck, but had now escaped and hung in a tangle. He had a rugged face, square at the jaw beneath his beard, still spattered with blood. A nose with a slight hook to it. A generous mouth held tight.

His eyes, as brown as his hair, held steady on hers. She could not see any fear in him. Then again, presumably he could not see her grief.

"I am Moira MacBeith," she told him, "and while my father, our chief, is laid up I will be in charge."

The brown eyes narrowed. He performed an inspection of his own, starting at her feet, marking the dirk at her side, and lingering on her hair. He said nothing.

Moira drew a breath. "The men fighting close by last night say you delivered the blow that injured our chief. Do ye own that?"

"Aye."

His voice sounded low and rough. Some guarded emotion flickered in his eyes. "You were there. Fighting. Dressed as a man."

"Aye, so?" She lifted a brow. "Your meaning?"

"'Tis unusual, that. MacLeod women do no' take the field."

"Mayhap because they are weak."

He did not like that. She saw his lips tighten further. Had he a wife back home waiting for him, one he loved right well? She supposed those of his kind were capable of love. If so, bad fortune to the woman. She might well never see him again.

"We need to speak together, Farlan MacLeod, and then I need to make a decision. Twill be up to me whether ye live or die."

Chapter Seven

F ARLAN DID NOT give much hope for his chances. This fierce, merciless woman who faced him had already established that he'd been the one to take her father out of the fight. Iain MacBeith must be sore wounded or he would be the one making decisions about the slaughter of a prisoner.

Aye, the blow he'd delivered had been sound.

They had no women of her ilk at MacLeod. Not to say their women were not strong and could not give as good as they got. They would take up weapons to defend their homes.

So far, none of them had marched out to battle.

He'd never seen a woman to match this one. Ainsley—aye, Ainsley had possessed her strengths. They had not included the tendency to brandish weapons. And by any road, she was gone.

His gaze strayed to the irons heating in the fire. Och, it had to be the irons, did it? He wondered if he could endure it without shaming himself. Aye, so he must.

The woman, Moira MacBeith, looked at Alasdair. "Untie him."

The hulking war chief did not hesitate. He drew his dirk and came at Farlan, cutting his bonds roughly and nicking the skin.

"Now." Moira MacBeith seated herself comfortably, taking the large chair that must be her father's, though she did not invite Farlan to do likewise. Alasdair remained standing also, his hand resting on the hilt of his sword.

Farlan calculated the distance to the door. Could he make it before Alasdair drew that weapon? Likely not. Anyway, once he got out beyond, he would run the gauntlet of the clansfolk and would likely be taken down by a woman wielding a stew pot.

"Why d'ye no' tell me, Farlan MacLeod, what ye be to your chief, Rory?"

Farlan shrugged. "A clansman, no more."

"Are ye sure o' that?"

He nodded.

She addressed the war chief. "This man, Alasdair, maun think we are stupid. He has no' the sense God gave a hen."

"It appears not." Alasdair's voice rumbled. His dangerous, dark eyes did not waver from Farlan's face.

Moira MacBeith leaned forward in her seat. "You were fighting close beside your chief last night, when you and your kind—" the word was a sneer "—came to steal our cattle."

"The battle ha' become heated. I fought where e'er I could." He wondered what they'd done with his sword. The old chief, Camraith, had given him that the summer he turned sixteen— had given one to both him and Rory.

He wanted that sword back, felt its loss like another wound.

"I do no' believe him," Alasdair growled.

Moira turned her head again, giving Farlan the side view that had initially betrayed the fact that she was a woman. Her profile looked delicate and beautiful. Her sentiments, when she turned back, did not. "Nor do I."

"I ha' seen this one before." Alasdair gestured roughly. "Fighting always beside Rory MacLeod in past battles. On his right hand, no less. I think he is a trusted companion."

"Are ye that, Farlan MacLeod?"

Farlan could not help flicking a glance at the irons, still resting in the fire. They would be white hot by now. A source of excruciating pain. "My chief trusts all the men who fight for him."

"No doubt, no doubt." She pretended to muse. "And some

more than others."

Aye, true. Rory had more than once placed his life in Farlan's hands. Which was why he must now withstand whatever he might be dealt.

"I wonder," she pondered aloud, "what Rory MacLeod would do should he receive a message saying we have ye in our hands."

"He would kill the messenger, o' course."

"Ye think so?"

He would curse first, Farlan's closest friend, long and bitterly. He would pace and fight the age-old battle between loyalty and common sense. 'Twould be best for him to let Farlan die here. But could he?

"He already kens you hold me. He would ha' seen me taken."

"So, he marks the fate o' every man in a battle, does he? No' just those who are important to him?"

"All his men are important to him."

She got suddenly to her feet, all restrained emotion. "I grow impatient of this. Alasdair, call the guards to hold him down. Bring the irons."

Farlan's balls tried to crawl up into his belly. He fought to keep the fear from showing.

He snagged Moira MacBeith's blue gaze with his. "Be ye no' woman enough to apply the irons yoursel'? Will ye make your big hound do it?"

She ignored the jibe. Alasdair called for the guards. When they came in, she said to them, "Strip him down. That wound o' his, I am thinking, needs to be cauterized. Mayhap after that, he will speak to us more readily."

⸻⸻⸻⸻

FARLAN REGAINED HIS senses slowly, a piece at a time. He remembered immediately who he was, but not where. Peeling his eyes open, he saw a chamber he did not recognize.

A piece or two fell into place on a rush of—

Pain.

The woman with the hard blue eyes. Questioning him as to what Rory might give for an assurance of his safety.

He'd held out as long as he could. Said nothing. Had striven to not even cry out.

Now he lay flat on his back upon a bare stone floor. No longer in the cowshed where he'd been confined earlier. This appeared to be a cell.

He wore only his kilt with the leggings beneath, his chest bare. His shirt, so he saw, lay flung across his feet. He could smell his own singed flesh.

Not much in the room with him. A piss pot. A bucket of what might be water. He lay opposite a door, which he did not doubt would be heavily barred on the outside.

He remembered it now, remembered her eyes coming at him, and the iron in her hands. He recalled her voice, as hard as those eyes. "Wha' are ye to Rory MacLeod? Friend? Blood?" *Friend, as close as blood*, but he had not admitted that. Somehow, he'd kept his lips sealed and had not broken. Not yet. He had no doubt there would be more.

He moved tentatively and gasped. His senses once more swam, the room seeming to turn around him in a slow, sickening circle.

He received another flash of her face—merciless and beautiful, accompanying the pain. By God, he hated her.

He struggled into a sitting position and took stock of himself. They'd left his wound open, likely so he could observe the damage. When he did so, his stomach heaved.

Well and for certain, it had stopped the wound bleeding.

He had seen Rory do the same to terrible wounds in an effort to save a man's life. Which was very different from what he'd just endured, though doubtless no less painful.

She'd done him a favor, Moira MacBeith. Curse the bitch.

Rarely had he felt such hatred, raw and bright. To be sure,

the members of Clan MacLeod hated those of Clan MacBeith, but it was on an impersonal basis. They were there to be overthrown so MacLeod might take their land.

It was not gut-wrenching or heartfelt, like what he now experienced. This filled him with a bitter taste, and was very personal indeed.

He struggled to his feet and made it across the floor to the pail of water. He'd meant to take a drink—his mouth felt dry as dust and contained blood. No doubt he'd bitten his tongue back there.

He ducked his head instead. It helped, but not much.

He wondered what Rory was doing right now, if he planned another raid. A rescue. *Do no' do it, my friend.* The words rattled around his head but did not escape the room.

Would Rory be able to abandon him? It would unquestionably be the wisest thing he could do.

Farlan wondered how long it would take Moira MacBeith to kill him. He wondered whether Ainsley would be there to meet him when he crossed over to the other side.

Chapter Eight

"THERE NOW," ALASDAIR said in a comforting rumble. A large hand caressed Moira's back with surprising gentleness.

Moira drew a breath and vomited again, into the basin. She had no idea who had left an empty vessel behind her da's big chair here in the hall, but she felt grateful for it. No sooner had the guards dragged the prisoner away than she'd been heartily sick into it.

She straightened up and wiped her mouth with the back of her hand. "They did no' see, did they?"

"The guards?"

"And the prisoner."

"Ah, now." Alasdair kept hold of her shoulder, his fingers scribing a half circle. "He was in no condition to see anything. Stone cold."

"Aye. But—" She gazed up into Alasdair's dark eyes. "I can no' afford to appear weak." Not even to Alasdair. But it seemed that boat had already sailed.

Alasdair MacBeith was a lot of things, a stern taskmaster to the men he trained. A devoted clan member. She'd once heard him say he was the chief's best weapon, held in his right hand. He was not soft nor did he coddle those around him. He'd done much to assure Moira and Saerla were prepared to take the field.

Yet, now she caught a flash of sympathy from him. "Ye ha' no' had an easy time, lass."

"Truth."

"Allow yoursel' some while to catch your breath."

Moira did not know if she ever would.

She drew away from him slightly. His hand fell. She dragged shaking fingers through her hair and turned to face him.

"I will tell ye one thing, Alasdair. I do no' think I can do that again." She might not be the most sympathetic of Iain MacBeith's daughters. She could not afford to be. That title must go to Rhian, and Saerla—with her intuitive knowledge—a close second.

But she had never before caused deliberate pain, not to man nor beast.

Alasdair studied her gravely. "Ye get used to it."

"I do no' wish to get used to it." Indeed, she did not think she wanted to be a woman who could get used to it.

What, she wondered suddenly, would this ruse she'd launched make of her? Och, what had she done?

Too late to go back on it.

"Do no' worry, lass," Alasdair rumbled. "I can undertake any further questioning. As I ha' been your father's right hand, I will be yours also."

Moira did not much like that prospect either. Farlan MacLeod might be their enemy, but he did no' deserve what he'd just received.

Even if he had delivered the blow that caused her da's death?

She thought of the heat of the iron, fresh from the fire. The stench of burning flesh. The way the color had fled his face when it was laid on. How his eyes had widened and then narrowed as he sought to endure the pain.

Not a sound had escaped him. And he had endured until the moment his eyes rolled back in his head and he went down like a felled stirk.

"What if he refuses to talk to us, no matter what persuasion we apply?"

"He'll talk," Alasdair assured her. "Ofttimes, the memory o' pain is more persuasive than the pain itsel'. He'll be thinking on that as soon as he wakes up."

Nay, she could not allow this. And yet—and yet, she now stood at the gate between MacBeith and all harm.

Alasdair lowered his voice further, although no one could hear. "Do no' forget, lass. He is the one who delivered the blow."

"I ha' not forgotten."

A strong man, Farlan MacLeod, and a handsome one. But the enemy all the same.

ALASDAIR WENT OFF to arrange the rotation of the guard that would stand watch on the hastily-assigned prison. Moira, left alone, took care to empty the basin, not wanting anyone to see. She must appear strong. Fearless. If she crumbled, so might the rest of the clan.

What should have been a quick visit to the midden, however, turned into a running series of conversations. Everyone she passed stopped her to ask, how fared the chief? How grave was his injury?

Grave, indeed.

Would he soon be up on his feet?

Not likely.

She said none of that, to be sure. Instead, she answered without answering.

Himself is under Rhian's care, and ye ken how skillful she is.

We will ha' to see how he gets on.

Clan MacLeod will never defeat us.

Aye, the slaying of the chief would be a defeat. Mayhap that was why, instinctively, Moira refused to admit to it. She could allow no chinks in their armor.

Knowing their chief lay dead would make more than a chink. 'Twould be a great, gaping fissure.

But och, Rhian, however skillful, could not raise the dead.

Moira ached to be alone, to take some time, as Alasdair had suggested, and lick her wounds. She had little hope of such a reprieve. She went instead directly to Da's chamber, since that was what the clansfolk would expect of her, and found Rhian there, chaffing.

"I canna stay here playing at nursing an empty bed," Rhian complained as soon as Moira came in. "I ha' work to do and other patients to tend. You tak' a turn, sister."

"I canna. I maun go to speak at the warriors' hall. They will be expecting news, and wondering if we mean to strike back for this—this dire injury to our chief."

Rhian glanced at the bed and away again. She was, or so Moira would have said, the calmest and most level-headed of MacBeith's three daughters, the lodestone that kept the rest of them in place. Just as Ma had once done, she dispensed comfort and reassurance to others.

Usually, Rhian carried serenity in her blue eyes. Now they appeared wounded, and her hair, which must have started out the day neatly braided, had escaped into curling, separate tendrils of deep red.

"I canna stay here. Moira," she repeated, "I shall go mad if I do."

Aye, the past day and night had been hard on all of them.

Moira said, not without sympathy, "We must each tend to our own tasks. Yours lies here. The clan expects it."

"They will also expect Fiona to help wi' caring for Da." Rhian's eyes grew intent. "Moira, we will ha' to tell Fiona the truth."

"Nay. Only we five can know."

"We can trust Fiona."

Most likely.

"She would not mean to give aught awa'. But you know what she is for chattering."

Fiona loved to talk. In truth, it made part of her charm. It had been she, speaking to her particular friends, who had given away that she'd been sharing Da's bed, a thing Da would have preferred to keep private. When he found out, he had merely rolled his eyes.

Remembering, a spear of panic passed through Moira's gut, stealing her breath. Fierce and strong as Da had been, he'd seen a humor in dark things—just like Moira herself—and could convey it to her with just a glance.

Never...she would never experience that again.

Rhian interrupted her thoughts. "Fiona has been here no fewer than three times already, begging to see Da. It feels cruel to put her off."

"Aye, well." Moira considered. "I will talk wi' Alasdair about it."

"Did ye get any information from the prisoner?"

Moira's stomach turned again. She shook her head violently.

"Sister?" Rhian eyed her with concern. "Ye do no' look well."

"He's the one who struck the blow, Rhian. The one who took Da's life."

"Oh."

"Still and all—we used the irons. It did no' make him talk. He—he held strong until he slipped unconscious."

"Here. Sit ye down." Unceremoniously, Rhian shoved Moira onto the bench that footed the bed and, with gentle fingers, pushed her head between her knees. "Take deep breaths."

"I canna." For the first time, here with her sister, Moira gave into the pain that had filled her since Da's death. "Every time I try to draw in the air, it hits a wall of pain."

"I ken. I feel it too, as if the ground has fallen awa' beneath my feet."

So it had. *It had.*

"Sister," Rhian crouched down to peer into Moira's face, "you are strong. You do no' ken how strong ye be."

"I shall ha' to be," Moira whispered in reply. She could not allow herself to crumble and fall, or so would MacBeith's defenses.

41

Chapter Nine

NO ONE CAME near Farlan for the rest of that day. A part of him felt grateful for it. He did not relish another round with the irons. Part of him languished in mental torment. His new prison allowed him even less contact with the world than had the cowshed. He could not tell what was happening beyond the stone walls, and frustration rose to staggering proportions.

From time to time, he caught footsteps outside the door and heard voices. The changing of his guard, no doubt. No one came in. Nobody brought him food. His only illumination was a few strips of light where the roof met the walls. Then, even that failed.

It was, as he came to understand, another form of torture. A man so confined could only let his mind wander to the worst of eventualities.

This could not end well for him, no matter what.

Och, aye, Rory might launch an attack, a rescue attempt. No doubt he wanted to. They had been fast companions since early childhood and had shared everything from bad jokes to their first battle wounds.

Rory had been there when Ainsley died—her and their wee bairn too, a son. Farlan hadn't been able to imagine how he could go on then. His courtship and marriage with Ainsley had been like a dream, fast and almost too easy. A spring flower, as he later thought her, spunky and beautiful, Ainsley had bloomed and perished too soon.

Rory had talked Farlan out of the conviction that he, himself, had killed her. His passion had, and his desire. Had he never touched her, she'd be alive still.

Rory had stayed with him through the darkness, had made him get out of bed in the morning, had set him tasks, even small mindless ones, to keep him occupied.

Like a tide, the grief had receded. Drilling at arms, organizing weapons, helping Rory plan for a future Farlan could barely see.

Now, though, in his confinement, the thoughts returned. It had been nearly five years since he had laid Ainsley in her grave with the small bundle in her arms. They had been mere children when they wed.

Going over it again, he found he still blamed himself. Mayhap he did not warrant anything better than Moira MacBeith's irons. Mayhap he did not deserve to live.

Nay, but Rory deserved better from him. What good was a weapon—for he was at least that to Rory—which failed when tested?

If he survived this, it would not be for himself, but for his chief and best friend.

Dark had fallen outside before he heard the bar lift on the door of his prison and someone came in. Hastily, he stumbled to his feet.

Two women came in. The first was the healer who had treated him before, the one who could only be Moira MacBeith's sister. She looked weary, with faint lines bracketing her mouth. She might, Farlan concluded, have come from the Chief MacBeith's bedside. He must live after all.

The second woman was Moira MacBeith.

She stationed herself with her back to the door and drew her sword. She did not look at Farlan as she said, "Mistress Rhian has come to treat your wounds."

Rhian, the healer, had brought a basket. She came forward

and gestured at Farlan. "Take off your sark."

He struggled out of the garment he'd donned when he woke and found himself alone, not without pain. He stood there trying not to shiver in the cool air.

Rhian MacBeith pursed her lips as she touched the gash on his arm, which, to Farlan, looked red and angry.

"That needs more salve."

When she looked at the wound on his shoulder, a small sound came from her. Not of sympathy so much as appalled dismay.

She glanced over her shoulder at her sister but said nothing.

Raising his eyes, Farlan saw that Moira did look at him now. Watching to make sure he did not strangle her sister, no doubt, while she was within reach.

Her blue gaze, cool and dismissive, followed the movements of Rhian's hands, down the long gash on his arm, and to the seared wound. It seemed to mark the rest of him also—his mucky boots, his kilt, the breadth of his chest and shoulders, his hair now in a mad tangle. She regarded him as if—but nay, nay that could not be interest. He did not want it to be. Though she might be attractive to look at, naught but hatred existed between them.

No one spoke while Rhian tended his wounds. Not until she finished, and Farlan had crawled equally painfully back into his shirt, did he speak.

"Am I to be fed?"

Moira MacBeith appeared to think about it. "I will ha' somewhat sent in."

Aye, and that made her point clear. He lived and died—ate and suffered—at her will.

Who would have thought it would come to this? A woman, even temporarily, leading clan MacBeith. He, at her mercy.

Yet—she was no ordinary woman, was she?

He wanted to know so many things. How the chief, her father, fared for he still felt how well that blow of his had connected. Whether—and when—she meant to question him again. Whether she'd heard from Rory yet.

He would admit to none of it and stood stolidly while Rhian returned her salves and bandages to the basket.

Then, once more refusing to look at him, Moira MacBeith gestured briefly to Rhian. "Sister, come."

They went out. Farlan heard the bar come down across the door and her voice instruct the guards.

Despair flooded him from the floor upward. He whispered what might be a curse or a prayer.

"Deliver me from this."

No one heard, save the walls. He doubted anyone listened. No one had when Ainsley died, and his wee son.

Still and all, he wished he could get a message to Rory. *Do no' come for me. Do no' take chances. MacBeith's daughters are canny. And I am but one man.*

Moira MacBeith took her time sending in his food. Indeed, he was dozing on the floor in the corner when it arrived, no cot or pallet having been provided. A guard brought it in and, as swiftly, left again.

It was good food, though, and Farlan devoured it ravenously. The body, it seemed, wanted to go on living even if the spirit was not so certain.

Either way, it appeared Moira MacBeith intended to keep him alive for a while yet.

Chapter Ten

"ARE YE QUITE well, Moira?" Rhian asked as they left the stone hut where Farlan MacLeod remained confined.

Moira quickened her step. Even at this late hour, she had tasks to complete. And anyway, if she did not move swiftly, folk would stop her to ask after the health of the chief.

In truth, she did not feel well. She was sick from lying, and from seeing that—that man. The one who had struck Da down. By God—by God, she did not know what to do with him.

If he was close to Rory MacLeod, as Alasdair insisted, Mac-Leod would no doubt make a bid to regain him, by sword or negotiation.

She supposed that meant she could not let him starve to death.

"Moira?" Rhian laid a hand on Moira's forearm and drew her to a halt. "What is it?"

"I do no' like lying. And I do no' like causing pain." Moira's own words surprised her. She had not intended to admit that. But she and Rhian were barely a year apart in age. Rhian knew her too well.

"I hope I do no' need to torture him again, even if he is the one who felled Da."

Her heartbreak sounded in her voice. She had not wept tears enough for the brave, strong, loving man who had occupied so much of her heart. She supposed Saerla had, up beside his grave. And Rhian?

Moira looked at her sister. Aye, the marks of grief lay strong in her face.

Rhian sighed. "Have ye taken time to eat anything today? Or to rest?"

Miserably, Moira shook her head. "I ha' no time for it. Now I maun concern mysel' wi' having something sent to the prisoner."

"Do that, by all means, but tak' something for yourself."

"I—"

"Moira," Rhian's gaze captured hers. "If ye do no' look after yoursel', where will we be?"

Always sensible was Rhian.

"Come to Da's room. We will talk out all that is worrying ye. No one will trouble us there."

"I maun give orders to strengthen the guard. Rory MacLeod may well launch another raid in the dark."

"Do that. Then come to me, in Da's chamber."

"I will, if I can."

Rhian's fingers tightened for an instant. "Sister, ye canna' lead the clan if ye go down."

Indignant now, Moira snapped, "I will no'."

"I should say ye are not far from it."

"Very well. I will talk to Alasdair and give orders for the prisoner to be fed—not too promptly, mind. Then I will come to you."

She found Alasdair on guard overlooking the gates. He shot her a measuring look as she joined him, and she wondered if she looked as weary as Rhian implied. If so, Alasdair did not comment on it.

"Anything?" she asked him.

"No' yet."

She gazed out over the open country, now cloaked by the night. Dark it was, with no moon and enough cloud cover to blot out the stars. A whole army could be on the approach, if they kept quiet, and there was no way to tell.

No wonder Alasdair was worried. And he would not be here were he not worried.

"You do think Rory MacLeod will come?"

Alasdair shrugged. "Aye. I'd bet my life he'll want the return o' his man. The question is, when?"

"He may try and negotiate his release."

Alasdair grunted.

"Ye do no' think so."

"I will be surprised if he does."

"I want rid o' Farlan MacLeod, Alasdair."

That made Alasdair look at her again. "He'll ha' a wealth o' information in his head."

"He's no' talking. We proved that."

"Och, nay, we barely made a start wi' him, Moira."

Moira squirmed inwardly. She did not want to go through what she had again.

Alasdair gazed at her with sympathy. "Why no' leave it in my hands, if ye ha' no' the appetite?"

She had not the appetite.

"What kind of chief is too lily-livered to face her actions?"

"Plenty, I do no' doubt. Anyway, Chief Iain is still chief, at least so far as the clan knows."

Moira said nothing.

"Lass, go and get some rest."

"Aye. You can find me in Da's chamber, if—" She gestured to the darkness.

"Verra well."

She made her way off. It had grown late and she encountered only a few guards who inquired after the chief, and she fended off their questions as best she could.

She found Rhian in Da's chamber, sitting beside the bed. A single lamp burned and, squinting her eyes at the bolstered mattress, she thought aye, someone might be lying there.

Or she could merely be stupid with weariness.

"Did ye fetch something to eat?"

"Aye," Moira lied.

"Then come ye in. Rest here, on the bed."

"I canna' lie there."

"Why ever not?"

"'Tis Da's bed. And Ma's."

"Neither o' them would deny it to ye. Rest now, while 'tis quiet."

That made Moira shoot her sister a look. "You, too, think Rory will attack."

"'Too?'"

"Alasdair thinks so. He's on watch."

"Then you can trust him to call ye if aught happens. Here. Sit ye down."

Rhian pushed Moira onto the edge of the bed, dragged off her boots, and took away her sword. Another push sent her lying on her back beside the bolster.

She tried to hang on to all that filled her mind, the tasks still to be done, the problems solved, the eventualities anticipated. But lying here felt an awful lot like being cradled in Da's arms. A gray fog descended on her and she fell into sleep.

And tumbled into a dream.

It took no time to get there. She gained no hint of rest before finding herself once more on the battlefield, in the very battle during which Da had fallen. The clamor and immediacy of it surrounded her. The loud clang of weapons striking shields, and cries of the men. She heard Da's voice—

She heard Da's voice.

In the dream, she turned her head and saw him. He lived still, and battled boldly as ever, his gray hair flying with his movements, and his eyes agleam. Alasdair fought beside him on one side, as on the other, did she.

They faced the knot of MacLeod warriors, though naught so orderly as an organized defense could be claimed. It was all a welter of noise, of danger, weapons on every side. Rory MacLeod fought directly in front of them, a roar bursting from his lips. He beat them back hard. And at his side—

Him. Farlan MacLeod.

Fear and realization seized Moira. He had not yet struck the blow. She had time yet to protect her chief, her da.

She leaped forward, her sword raised. She placed herself between Da and the battling MacLeod. She didn't know by what miracle she'd been given this chance. But she would defend Da this time, even if it cost her own life.

At that instant, it did not feel like a dream. Too real, too desperate, bright with noise and pain. Her heart thudded in her ears and her breath rushed through her lungs. She fastened her eyes on the enemy.

The enemy. Despite the furor all around them, he seemed to be all she could see at that moment.

Brown hair streaming, muscles tense. Face set in a grimace of concentration. His eyes—fine, brown eyes—clung to hers as he raised his already-wetted blade.

She set herself, heels planted in the turf, to withstand the blow that must come. Without question, he was stronger than her. She, though, fought by a holy determination and duty to defend her chief from what must come.

He would strike. A killing blow.

She raised her sword to meet his. But his blade halted in midair. His lips moved as if there, in the midst of the battle, he spoke to her. To her alone.

Astonishment froze her blade also. Whatever words he spoke, she could not hear for the clamor all around them. But he thrust his sword back into its scabbard—there in the heat of the battle, he did—stepped closer, and seized her forearms.

And she could feel him, the grasp of his fingers fierce and desperate. The heat coming off him. She saw the expression in his eyes—wide, brown eyes staring into her own—as he spoke again.

"Nay, lass. Nay, we canna."

She should strike at him, slay him. This was her chance. She needed to swing up her sword from her side and deal a mortal blow. If she did not—

She would lose her da.

Yet his hands held her arms in place and she could feel the emotions that filled him, all desperate certainty.

"Do no' kill me, Moira, or how will we e'er be together? 'Tis our destiny."

Her heart now struggled to beat in her breast. He could not be her destiny. He was the enemy.

A trick it must be, to coax her into failing to defend Da.

Again.

Yet she could feel that something inside him reached out for her. More than hatred. More than fear.

"Nay," she shouted into his face. "Nay, it canna be."

"Do no' try and fight me, lass. For ye are meant to be mine."

Chapter Eleven

"**M**OIRA? MOIRA!"

Rhian's gentle fingers roused Moira from the dream that did not seem like a dream. It went to pieces all around her, breaking apart like a pot that is dropped on a stone floor, the sounds of the battle the last thing to let go of her.

She found herself on her back in Da's big bed, foundering as if she'd just surfaced from deep water.

Rhian leaned over her, face wreathed in concern.

"Moira, my love, 'twas but a dream."

"I—" Moira could manage no more. Tears filled her eyes and her throat. She choked on them.

"Och, my dear."

To Moira's surprise, Rhian climbed into the bed with her, pushing aside the bolsters that played at being Da, and held her tight. Moira wept.

She wept.

A storm it turned out to be, a violent one that Rhian did not try to staunch. She did croon as Moira wept on her shoulder, called her *dear* again, and clutched her as if to drag her back from the edge of an abyss.

Not until the storm played out into hiccups did she repeat, "Moira, my love, 'twas but a dream."

"I failed him, Rhian. I was there at his side. I should have been able to protect him. I failed."

"Lass, ye did all ye could."

"No' enough."

"Is what we can do ever enough? I was unable to save Ma when she took so ill."

"You were but a girl then."

"One already well-versed in the study of healing. Would ye blame me?"

"Nay." Moira palmed the tears from her face. The wound that marked her right cheek stung.

"Then how can ye blame yourself?"

Gently, Moira pushed her sister away and sat up. "Ye do no' understand."

"Truly?" Rhian's blue eyes met hers, sane and steady. "Ye will say that to me?"

"My sword was there. It should ha' made the difference."

Rhian sat up also, beside Moira. This reminded Moira of days long gone when all three of MacBeith's daughters had slept in the same bed. Rhian at the wall to keep the damp at bay. She, Moira, on the outside to fight off any monsters that might show their faces in the dark. Fey Saerla in between them, holding on to the good spirits.

"Tell me about the dream."

"I do no' want to." Moira did not want even to think about it. That man, holding fast to her. The emotions she'd felt from him.

"Come, sister. Twill serve to put the horror at bay."

"I was back in the battle."

"Aye, so I could tell."

When Moira said no more, Rhian asked, "Did—did Da fall all over again?"

No, he had not. Farlan MacLeod had failed to strike the blow. Because he'd had hold of Moira instead.

What did it mean? He'd spoken of destiny. Moira wasn't certain she believed in destiny, though Da had, and she suspected it was bred in her bones. It might well show up, if all else was stripped away, muscle and bone.

"I maun go and check on the guard."

"Rest a while yet. 'Tis nearly morning. Just lie quiet."

Moira obeyed her sister's bidding, but she did not sleep again. She feared a return to the dream. Yet it hovered like an evil mist, crawling around the ground behind her.

Rhian did doze, one arm curled over Moira in a gesture of valiant protection. So Moira lay still a while for her sake till a knock came at the chamber door.

Then she slipped from the bed and went to answer it.

Saerla entered, moving in that way she had, like water flowing.

"Your cheek is bleeding." Her fey blue eyes examined Moira with compassion. "And ye do no' look entirely well."

"Nor do you, yoursel'." Saerla, the prettiest of MacBeith's three daughters, just as she was the youngest, now had lines in her face, ones that had never been there before. And her dreamy eyes held a measure of desperation Moira shared.

"I do no' think I am well entirely." Saerla cast a look at Rhian, now awake and sitting up in the bed. "Moira, we shall ha' to do something about Fiona. She is, well, persistent."

"Aye, so." Persistence could well be Fiona's name. It was what had gotten her into Da's life, and quite possibly his heart. "She is naught if no' that."

"I just encountered her when I was on my way down from Da's grave."

"Ye went there again?" Rhian frowned. "Saerla, 'tis dangerous, that. If anyone questions why—"

"They will no. All the clan kens I go there to speak prayers. For the benefit o' the clan in fact. 'Tis a holy place, where he lies. Besides..." She broke off.

"What?" Rhian prompted.

"He is there. Da is." Saerla sat on the edge of the bed and spread her hands. "I can feel him when I'm there."

Moira might have scoffed had she not long ago given up

scoffing at her sister's fey pronouncements. Saerla knew things. Moira sometimes thought she picked them up from the very air, of from those stones up on the heights.

Anyway, how dare she scoff after fancying she could feel what lay inside the mind of the man who'd slain Da?

Saerla looked directly at Moira. "He is proud o' you, Da is. For stepping up to lead us."

That caused tears to come once more to Moira's eyes. Truth, or fancy? Did it matter? They were words her heart desperately wanted to hear.

Staring into Saerla's misty eyes, blinking the tears from her own, she asked, "Have we done the right thing?" She'd been so sure when they'd brought Da home. When they'd laid him in the armory. When she'd needed with all her being to hold the fabric of their world together because the very weave of it lay sundered.

Now the complications came creeping in. Fiona. Fear of discovery. The accursed prisoner.

Saerla, who possessed her own brand of honesty, said, "I do no' ken if we have done right or wrong. But the choice is made now. We will ha' to tell everyone the truth eventually—that he is gone."

For the space of a score of heartbeats, the room held silent, the three of them united by a truth their minds could not accept.

"For now," Saerla went on softly, "I say we should tell Fiona."

Moira looked at Rhian. "And you?"

Rhian, who lived by an inner certainty and very rarely had difficulty making up her mind about anything, hesitated. "I am worried about Fiona's reaction. She may well agree to keep our secret, but you are right, Moira, grief could overset her. She will wail and moan, unable to hide her sorrow. I agree that aye, she needs to be told. She's been here to the door more times than I can count and is frantic to help care for Da. But I do no' ken if she will be able to hold her tongue."

Moira turned her head and looked at the bed. The bolsters

had been pushed aside along with the coverlet, so it looked no more than an empty resting place.

Gone. He was gone.

And the man who had killed him lied to her in her dreams.

"For now," she whispered, "for now let us keep it among us five. Tell Fiona Da sleeps most of the time."

"I tried that. She asks to sit with him while he sleeps."

"Tell her he has asked to be cared for by his daughters."

It would hurt the woman's feelings, but how could she argue it?

Rhian nodded. "We will ha' to spell one another here. I cannot spend all my time shut awa' either. There are other wounded to be tended, and a household to run."

"Aye." They had locked themselves into a cage of sorts, had they not? Moira should be keeping watch at the gate. Rhian should be minding her hearth. Saerla—

"You two go," their youngest sister said. "I will stay a while. But aye, we maun find a way to tell the others, and soon."

Chapter Twelve

F ARLAN WOKE TO the dim air of the enclosure and lay with his eyes wide, shivering. He lacked either pallet or blanket and lay sprawled flat on his back, prey to the chill. But nay, it was not the cold that had awakened him.

Every muscle quivered with alarm. With awareness. With a kind of fascinated horror.

He sat up and dragged a breath into his lungs. A dream. It had been nothing more than a dream. Yet he'd never in his life had one like to it.

Back in the battle he had been, in the thick of it with all the accompanying sights and sounds. Once more, he fought by Rory's side, as ever his staunch right arm. They faced Chief MacBeith and a small band of his men. And despite the fact that others of both clans fought around them, he was convinced the battle would turn here, among these few.

A figure leaped forward, imposing itself between Farlan and Chief MacBeith. All fierce eyes and sweeping sword was this MacBeith warrior. But now, Farlan knew her.

Not an unnamed opponent at all, but Moira MacBeith.

There in the dream, surrounded by horror and death, conviction swept through him. It worked up his body the way a wave fills the rock pools of a shore, unstoppable. He knew her, every inch of her, body and soul. Not the enemy. But his destiny.

Madness, a kind he'd never before experienced. Yet it made him thrust his sword into its scabbard, deep. It made him reach forward and grab hold of her forearms.

There amidst the clamor and the stench of death, he gazed into her face. He spoke to her in his mind. *"Do no' try and fight me, lass. For ye are meant to be mine."*

Her gaze widened with shock that he would touch her, beautiful eyes of blue surrounded by long, reddish-brown lashes. The cut on her cheek, not long inflicted, trickled blood. He didn't see her beauty, though, as much as feel it. He could feel her steadfast spirit—that of a warrior—feel her strength and the kindness beneath it all.

She must not hear the words he thought at her. How could she? They but resounded through him. His fingers tightened on her arms and his heart yearned for oneness with her such as he'd never known.

This woman, aye. This one spirit. His destiny.

Protest arose in her eyes, bright and warlike. He felt that too, as if the emotion were his own. He had to make her see—

They could not spend their hate on one another. Or how might they ever be together?

Farlan shook himself as he emerged from the dream, the way a dog does in the wet, and the bright, devastating scene retreated a little. Still, it lurked there inside him, not quite gone.

He drew up his knees and pressed his head to them. His battered body protested, and the wound on his shoulder pulled tight.

A dream. Just a dream, a fancy. No more. A man might dream anything, especially a man under duress who likely ran a fever. One who did not know if he would live or die.

He could have no connection with Moira MacBeith. Aye, she might be attractive in a way that had naught to do with beauty, and that called up in him an almost visceral reaction. She was also the enemy. She had pressed a white-hot iron to his flesh.

There could be no more between them than hate.

Ye are meant to be mine.

Had he said that to her also? Had those words been part of the dream?

He must indeed be fevered. A fever dream it had been. A product of being trapped here, of not knowing what was to come, whether she'd decide to question him again or kill him this very day.

And yet—and yet he yearned to see her. Against all reason, he did. His very soul cried out for it. He longed to go and pound on the door, call to the guards. Demand she be brought here to him.

Aye, and what would he say to her then? What, when he gazed into her eyes—the eyes of a warrior—and sanity returned.

He paced the limited space of his prison; he chaffed and he wondered while the light of a new day trickled through the seams in the roof. He fought back the feelings inside, the way he might fight an opponent in battle. Those feelings retreated, aye, they did. But like the dream, they refused to flee.

ALL DAY LONG, Moira fought the impulse. She took care of any number of tasks. Spoke at length with Alasdair regarding the stationing of the guard. Checked their supplies of food and weapons in case of siege. Relieved her sisters in Da's chamber and fielded scores of inquiries about the chief's health from concerned clansfolk, who included the persistent Fiona.

Fiona, a strapping sort of woman with fair hair going to silver, was not used to being refused much of anything. Her hazel eyes questioned Moira far more intently than her words, and Moira felt lucky to escape her.

Through all this, she held strong, refusing to visit the prisoner's pen. Indeed, the impulse rode her mercilessly. She told herself she could question Farlan MacLeod again at any time. She could go in company with Alasdair and try to batter some useful information from him. The very prospect turned her stomach.

She could accompany Rhian there to check his wounds, for it would never do to send her sister in alone. A dangerous man was their prisoner.

His hands, clutching her forearms in the dream. The heat of him, and the way she could sense his emotions.

All fancy. He was but an ordinary man, and an enemy to boot. The man, moreover, who had struck the blow that killed her father.

By midafternoon, she concluded she must be going mad. Enemy or no, she could not get the man—or the accursed dream—out of her head.

She gave no orders for his care. She told no one to take him food. He did not deserve her thoughts or her concern.

The weather, as if to match the turmoil inside her, turned fretful. A wind came up the glen, one that spoke more of winter than of spring, and rain hovered in the offing. When it came, it would make a clatter. Would Rory MacLeod choose such a time to attack?

Knowing they must be ever vigilant, she made a round of the guards. Her da had always done this, checking on each man as a father might.

Men turn restless when stationed in one place, he'd often told her. *They tend to become careless and sometimes fall asleep.*

He'd always assigned them in pairs when he could. So she found them now, all around the battlements of the keep and outlying from it in every direction.

They had not become careless and had not fallen asleep. Instead, with their eyes trained on the windy darkness, they spoke to one another in tense voices and came to attention when they saw Moira.

"Anything?" she asked each pair with a jerk of her head toward the open country.

Each answered in the negative, though the expressions in their eyes argued they felt the same uneasiness as she.

"Will Rory MacLeod attack soon? Ha' ye got any word out o'

that man o' his?"

"Naught yet. Naught sure," she told them in turn, "though I ha' a feeling Rory will make his move."

And then they inevitably asked after their chief, as indeed they would a father, and she found herself forced to lie over and over again.

She met young Calan stationed on the west wall, where the wind blew coldest. He and his partner stood huddled together, and both started up when she appeared out of the darkness.

"Och, Mistress Moira, 'tis yoursel'," said Lachlan, an older fellow.

"Anything?" She rested her eyes on Calan, her concern spiking. Calan looked the way she felt, wretched and uneasy. She wondered if the expression in his eyes mirrored her own.

"Just dark and rain," Lachlan answered. "'Tis hard to see aught at all, wi' the wet in our faces."

"'Tis just why Rory MacLeod would choose such a time." She touched Calan's arm. "Are ye well, Calan?"

He nodded, his lips pressed tight as if he kept back all he wanted to say.

Lachlan had no such hesitation. "How fares the chief?"

"Resting quiet for now."

Calan made a sound in his throat. Lachlan brightened. "That is good. As my wife always says, sleep lends much healing."

"Aye. Rhian is keeping watch on him."

"Well then, we canna ask for a better one to tend him than Mistress Rhian."

"Stay vigilant."

What if Calan crumbled and spoke to his companion about what had truly happened? Moira could not help but wonder as she climbed down from the walls. The lad appeared shaken to his soul.

As was she.

Mayhappen 'twould be best if it came out. A terrible shock to all, aye. Yet secrets were hard to keep, and she found it a torment keeping this one.

So long as Rory MacLeod, out there somewhere in the dark, did not find out their chief lay dead.

Chapter Thirteen

N O ONE CAME near Farlan that whole day, either to provide food or care. Indeed, no one peered in to see whether he still drew breath. The dirty water in the one bucket dwindled, and the other, which he was forced to use, reeked. His bones ached from lying on the hard floor and he experienced waves of cold and heat.

He could hear rain dashing on the outside of his prison and the wind shrieking about the roof. Just the sort of night Rory loved best for an attack. Would he come? Had he already? Hard to hear much above the wind.

He might be forgotten here, and starve to death slowly.

No such worry, he assured himself grimly. He would go mad first. Climb the walls. Such confinement and isolation were crueler than any wound.

Aye, and Moira MacBeith was a clever lady if she sought so to break him.

He wondered over and over again what Rory would do. He knew the heart of his friend. Sometimes hasty, and even reckless, it carried a flame. Loyal to the death, he placed his clan above all else.

Every member of it.

But if he mounted a raid in an effort to get Farlan back, he could fail. Stealing a few cattle was one thing. Dashing himself against the stones of this keep was another.

Iain MacBeith, even if he lay injured, would be ready for any such attempt. He would direct his daughter from his bed, unless he was already up on his feet.

Unless he was dead.

Farlan shook his head and spoke aloud to himself. He'd been doing that more and more, just to hear a voice.

"Nay, the old man is tough as aged leather. He staggered back, aye, when I struck him. But he did not fall, and did I no' see him move off upon his own feet?"

Not knowing was hard. Not knowing whether the bulwark of Clan MacBeith still stood. What Rory might take into his head to do.

When Mistress Moira might return.

He tried to sneer over that last and attempted to tell himself he did not care. The dream had been but a dream. He hated the redheaded vixen.

Dangerous, she was. To his peace of mind and to his life.

By morning when the wind died, he'd convinced himself she intended to let him starve to death. Only then did he hear voices and a rattle at the door.

His soul leaped within him. Was it her? To be sure, when the door creaked open and a woman entered, he felt certain of it. She wore a long gray cloak against the wet, but he caught a glimpse of red hair beneath the hood.

But nay, nay—this woman did not move like Moira Mac-Beith, with a warrior's unthinking confidence, and did not feel like her. When she threw the hood back onto her shoulders, he saw it was the healer, the one called Rhian. Her sister.

Rhian swept him with a look from assessing eyes and wrinkled her nose.

"It stinks in here. Drachan, will ye change the bucket? And bring more clean water."

The guard grumbled over it, but obeyed. Rhian placed the basket she carried on the floor, and regarded Farlan still more closely.

"How d'ye feel?"

He told himself she asked the question out of nothing more than duty. Apart from his value as a prisoner, she did not care if he lived or died.

Yet she stepped up and laid a cool hand on his forehead.

"You are burning wi' fever."

He shrugged. Did it matter?

She had left the door open a crack after the guard carried out the stinking bucket, and sweet, cool, damp air came sweeping in. His eyes strayed there.

"Do no' try it," she warned. "No' unless ye wish to end impaled on a blade."

It might be preferable.

"Did my chief attack last night?"

Her blue gaze moved to his, inquiring.

"'Tis almost impossible to hear aught in this damned place."

She nodded. "Ye maun be afire wi' frustration." No sympathy colored the words. Merely an observation. "No attack last night, though we were ready. No word at all fro' your chief."

"I tried to tell that other woman, your sister? I am of no particular importance to him."

"Aye, Moira is my sister. Busy wi' our defenses she is, the now. If your chief does come, we will be ready. Take off your shirt."

He did so, moving stiffly and with pain.

The wound on his shoulder, the one Moira MacBeith had cauterized, seemed to be healing cleanly, though it hurt like fire. The long cut on his arm, dealt by a filthy blood-encrusted blade, showed puffed and red.

"Ah now," Rhian murmured, "this looks bad. It maun be causing ye a might o' pain."

He shrugged again.

She worked over him, there in the middle of the cheerless cell, with careful, gentle hands. Not one to inflict pain, this woman. Unlike her sister.

They might look alike—the same broad foreheads and mops of curly red hair. The same blue eyes. But those eyes held vastly different expressions. Rhian seemed steady and measuring. Her nearness did naught to arouse him.

Did Moira arouse him? His anger alone, surely.

The guard who brought fresh water and an empty bucket hovered in the doorway, watching carefully while she finished treating Farlan's wounds.

Farlan might well seize her by the throat. He could threaten to strangle her. Try to use her as a hostage in bargaining his way free.

He did not doubt Moira MacBeith would value this sister of hers with the gentle hands.

Yet one of the guards blocked the door. The other waited beyond with his sword at the ready. And Farlan found he did not want to harm Rhian MacBeith.

"There now. I will ha' a draught sent in for the fever. And some food. Ha' ye been fed?"

He shook his head.

She glanced around the barren cell. "Ha' ye no blanket?"

"Nay."

"I will see what I can find."

He did not want to feel grateful to her, this second of Iain MacBeith's daughters. He glared hard.

She gathered up her basket and turned to leave.

"How fares your chief?"

That made her freeze before she swung back to face him. "Why d'ye care, MacLeod?"

It was the first aggression he'd received from her and, aye, it made her look more like her sister.

"I saw him take a wound on the field."

"Aye, so." Her eyes fell. "The time I spend here takes me awa' from caring for him."

"He will recover then?"

That made her stare at him once more, uncompromising. "As ye will discover, Master MacLeod, 'tis a very hard prospect indeed to keep a MacBeith down."

Chapter Fourteen

"**I** TELL YOU fairly, sister, if he is no' kept in better conditions, ye will likely lose him."

Lose him. Farlan MacLeod, Rhian spoke about. But Moira had never had him to lose.

She stared at Rhian, who'd just come bustling into Da's chamber with her cloak wet from the rain, and her basket filled with soiled bandaging. Moira had snatched a wretchedly brief few moments of sleep once again in Da's bed, while supposedly watching over him. Doing so felt—well, oddly comforting.

Now her thoughts were muzzy as she sat up.

Blatting about the prisoner, and right fired up about it, was Rhian. Moira sometimes thought mercy had been bred into her sister's very soul, and while, aye, there was a place for mercy, she wasn't sure this was it.

"He's a prisoner," she croaked. Thank God and all the saints she hadn't dreamed of him again in her few moments of reprieve. "Besides, he's a big strong lout o' a man. He will no' perish o' a few wee wounds."

Rhian put her head on one side and considered. "He is a big strong man." She swept Moira with a glare as if wondering what she meant by the words. "But they are no' wee wounds, and poisoning is no respecter o' height or muscle. He already has the fever, I am telling ye."

Fever. Aye, and Moira had seen that take many a strong man. She crawled from the bed onto her feet. "So? Ye ha' treated him, ha' ye no'? He will soon be well."

"Mayhap. Mayhap no."

Moira shrugged. She hurt from head to toe and was weighted down with grief.

"Did ye no' mean to feed him either?" Rhian continued.

Had he not been fed? Surely she had given the order. Moira struggled to remember. "I must ha' sent something in."

"Ye must not. Never mind. I ha' given the order for food and a blanket."

"A blanket?" Moira squared off against her sister. "Our own injured need those."

"There are enough in store to afford him one. As ye well know. Ye spend enough time counting up our stores."

"'Tis good to know what we have, in case of siege." That had been much on her mind. If Farlan was important to Rory MacLeod and he launched a siege, would they have enough? Of food. Of weapons. Of supplies? "Anyway, he is no' our guest, this MacLeod."

Rhian, clearly annoyed, shrugged one shoulder. "Let him die then. But do no' expect me to stand by while ye do."

Moira stepped close, touched Rhian on the arm, and reminded her, "Sister, he is the one."

"Eh?"

"The one who struck the blow. The blow that took our da's life."

"So ye did say."

Moira gestured angrily to the messy bed. "He killed our father, and ye want to waste your kindness on him."

Rhian swung to face her. "Is it a waste? Is decency ever a waste? Are we to lose that also?"

Moira bit her lip. Anger rose inside her, like vomit.

Rhian sounded angry also as she rushed on, "Ye do no' understand. I do naught for the MacLeod's sake. But hatred and ugliness are bad for a person. I do no' want to harbor a soul that indulges in either."

"Nor do I!" Moira returned indignantly. "But I find mysel' having to step up. To think o' others besides mysel'. If Rory MacLeod comes, 'twill be I meeting him at the gate."

"I ken. And I would I might tak' more of that burden fro' ye. Just, sister, do no' lose yoursel' in the doing."

"I am willing to sacrifice mysel'. If I must."

Rhian nodded somberly. "Anyway, I will mix a draught and send it in to the prisoner. If ye want any information from him, though, ye'd best ask for it sooner rather than later."

Was the MacLeod so gravely ill as that?

All day, as Moira went about her tasks, the question haunted her. She figured she should go and set eyes on him. She found any number of excuses, though, to keep from doing so. A meeting with Alasdair about increasing the guard. A meeting with the council regarding the state of the supposedly-recovering chief. A party sent out to gather the rest of the cattle and bring them in close for safety.

Alasdair seemed as unsettled as she. Even when they met on the battlements, he could not keep his eyes from the horizon long enough to speak to her.

"I ha' a feeling in my bones," he confessed, "that he'll be coming, Rory MacLeod. Coming for his man."

"Ye think so?" Moira allowed her gaze to follow his, prodding every feature of the familiar landscape. "When?"

"Aye, that is the question, is it no'? I think I will stay on guard tonight."

That made her regard him with alarm. A giant of a man, Alasdair might be, one who possessed a loyal heart. Even such a man needed respite.

"Have ye taken any rest?"

He gave an almost soundless laugh. "Me? Ye be a fine one to ask."

"I caught some, while sitting wi' Da."

"Och, aye." To her surprise, tears flooded his dark eyes. Over the years, Moira had seen Alasdair in many moods. Angry. Determined. Unflinching. Grief looked shocking on him.

She told him, "You had best grab a few moments while ye may. If an attack does come, or God forbid a siege, there will be little rest for ye. I will keep watch at the gate tonight." She widened her eyes at him. "You trust me, surely."

"Like none other." To her surprise, he touched her elbow lightly. "Lass, I've been meaning to say—"

They were interrupted before he could finish by a man with a question about the stationing of the guard. Moira went off and left Alasdair to it.

By the end of the day, she ached with uncertainty, with dread. Her conversation with Alasdair haunted her, as did that with Rhian.

Late in the afternoon, she came across Saerla, training with other warriors, including Calan, in the forecourt. Saerla once more wore a warrior's garb, her hair tightly braided, and moved with the fluidity that marked all her actions.

Fey as a wind from a fairy mound, Saerla might be. But when she gave herself to something, she did so completely.

This, so Moira guessed, was her way of being prepared if the worst happened and Rory MacLeod attacked. Moira watched her sparring with young Calan, admiring Saerla's capability. And yet—

As they'd just learned, anyone could be struck down. Even those she could not imagine losing.

Would she lose Saerla, or Calan, or Alasdair in the next battle? Would she lose her own life? There must be a way to prevent it.

Dark had not yet fallen across the glen when she went again to the prisoner's pen. She told herself she did not want to go there, but it was a lie. She might not wish to face off with the man who'd killed Da, but—like Saerla and Alasdair perhaps—she wanted to be sure of her weapons.

She found the guards playing at draughts. They got to their feet when they saw her.

"Mistress."

"All quiet?"

"Aye, as the grave."

That caused enough alarm for her to hurry inside. She found the prisoner sitting on the hard floor—to be sure, he had nowhere else to sit. An empty cup and bowl lay beside him. Rather than lying upon the blanket Rhian had sent in, he sat with it wrapped around him.

Aye, it was cold in here where the sun did not reach. He deserved no more.

He stumbled to his feet when he saw her and stood with the blanket hanging crookedly around him. One glance behind her revealed he wondered who else might come in. Others of the guard, to provide a beating. Or Alasdair with his irons.

Moira examined him swiftly for the signs of fever, but could mark none.

He still looked strong and stalwart, a large and—were she honest about it—handsome man.

A sick feeling crawled up from her belly. An accursed MacLeod, who had killed her da.

She gave him a tight smile. "Do no' worry, Farlan MacLeod. I ha' no' brought the irons. I want for us to speak together, nothing more."

Chapter Fifteen

A S SOON AS Farlan laid eyes on Moira MacBeith again, the remnants of the dream stirred inside him.

He'd been doing his utmost all the while not to think about her, shoving away the details of that accursed dream he'd relived so many times he felt fair sick from it. The thing was, shut away here in this dim cell, he had little enough else to think about. The woman fair haunted him, and thinking of her brought other wild thoughts.

How it would feel to touch her, in truth. To kiss those lips. To feel her heat. Because aye, he could tell from a glance there would be fire beneath Moira MacBeith's tightly held exterior.

Now she came to him like an answer to his unadmitted longing and stole all his words away.

She still wore the dun-colored gown, or another just like it. Plainly clad she might be, but she needed no adornments. Her eyes glowed like two jewels, and she brought with her an energy that outshone any trappings.

A funny thing about this woman, if anything about his wretched situation could be considered funny. Bright as he remembered her, her actual presence cast memory into the shade.

There could scarcely be a worse woman for him to desire. Yet this was no ordinary desire he harbored. It was something far different. Far more.

He shifted on his feet and waited. Why had she come?

Her gaze swept the cell. "I see ye ha' been fed. How d'ye feel now?"

Solicitousness? Was he to suppose she cared? In truth, he felt better, stronger.

"The healer—your sister?—sent a draught. For the fever."

"Aye?"

"It helped." He swallowed, wondering. Was that what she wanted? Or did this vibrant woman who he sensed might mean so much to him want him dead?

"Sit down," she ordered, her hand hovering at the hilt of the sword she wore.

A sword. Strapped on over a dress. He should not find that arousing, but did.

He obeyed. To his surprise, she sat down also on the floor opposite him.

"I want to talk to ye," she announced. "Honestly. And I want ye to talk to me. Tell me how I might use ye to negotiate a peace."

Farlan might have fallen over backward had he been any more surprised. They were the last words he expected from her.

"Peace," he repeated. Between the MacLeods and the Mac-Beiths. The word *destiny* echoed in his head.

She made a face and spread her hands upon her knees. "I ken fine 'tis a shocking notion. How long ha' we been at odds wi' one another? Since our grandsires' time?"

"Longer than that." Farlan struggled to figure it. He'd been raised on the belief that the MacBeiths were intractable, stubborn wretches who would stick a dirk in your back as soon as look at you. They believed as firmly, no doubt, that the MacLeods were savages—upstarts still after a hundred years or so.

"I do no' ken whether such a peace is possible. Anyway, should it no' be on the Chief Iain MacBeith to negotiate such a thing?"

Something flickered in her eyes, and was as swiftly gone. "My father will be laid up a while yet. I act in his stead."

So, what she wanted was breathing space, time during which her chief could grow sound. Aye, it made sense. But Rory—Rory was a man to move on any perceived advantage.

Rory must have seen Iain MacBeith take that wound on the field. Indeed, Farlan was half surprised he hadn't already moved to attack.

She leaned toward him slightly. "Tell me how to deal wi' your chief. It could well mean your life."

Was there a chance of him getting out of this? Freed from this cell. Away from these conflicting emotions?

"Rory wants your lands."

"He may want your safe return more."

Regretfully, Farlan shook his head. "I do no' think so. He may, aye, be willing to negotiate once all the glen belongs to him. Gi' ye and your people a portion of land where ye might live subject to him."

She snorted. "That will never happen."

Farlan shrugged. Believe what she would, it was Rory's intended goal.

"Tell me, will he no' gi' me a guarantee o' truce in return for your release?"

So that was what lay in her head. Ah, Farlan longed for it, but again, he shook his head. "I fear not."

"Should I send a messenger to him wi' such an offer, will he kill the man?"

She was as stubborn as she was strong. "Nay. Whatever ye believe o' us, we do ha' some moral convictions."

"I will go now and prepare the message to be sent in the morning." She rose to her feet. "Rest easy, Farlan MacLeod. This may be your last night beneath Iain MacBeith's roof."

She might well hope for it, as might he. Farlan had his doubts.

He stumbled up in her wake, and when she turned to the door, he stretched out a hand. One she did not see.

Do no' go, lass. Do no' go from me.

Did her narrow back tense? But nay, she could not hear words he hadn't spoken. She responded only to her own thoughts.

She went out with a swirl of red curls, and another of brown wool, leaving him—

Devastated.

Only because he hated being pent up here. Only because, with her gone, he once more fell prey to his thoughts. What would Rory do? What did fate intend for Moira MacBeith to mean to him?

Naught. Naught at all. She was the enemy.

Destiny. The word chased around in his head, in his heart. He paced the confines of the pen until he could do so no longer.

She said she wanted peace. Yet, even when she went from him, she afforded him none.

>>>><<<<

MOIRA PAUSED AS soon as she left behind the men standing guard at the cell, and drew in several deep breaths. The atmosphere inside the chamber had been—

Well, she did not know that she had words for it. Such a place should feel confining, and it did. At the same time, it contained a subtle energy that satisfied her in ways she could not hope to explain.

He was there. Farlan MacLeod.

MacLeod. The very name should make her shudder. When she'd been small, their nurse, Cara, used to say, "Ye lassies be good now, or the dread MacLeods will get ye."

Bugaboos, they had been. Fearsome monsters that ate children. Of course, when she grew she found out they were just men who harassed and attacked her own folk, seizing cattle and damaging vital supplies. Thieves and raiders who sought to steal the very land upon which they stood.

Men, aye, but bugaboos all the same.

The man back in the cell was among the worse of them. Close to Rory MacLeod, who possessed none of his father's common decency. Above all that—

He had killed her da. Put an end to his kindness, stilled his great laugh, and his mighty heart.

She, upon whom the safety of this place now rested, could not possibly have feelings for that man. No sympathy. No understanding.

Except, she did.

Standing there in the dark, she twisted her hands together. She remembered pressing the white-hot iron to his flesh. She'd felt his body tense, felt his will rise as he set himself to endure what could not be endured. She'd experienced the release right along with him when his eyes had at length rolled back in his head and he became senseless.

Aye, well, all that meant was she must share more of Rhian's sympathetic spirit than she'd guessed. Or maybe she possessed a hint of the fey, like Saerla, that could see inside the man.

He was just a man. And she needed rid of him if only for her own peace of mind.

Resolved upon it, she thought about a messenger she should choose to send. The very prospect felt like assigning one of her children to risk of possible death. She could think on it while she kept watch tonight, as she'd promised Alasdair.

A shout came from up ahead, in the direction of the gate. Another echoed it from along the ramparts.

She lifted her skirts and ran.

Chapter Sixteen

A LASDAIR REACHED THE gate ahead of Moira. Even as she clambered up, half tripping on the hem of her dress, she saw his hulking form and heard him shouting orders. A measure of relief took root inside her.

She scrambled to where she could look out, which landed her beside him. "What is it?"

A number of warriors crowded the ledge up here and Moira could feel their alarm. They muttered and shifted in place, their weapons at the ready. She drew her own sword from its scabbard. Thank goodness she'd worn it for her visit to the MacBeith's cell.

One of the guards spoke. "We saw movement. Dairwin did. Ye ken fine, Mistress, how sharp his eyes be."

"Aye." She spoke also in a hush. "Attack coming?"

"Maybe."

Looking out over the familiar fall of land from the level place where stood the keep, about halfway up the brae, she saw only darkness. After midnight it must be, and a dark night without any moon. If she narrowed her eyes, she could just see clouds scudding from west to east, darker shapes against the black sky, and here and there the brief gleam of a star between.

A fine night for an attack.

As Da had frequently told them, it never did to underestimate your opponent. And they'd learned since old Camraith's death,

Rory MacLeod was a canny and determined man. Not so straightforward as his father. And perhaps less likely to let things ride.

More than likely, he'd decided to move on a night black as the pit of hell.

"Have we got all the cattle inside?" she asked, though she knew Rory had not come for cattle, not this time.

"Aye."

"I can see naught."

"There, Mistress." One of the guards, as she realized when he spoke, was young Calan. Och, it would be—he who shared her secret. "O'er where the rill runs down. We saw them slippin' across."

Them.

Moira still saw nothing. Eyes wide, she listened to the darkness, and to her instincts. Something was there.

"Attack," she whispered.

"Attack!" Alasdair bellowed it an instant before they appeared out of the dark. Two men running hard with their shields in front of them. Then three more. Half a score.

"Torches! Bring more torches. Call the men! Get them up here." Alasdair bellowed orders. He turned to Moira and seized her shoulders. "You go down."

"Nay. This—this is my place."

"Ye ha' no shield. No—"

"I ha' my sword."

"Moira, please." A hard emotion looked at her from his eyes. "Ye be too important to risk. Go now."

He half forced her behind him away from the gate. Protest filled her to overflowing. This was her place. Hers to defend. Stubbornly, she stood her ground.

Men rushed past her, hurrying straight from the armory. More than the walkway up here could hold. Bowmen climbed up, streaming by her.

She could hear the attackers now, howling like a pack of wild dogs. Her mind roamed over this place she loved. Where were her sisters? Rhian would be in Da's chamber, aye. But Saerla? What if she'd gone back up the brae to the stones? What if she got caught out?

The thought made her breathless. So dear to her, her sister was. The very idea of losing her—

She saw Saerla then, hurrying toward her with a bow in her hands. Aye, Saerla was clever with the bow. Saerla, focused on climbing up one of the stone risers to the ramparts, did not notice Moira there.

They would repel whatever Rory MacLeod threw against them. All would remain safe.

She pelted off against the tide of defenders, fighting her way to her own quarters where she picked up her shield, not taking time to change into her warrior's clothing. On the way back, she swung by the cell.

"Mistress Moira," called one of the guards, "what is happening?"

"Attack. Stand firm. Guard the prisoner at all cost."

"They will no' break in, surely?"

She pelted off. Surely not.

Thank the holy God for Alasdair, she thought as she rejoined the confusion at the gate. He'd taken control and bellowed orders at the men to spread out, to take orderly stations. To keep their heads.

Torches already ranged all along the ramparts, throwing precious light to dispel the attackers' cover of darkness. She could see their men firing arrows, though in all the din she could not hear the twang of the bow strings.

She pushed against Alasdair, who half blocked the walkway. "Let me through."

"Nay. We ha' men enough on the walls already."

She tapped him with her shield, not a blow but enough to emphasize her words. "It is my place."

"Let me lead this." He glared into her face. "Let me fight it for ye, lass."

Nay.

But she could not argue it then. He turned and scrambled forward to the rampart over the gate.

Heart pounding hard enough to rattle her teeth, Moira pushed past the intervening men and followed.

She cursed her skirts that wanted to trip her up. It made much more sense to dress in leggings like a man. When she reached the top of the wall, she saw—

Not a small force of attackers, this. No raiding party Rory MacLeod had brought. These spread out like a dark tide lapping at the stones of this place she loved. Fury rose in her heart and a wild desire to defend.

Despite the light from the torches, she could not estimate the number of attackers beyond a multitude. They moved in and out of the shadows like wraiths.

The bowmen above the gate hesitated to fire, and Moira saw why. Targets blended with the shadows, moved and faded.

All except a dark knot of MacLeods who battered the gate itself.

Hard to fire on them, though, as they were directly below and they had their shields raised above their heads.

Rory MacLeod would be there. The spearhead of this attack.

Moira thought of him, for she'd seen him many times both in skirmishes and when he'd met with Da in the company of his own father in past efforts to negotiate. Of course he'd been younger then. A tall youth with glossy black hair tied in a tail, and startling green eyes. They said, since his father's death, he'd turned vicious and merciless.

They said much of the MacLeods.

She leaned out as far as she dared to try and glimpse the action below. A hand on the back of her dress hauled her in again. Alasdair.

"What did I tell ye?"

"You do no' tell me, Alasdair!"

"Curse it all!"

"Will the gate hold?"

"Aye. Now use some sense and get ye back."

No time for further words. The MacLeods had brought their own bowmen and began to fire back from the shadows, using the torches to find their targets. A range of shields formed above the battlements, Moira's among them. She found herself next to Calan, who stared into her face with wide gray eyes.

An arrow embedded itself in Moira's shield with a thud. Others sailed over them. Someone behind her cried out.

The group of MacLeods below began to batter the gate. If they broke through—

If they broke through, it would go hand-to-hand. The defense would move from wood and stone to muscle and bone.

Another arrow found its way between Moira and Calan, though they stood shoulder to shoulder. He cursed and shifted to better cover her.

The defenders could not lower the wall of shields long enough to fire back. And she could hear—

Someone hollering below. The MacLeods had ladders. They'd begun to climb.

Calan lowered his shield at the same time she did. An ugly face appeared at the parapet, a MacLeod warrior climbing up with his sword in hand. Calan started forward, but an arrow came over the stones and took him in the arm.

He cried out and staggered. Moira leaped into his place and swung her sword at the attacker's head.

Curse her skirts anyway that wanted to trip her, and her long hair that swung into her eyes. Astonishment at facing a woman, however, caused her opponent to hesitate. She swung for his head and he tumbled off the ladder.

No time to fall back and see how Calan fared, for another MacLeod warrior scrambled up to take the last one's place. Hollering, grunting, and cursing now engulfed the ramparts on both sides. Hell, there in the dark of night.

How many of them were there? She wondered as she threw off her second man.

And then—

A fierce call came out of the gloom, one that cut through all the other voices.

"Iain MacBeith! Step up and face me!"

Chapter Seventeen

R ORY MacLEOD CALLING, so that had to be. Demanding a
word with Da.

Moira threw herself onto the rampart above the gate only to
be bumped aside roughly by Alasdair.

"Nay."

"Iain MacBeith, show yoursel'!"

With the call, the fighting died back. A rough silence, devoid
of all but groans and curses, took hold. Moira's heart pounded in
her ears.

Alasdair shook his head at her. "Ye canna let him see ye."

"Why not?"

He did not answer. Instead, he took the place directly above
the gate and called down, "Rory MacLeod?"

"Where is your chief?"

"He is here," Alasdair called back. "I speak for him, the now."

"Tell him I want the prisoners ye hold."

"We hold but the one, Farlan MacLeod," Alasdair shouted.
"The other man died."

"I want ye to hand him over."

Ah, so Farlan was important to Rory, enough so for him to
launch this attack. At that moment, the knowledge caused Moira
both satisfaction and alarm.

"Ye may want what ye will," Alasdair countered. "Why

should we surrender a prisoner taken in fair combat?"

Moira, peering over the stones at Alasdair's side, could see Rory glaring up at them. The air was not so dark as it had been; the night came to an end.

He wore a leather helm and leather armor over the MacLeod tartan. What she glimpsed of his expression looked fierce and unyielding.

"Give him up, else we will take this place down."

"Ye canna!" Alasdair bellowed. "D'ye think MacBeith so weak as that?"

"Ye'll give in, in due time. You'll need fuel for your fires and food for your table. You'll need the free air after a month or so o' siege. Hand him over, and it ends here."

Moira pushed up on her tiptoes, clutching at the stones. "Are ye talking of a truce, Rory MacLeod?"

His eyes narrowed at her. Aye, she could see him clearly now. The strong, stern face. The eyes bright with antagonism.

He took in her appearance, the tumble of curls, before he sneered. "I am no' talking a truce, merely a temporary cessation o' the hostilities."

Aye, for how could there ever be peace between them? How, when this man desired their lands from Loch Bronach all the way to the holy stones?

Where Da lay.

"Ye want your man back? Whole?" she shouted.

"I do, and will ha' him."

"Then ye can guarantee a peace. Or go wanting."

Murmurs started up in the crowd behind Rory. Like an echo, it spread behind Moira, among her own men.

Rory snarled. "Ye maun be mad, woman."

Aye so, perhaps she was.

"It will ne'er happen and," he shouted it like a curse, a promise, "harm one hair o' Farlan MacLeod and ye'll ne'er know a moment's peace again."

They withdrew then into the encroaching morning, a hail of

arrows chasing them on their way.

"Do we open the gates?" Moira asked Alasdair. "Do we pursue them?"

"Nay."

Indeed, if they did, a pitched battle would ensue and her men were ill-prepared, half caught in their night clothes.

No matter. Their walls had held strong. Everything she loved remained safe. *For now.*

She drew a breath that felt like her first in far too long.

"He'll be back," Alasdair declared. "And back again till he gets his man. It seems the bastard has a shred o' loyalty in him after all."

"Perhaps we should hand Farlan over."

"Wi'out getting something for him? Nay!" Alasdair turned on her. "And wha' were ye doing, talking o' peace? It makes us look weak."

"'Tis what we need, wha' will make us safe."

Alasdair spat over the wall. "It can ne'er be while those curs share our glen."

He stomped away from her, still bellowing orders. Upset with her, he was. Yet he had to acknowledge that negotiations were hers to make. Whether he agreed with her goals or no.

He must acknowledge that she was now in charge.

She turned to find Saerla at her side. "Sister, are ye well?"

Moira nodded woodenly. "And you?"

Saerla shrugged. "Who is this Farlan MacLeod that Rory wants him so badly?"

"His friend, so I do believe."

"Aye, well, you had better consider handing him over. For I can feel naught but iron in that man." She jerked her head over the wall, where Rory had withdrawn.

"Aye." Rory was not his father, who had met mind-to-mind with Da. Who had kept from destroying his neighbors. That was certain. "Alasdair is angry. He thinks me weak."

Saerla gave her a sweeping glance. "He knows better than

that. Come, sister, let us get down fo' here."

Moira did, while trying to disguise the fact that she trembled in every limb. Reaction, she told herself, no more. It took her that way sometimes.

But to the folk who gathered around her, she needed to appear strong.

"Mistress, when will Himself be back on his feet to lead us?"

Ah, and did these men agree with Alasdair that she was weak?

"I do no' ken. He is resting." Quietly, she hoped, up on the rise.

Others, members of the guard, expressed their concern about their families, some of whom lived on outlying plots of MacBeith land, distant from these encircling walls. The MacLeods had in the past directed raids there and had stolen cattle. But Camraith always held his hand from killing the innocents who lived there, or burning their homes. And such raiding parties had often been intercepted by MacBeith defenders on their lengthy way home.

Rory, as she'd just seen, was not Camraith, and in order to win back his man, God alone knew what he might do.

She stared into the faces of her men and sought not to let on that she shared their fear.

Should she order all the outlying clan members to come in? There was scarce enough room, and if it came to a siege, doubtful enough supplies.

"Set up a watch," she told Bean, who happened to be standing by. "Let no MacLeod party cross onto our lands at any cost. If they try, we will go after them."

"Aye." He hurried away.

It took time before Moira could escape the others asking after Da. At last, Saerla took her arm and addressed those gathered around them.

"We go now to tell the chief all that has taken place. He will be waiting."

The men let the two of them pass then. Neither of them spoke to the other along the way.

Saerla, as Moira well knew, possessed a mind quite unlike his. Fanciful and whimsical, focused on a world beyond their own, she followed her own truth. That was not to say she would hesitate to lie as she had just done, but she hated doing so, and Moira could feel her tension.

She never spoke until they reached Da's chamber. "We can be alone here if nowhere else. Gather our thoughts."

Rhian leaped up from the bench beside the bed when they came in, face stark white and eyes dark with worry.

"What has happened? I heard—"

"Rory MacLeod at the gates," Moira finished for her. "Wanting the return o' his man. Curse him."

"Gone now." Saerla answered Rhian's unspoken question.

"What will ye do?" Rhian helped Moira to the bench. "Gi' up the prisoner?"

Moira sat with a sigh and forced her fingers through her hair. "I do no' see how we can. He makes a powerful hostage—as has just been proven. And I do no' see Alasdair agreeing to surrender him. Alasdair is certainly furious wi' me." And she with him.

She could not afford to be at odds with her strongest supporter.

Rhian knelt beside the bench and smoothed the skin of Moira's arm. "'Tis no' Alasdair leading us though, is it? 'Tis yoursel', Moira."

Moira dropped her head. "It should be Da! Och, how I wish he were here."

"And I," Saerla said softly.

"And I," Rhian agreed. "But we canna have that wish."

Wretchedly, Moira said, "I do no' ken what to do. I want to force a truce wi' Rory MacLeod. Och, I ken fine it will not be for good, not if the man has his sights on our land. But we need a span o' time wi'out him battering our gates so we may find our feet. And we can tell our people that Da—Da is gone."

"Aye," Rhian breathed.

"Farlan MacLeod makes a powerful weapon, but I am no'

sure how best to use him. Should I hand him over in exchange for a promise o' peace? Or hold him hostage to try and assure Rory will no' destroy us?" She raised her eyes and regarded her sisters one after the other. "Wha' do ye suppose Da would ha' done?"

Neither of them had an answer for her, and she could find none in her heart.

Chapter Eighteen

R HIAN WENT OUT soon after to make her rounds and tend the wounded, leaving Saerla and Moira alone. Even though she ached with weariness and had collected a number of new scrapes and bruises, Moira could not rest. She paced the floor of Da's chamber, listening to the passing footsteps outside, and knowing she should go out there, show herself in an attempt to exert order.

Saerla sat beside the window, her face turned toward the new morning, which showed gray and windy with rain in the offing. She appeared to be praying.

Moira wished Saerla would come up with some answers, fey ones or otherwise. She would be willing to take wisdom from anywhere right now.

She wanted to be strong for her people. She also wanted to be canny. In the unequal battle against clan MacLeod, she had few weapons and would not give up one of them.

Besides—besides, Farlan MacLeod was the man who had struck Da down. Did he warrant being handed back to his chief without serving any punishment?

She turned her mind away from the memory of white-hot iron meeting torn flesh. Aye, she had caused him to suffer. He languished still without light, sufficient food, or other comforts.

Not enough. He had taken Da from them.

What would be enough? She asked herself that as she turned once again and continued pacing. What torment could pay for what they had lost?

None.

She had promised Da when he lay dead in the armory that his daughters would step up and not fail him or the clan. She had to find her backbone. She was the closest he had left to a son.

"I canna stay here," she told Saerla at last.

As if startled from a trance, Saerla jerked her head around, eyes wide and misty with dreaming. Had she sought a vision?

"Sister, ye need rest. Stay here a while, try to sleep."

"Sleep?" Moira gave a harsh laugh. If she slept, she might dream once more. *Of him.* "There is far too much to be done. Ye will stay?" She gestured to the empty bed.

Saerla nodded.

They must tell the truth soon, she thought as she hurried down the corridor toward the main hall. Announce to the clan that their chief was dead. Och, what a blow that would be! And if Rory MacLeod found out—

She must locate Alasdair. Talk out their differences. She needed him on her side, his great strength at her call.

He was not in the hall, which echoed to her steps, empty. Outside the wind blew hard. A crowd of guards thronged the gate and paced the battlements. None of them was Alasdair. Folk hurried around with frightened expressions. Only a few stopped to ask after their chief.

Three guards stood at the door of Farlan's cell. She paused there to ask, "Has he been fed?"

They shook their heads.

"One o' ye go get him something." On impulse, she gestured to the others. "Let me by."

Some light would be helpful, she decided as she stepped inside. She could barely see Farlan as he scrambled up from the corner, wrapped in the blanket the merciful Rhian had given him.

Aye, it was cold in here. And him, a man with a fever. A

valuable prisoner with a fever.

"Mistress," he said hoarsely. "Wha' is happening? I heard sounds o' battle."

"Your friend, Rory MacLeod, came calling. He verra much wants ye back."

⤜⤛⤛

FARLAN EYED MOIRA MacBeith cautiously. She looked exhausted, and a few new scrapes and abrasions had joined that already on her cheek, the one that would doubtless leave a scar.

At the sight of her, a strange thrumming started up inside him that kept time with his heartbeat. He hated the woman, aye.

Only he did not.

"Will ye gi' me up to Rory?" To him, it seemed the best thing she could do. Rory possessed the greater numbers, and thus greater strength. If he'd set his mind on getting Farlan back, he would come again and again to storm her walls.

She had her own brand of strength, aye—he could feel that. Would it be enough?

She lifted a brow at him. "Is that what ye suppose I should do?"

He shrugged. "I tell ye fairly, Rory will no' give up."

"Important to him, are ye?"

Why try and deny it any longer? Rory had already showed his hand. "We are good friends. Rory MacLeod, whatever ye might think o' him, has a loyal heart."

"I think he's a monster. All o' us do."

"Ye're wrong. He has a load of ambition and intentions passed down fro' his forebearers. He feels he has a duty."

"To conquer us."

"To hold all this glen."

A sneer crossed her face. "And you, Farlan MacLeod? Wha' d'ye think?"

92

A good question. He had often—if only in his own mind—derided the necessity of clan MacLeod dashing themselves against MacBeith's swords again and again. It caused a wealth of pain and death. Having met this woman, he found he wanted even less to be at odds with her.

But he knew Rory, had heard him arguing endlessly with his father about intensifying the feud. Overthrowing the MacBeiths and giving them a choice—leave Glen Bronach or live subject to MacLeod rule.

"I think," he said slowly, "if Rory does tak' that path, there will be very little left in the end for him to overthrow." This woman would not bend. Whether her father would—aye, that was another matter. "Wha' does your father say, Mistress?"

An agonized expression crossed her face, just a flash of one, and was as quickly gone. Hard to catch in the dim light, Farlan nevertheless knew.

Chief Iain MacBeith was dead.

The conviction found him whole. And aye, it explained so much. The hard blow he had delivered to the old man. The fact that she, MacBeith's daughter, seemed to be making all the decisions and had just come from battle.

She did not want him to know MacBeith was dead. Moreover, she did not want Rory to know. Which meant if he had any hope of escaping his imprisonment, he could not let her guess he had tumbled to the truth.

He blinked at her. Carefully, he said, "Ye would be best sending me back to Rory now. If I die here, he will ne'er forgive it."

She narrowed her eyes. "Are ye likely to die here?"

Should he lie to her in turn? Pretend the fever still held him in its grip? But nay, the draught her sister had sent in had helped, and if the healer came back and examined him, the truth of it would out.

"These are scarcely hospitable surroundings."

"Ye are no guest."

He said nothing. She took a step closer to him. "Let me speak plainly, Farlan MacLeod. You are the best weapon I ha' to hand, and I do no' ken if I should give ye up so easily. Wha' I would like to do is forge a truce wi' your chief. D'ye think if I hold out, he will want ye back bad enough to gi' me that?"

Farlan did not know. Rory must want him back, aye, but he was set on finishing a task set by his grandfather. When Rory was set on something, it was neigh on impossible to distract him.

He looked Moira MacBeith in the eye. Pushing his conviction, he asked, "Wha' does your chief, Iain, say? Surely ye ha' discussed my imprisonment wi' him, in light of all that has happened here this night."

A rattle at the door saved her from answering. The guard she had sent for food came in, carrying a bowl.

Moira turned away abruptly, and even as the man handed Farlan his food, went out the door. *Without answering.*

So, Farlan thought as the door closed behind Moira and the guard, she wanted peace.

Good luck to her then.

Chapter Nineteen

I T STILL SEEMED wrong sleeping in Da's chamber, but it had come to be the only place Moira could be alone, away from the endless questions. Besides, with her there supposedly tending the recovering chief, Rhian had an opportunity to be off tending those newly wounded at the gate and on the walls.

Rhian looked tired, and no wonder. Moira, easing her body down on the bed in place of the bolster, felt weary to the bones.

If only her mind would let her rest.

Instead, the thoughts came crashing in. Worry for the safety of the clansfolk at their outlying dwellings. Could she sufficiently protect them? She wondered what Rory MacLeod would do next. Fretted about whether she'd lost Alasdair's support.

She contemplated what she should do with Farlan MacLeod. He was dangerous to keep. And dangerous to give away.

The thoughts and worries washed over her in waves, pounding at her in time with her heartbeat. Was she strong enough for this?

She must be.

Sleep came, and she tumbled into it, deep.

She stood on the rise above the stronghold, up on the height where they'd buried Da, with all the glen spread out below. She could see Loch Bronach, its waters silvery in the bright light, and all the hills stretching away like shaggy beasts hunkered down.

She could see the keep below her, looking over small, and the land spread out on every side.

She could see an army on the move, approaching. An army on the attack.

Nay, nay, and nay! What was she doing here, so far from her post? How could she get back in time before Rory MacLeod's men reached the gate? Before he took from her all she loved?

Why had she come up here where she did not belong? This was Saerla's place. Moira belonged standing strong as she could at the gate with her sword in her hand.

Defending all she loved.

Och, and she did love this place. The light, glinting off the loch, and the rough turf beneath her feet. The rock and the bone. Even the wind pushing at her here on the height that smelled not of the approaching death but of the distant sea, and wind thyme.

Her strength lay in the rock beneath her feet, in the air she drew into her lungs.

"Moira! Moira MacBeith!"

The call came not from the glen, but behind her. She turned and the wind blew her hair in her face so she could not see. But she knew his voice.

She knew.

He came out from among the stones, stepping swiftly. He looked vital and well, and she thought—madly—that aye, his fever must have passed.

What was he doing here, up among the stones instead of in his cell or fighting beside his chief?

Because he remained prisoner no longer. Something had occurred to free him.

He walked forward and stood beside her, gazing out over the valley. He wore his hair loose. Like hers, it streamed in the wind and played around his shoulders. Broad shoulders. A handsome, rugged face. Brown eyes steady on the scene below.

"Ye might stop all this, ye ken, Moira."

"This?"

He waved a hand. "The fighting. The anger. The hate."

"How?" The enemy was nearly at the gate and she, here with him where she should not be.

His gaze captured hers, warm brown eyes full of wisdom. Of compassion.

"Stop wi' the hating. Stop seeing us as the enemy. Stop wi' me, first. I am no' your enemy. I am your destiny."

Moira awoke in her father's bed, so filled with conflicting emotions she could scarcely breathe. She strove to push the dream away from her, but the strands of it clung to her yet.

Och, the way he made her feel, this man, standing beside her. As if, aye, the two of them stood removed from the immediacy of their lives and so could be peaceful and honest with one another.

She crawled from the bed and stumbled to her feet. Rhian had not yet returned. She should stay here pretending to tend Da, yet being penned up this way frustrated her.

She needed to go and find Alasdair. Work things out with him. She could not manage to lead the clan without his support.

Rhian came in a short time later, her basket empty, and looking still more exhausted than before.

"You take a turn and rest," Moira urged her. "Ha' ye seen Alasdair anywhere?"

"He is patrolling the walls. Keeping watch."

"I maun go and speak wi' him."

It took her an hour's tramping to find Alasdair. Everywhere she inquired for him, she was told he'd just gone.

At last she found him at the armory. She could not so much as glance into the building without seeing Da's body stretched out on the floor, and as she stepped in, a superstitious shiver pricked her skin.

Alasdair had one of the younger men with him. He shot Moira a measuring look before sending the lad off to the blacksmith with a number of weapons for repair.

"We need to talk," Moira said. "I ken fine ye be angry wi' me."

"I am no' angry, Moira."

But his dark eyes refused to meet hers and he kept sorting through the weaponry, pretending she was not there.

"I've had a dream." It wasn't what she'd meant to say. She intended to be fair and reasonable, to tell him they must work together for the benefit of the clan.

The dream still weighed on her so heavily, though, it wanted to come pouring out.

He did look at her then. "A prophetic dream?"

"I do no' ken." She hoped not.

"I thought that was Saerla's bent."

"I saw Rory MacLeod coming to attack us wi' a huge mass o' men."

Consternation flashed in Alasdair's dark eyes.

"The full might o' his clan it looked to be. Alasdair, he has ne'er done that before, come at us wi' all his might."

Alasdair frowned and rubbed at his forehead. Had he taken any rest?

"Ye do no' ken, lass, that this dream was true. It might be your fear and dread bringing such a thing to ye."

So it might.

"I canna' deny," she confessed to him, "I am afraid. Alasdair, I know ye do no' agree wi' the way I want to use the prisoner, Farlan MacLeod. But what if we tried to negotiate over his release?"

"Release?"

"Tried to get something in return for him. A truce. A period o' time when Rory will no' beleaguer us so we might tell the clan about Da, and gain our feet."

"A truce. Given his superior numbers, wha' makes ye think Rory MacLeod will agree to any such thing?"

"He wants the return o' his friend. He just proved that. If he will talk wi' me about it—"

"Ye—ye want to meet wi' Rory MacLeod!"

She did not want to. She feared she must. "There is no one

else."

"Ah, lass, he will chew ye up and spit ye out."

Did Alasdair truly have so little faith in her?

Slowly, he shook his head. "I say kill the prisoner and send his bones to Rory MacLeod as a message."

"Is that what Da would ha' done?"

"I do no' ken what your father would ha' done. He is no' here to tell me." For an instant, terrifyingly, tears filled Alasdair's eyes. "I say we can show no weakness. Negotiating will do just that. We maun see to our defenses—especially if this dream o' yours be true." He gestured at the weapons. "I say we bring everyone in from the outlying farms. 'Twill be tight for a time, especially wi' the animals. But if Rory MacLeod wants war, 'tis what we will give him."

Moira did not want war. She had to think this through, all the ins and the outs of it.

Because everything depended on the course she chose.

Chapter Twenty

S HE CLIMBED UP to the height, to Da's unmarked grave, because she believed it the only place she could be alone. It also made a fine place from which to keep watch on the whole of the glen. On a clear day like this one, she could just catch a glimpse of the MacLeod stronghold in the distance, looking deceptively innocent and harmless lying in the sunlight.

She realized her mistake almost at once, for being here recalled the dream in full force. She almost expected Farlan MacLeod to step out from amid the stones.

No one was there, not even Da, though Saerla insisted she found him here. However, no sooner had Moira taken up a stance when Saerla herself came up the rise.

Moira loved her sister, indeed she did. Saerla had always been the wee girl with the dreamy eyes and a way of knowing what could not be seen. No one had been more surprised than Moira when, having taken up the sword following Arran's death, Saerla followed her example.

Moira had always thought of her younger sister as gentle, perhaps a bit otherworldly. All that ceased when Saerla had a blade in her hand.

Indeed, she came now wearing her leathers and with her sword strapped on, clearly straight from the practice field. She looked unsurprised to see Moira here ahead of her.

"Sister."

It occurred to Moira that Saerla might be a fine one to talk to about the dreams. Were they a mere reaction to the pain of losing Da? Or did they hold true meaning?

"I came to snatch a wee moment alone."

"Would ye like me to leave?"

Moira shook her head.

They stood for several moments shoulder to shoulder, gazing out.

"'Tis so beautiful," Moira murmured.

"Aye. It looks like a cupped hand, so I always think. See—the fingers folded up are the mountains. The loch lies there at the center. Over on the thumb is—"

"MacLeod."

"Aye. Or as Da might say, a wart."

Moira laughed reluctantly. It sounded rusty.

Saerla stepped closer and put an arm around Moira. She came only to Moira's ear, being the smallest as well as the youngest of MacBeith's daughters.

"I can feel your agony. Your pain."

"I do no' ken wha' to do. Saerla, ha' ye Seen anything that may help me?"

"Nay."

"Can ye no' look ahead for me?"

Saerla smiled sadly. "Ye ken fine it does no' work that way, at least no' for me. Knowing comes seeping in like—like the mist seeps over the ground, or not at all."

"And dreams? Ye sometimes ha' dreams."

"Aye."

"Have ye had none since Da died?"

Saerla shook her head of tight curls. "I wish I would dream o' him, but I told ye, I feel him here. Why d'ye ask?" She turned her head and her wide, misty blue eyes gazed into Moira's. "Ye've had dreams. O' Da?"

"Of the prisoner, Farlan MacLeod."

Saerla's brows rose. She said nothing, but her gaze cooled. "Him."

"Him what slew Da."

"What sort o' dreams?"

"Confusing ones. There've been only two so far, but I get the feeling—the feeling there will be more if I do no' heed wha' he says."

"Wha' does he say?"

Moira clenched her fists tight. She did not want to repeat the words.

"Moira?"

"Och, he says we are meant to be together, he and I. That it is destiny."

Saerla took a moment to absorb that. When she said nothing, Moira added, "But he's the man who—"

"Killed Da."

Saerla spoke the words softly yet they seemed to whisper through the air all around them.

"Perhaps, sister, ye are merely attracted to the man. He is no' ill-favored for a MacLeod."

He was not. In truth, had all been different, Farlan was the kind of man who might snatch Moira's interest. Tall, strong, and utterly masculine without bragging about it, with those steady brown eyes.

Over the past years since Arran's death, Moira had spared little interest for men. There had been those among the clan, and especially her fellow warriors, who looked her way. A few of the bolder ones had even acted upon the attraction, asking her to walk out with them. She'd been utterly focused on helping Da, on filling the gaping hole Arran had left behind. As a result, she now found herself past the age when most women wed.

And men had stopped approaching her.

She had to admit, if one of them had come to her looking like Farlan MacLeod, with the same breadth of chest, the same rugged features, and that quiet strength, she might have been tempted.

Because there was just something about the man.

The MacLeod. He who'd killed her father, her chief.

Impossible.

She said, "I do no' think that's it. This does no' feel like—like mere attraction. In the dreams, 'tis as if I can feel wha's inside the man. How can I tell if these dreams are true foretelling or just dreaming?"

Saerla shrugged. "'Tis no' easy, since we dream such strange things at times. 'Tis as if while asleep, we give our thoughts permission to play out all the madness."

"It is madness, aye, that he and I should ever mean something to one another. He is the enemy."

"Aye." Saerla smiled wryly. "The only man wi' whom 'twould be worse to fall in love is Rory MacLeod himsel'."

"I am no' falling in love wi' Farlan MacLeod."

"Of course not."

"And I need to get my mind clear, decide wha' best to do for the sake o' the clan. Farlan MacLeod is an advantage I might use to strengthen our defenses. For in the second dream, Saerla, I saw—I saw Rory MacLeod's army on the move."

"Ah. So ye came up here to look."

Perhaps she had after all. She waved an arm wildly at the glen. "Down there, I ha' no chance to think. There's always someone stopping me to ask after Da. Fiona, begging to visit him. I'm constantly reminded we're lying to all o' them."

"Aye."

"Alasdair thinks we should slaughter Farlan MacLeod, send his bones back to Rory as a message."

"Ye do no' agree?"

"I'm no' sure 'tis the best use o' a weapon when we ha' so few to hand."

"Besides," Saerla added softly, "how can ye kill him when he may be your destiny?"

"Och, Saerla! Do no' say it aloud. I am no' even sure I believe in destiny."

"I do." Saerla gazed out over the valley, and for an instant her eyes turned misty and utterly fey. "I believe each o' us may ha' several destinies laid out before us like—like pathways we may choose. Some lead to braw places and some to terrible ones. The thing is, the thing is we canna always see which is which before we maun choose."

Farlan MacLeod could not possibly lead Moira to any good place. Absurd even to consider it.

She swiveled her eyes to her sister. "Ah then, what is your destiny?"

"I ha' not seen all of it yet. Right now, I am a warrior, but that will no' last. I am a Seer, always. Perhaps I will lead our folk out o' the darkness."

Unexpected tears flooded Moira's eyes. *If only.*

"Lead me." She whispered the plea and Saerla brightened.

"Sister, there's one better than I here to lead ye. Let us talk wi' Da."

Chapter Twenty-One

S AERLA TOOK HOLD of Moira's hand and led her back from the edge of the rise to Da's grave. When they reached the place, Moira backed off a step. "Nay."

"Aye, sister. Ye did no' believe me when I told ye, but he is here. His spirit, or a part o' it, lingers. He speaks to me."

Moira shivered. Aye, this was fey business indeed. Much as she adored her da, she was not sure she wanted to encounter him at his grave.

In a flash, she saw him again as she last had, sprawled on the floor of the armory with his life's blood staining his plaid.

Farlan MacLeod had done that. How could she even imagine—

"Come," Saerla insisted, and pulled her down to kneel over the sundered turf so they faced one another.

"Quiet," Saerla whispered. "Quiet yoursel'."

That was just the thing, was it not? Moira could not be quiet. The very peace of her existence had been stolen from her. Ever since Da's death, she'd been on constant alert, guarding. Even in sleep, she found little rest.

But Saerla raised her face, and her expression turned serene. How bonny she looked, Moira thought, with the light making a halo of her bright hair. She still clutched one of Moira's hands, and Moira could feel the intensity of her questing spirit.

"Da? Are ye here wi' us?"

A thrill of mingled distress and longing poured through Moira. Did she want this? To perhaps feel what Saerla felt, to see what she saw?

She half expected to sense a stirring from beneath the sod where lay Da's decomposing flesh and bones. The prospect fair terrified her. But that did not come.

Instead, the air stirred all around her, seemed to warm and to dance with sentience. With humor. *With love.*

She knew him then. *Da.*

Of course he would come with warmth. Though she'd never realized it before now, it was what Da had always carried within him, and had brought to each of them. The warmth of strength. A warmth of comfort, of belonging.

She caught her breath and held it. This could not be happening. It could not.

"Da," Saerla said softly, aloud, "ye ha' left us, yet no' left us, as we can feel. Our Moira, she now carries a heavy burden. If ye might lend her strength and wisdom, we will be that grateful."

Strength and wisdom. Aye, those he had always possessed in plenty.

Moira felt a sensation, as if soft air passed over her hair in a caress. The touch of Da's hand? But she could not see him.

"I want to see him," she half wept, her heart breaking asunder.

"Nay, ye need to believe. Believe he is wi' us, wi' ye all the time."

Believing was hard. Especially now.

"Ask him, what maun I do about Farlan MacLeod?"

"Da, Moira has had two dreams that trouble her, ones wherein Farlan MacLeod—he who delivered the blow what took ye down—has told her they are destined to be together. Truth, or fancy? Can ye tell us?"

Moira's chest hurt from holding her breath. She gasped and, pulling her hand from Saerla's, wrapped her arms around herself, waiting for an answer.

The air grew brighter around them, the top of Da's grave bathed by a ray of sun. She heard nothing.

Saerla's expression changed, grew thoughtful as if, aye, she listened.

"What?" Moira rasped hoarsely. "What?"

Saerla looked at Moira. Her eyes no longer appeared completely sane, and they seemed to gaze through as well as at her sister.

"The MacLeod is right," she spoke in a faraway voice. "He is your destiny."

THE TROUBLE WAS, Moira could not accept it. Even after she returned to the stronghold and to the scores of well-wishers who stopped her to ask after Da, when she helped organize messengers to go to the outlying areas and bring in the clansfolk, as she strove to make provisions for them, her mind continued to flail at her.

Would her da say such a thing? That the very man who had killed him was his daughter's destiny?

Besides—besides, had Saerla not said there might be more than one destiny, and choices to be made between them? That some paths might lead to terrible bad places?

Farlan MacLeod might be one of those.

Then why would Da point her toward the man? Had he done so? Or was this some wild fancy on Saerla's part, masquerading as foretelling?

Aye, Saerla was a Seer, no question of it. But must every vision be accepted whole? Had Saerla truly heard Da's spirit speak? Moira had heard naught.

Nay, but she had felt him. The warmth. The love.

Indeed, that might have been her own longing insisting he

was near.

She could not decide. She could not. But och, how she longed for her father's warm presence that she'd felt upon the rise.

Throughout that day, as she stumbled through her duties, her mind pondered it. How? How could any MacLeod clansman, and in particular one who had killed her beloved da, be her destiny? She remembered the expression in Saerla's eyes when she'd made the pronouncement. She wanted to find Saerla, to ask her again if it were so.

She wanted to go to the prisoner's cell and set eyes on him.

That last impulse bothered her the most, and proved horridly distracting. She had no time for such distractions, and by the end of the day, teetered hard on the edge of exhaustion.

She had not encountered Saerla again and had only glimpsed Alasdair in passing. Neither had she succumbed and gone to visit the prisoner. She did, at last light, stop by the watch above the gate.

She found two of their senior guards on duty there, both with their eyes fixed steadfastly on the distances.

"Anything?" she asked them.

Geordie grimaced. "A handful o' deer, Mistress, and a fox running. No accursed MacLeods."

She gazed out also, her gaze narrowed. "Keep good watch. Now that the shadows are gathering, they may well come."

"Aye," said the second man, Seumas. "My eyes are already playin' tricks on me."

"Mayhap ye need to take a rest, both o' ye. Go and get two replacements. I will stand while ye do."

Geordie refused to leave, though, and stayed with her while Seumas hurried off. "I am good to stand a while yet, Mistress. The thing is, I do no' want to cry a false alarm and get all the keep riled for a shadow, or a deer. At the same time, if they come creeping, I do no' want to give the alarm too late."

"Aye." It was a difficult situation. How long could they live this way, with every nerve on edge?

"Go and get some rest," she insisted when Seumas arrived with not one but two replacement guards he said Alasdair had sent.

She needed to follow her own advice. She should go to Da's chamber and see if Rhian needed a respite. Try to snatch a few hours' sleep and hope she did not dream.

But her course there took her past the prisoner's pen, and when she reached it, her feet dragged to a halt.

Folly to go inside. A wise woman would just keep walking.

Chapter Twenty-Two

I N THE DREAM, he walked alone through the early morning. He could feel the sweet, cool air against his cheek, smell the fresh tang of wild thyme. He could hear the birds singing their first songs even as the sun rose, shedding golden light.

He knew this ground beneath his feet. The rough turf dressed in bracken and heather. He recognized the mountains in the distance. He had lived in this glen all his life. Run at the side of Rory and his cousin, Leith. Laughing. Getting into mischief. Just a wee bit wild.

Now he walked steadily away from all that, out into the broad palm of the glen. A sense of urgency filled him. He went to meet with someone.

He could not see her yet, only the new light dancing over the turf and the loch to his left. Would she come? Would she dare to walk out, turn her back on all she knew even as he now did? Dare come to him on faith?

She was a woman who dared. And with all his heart, with everything in him, he wanted her to take this chance.

If he turned around, he would still be able to see MacLeod's stout stronghold sitting on the hill like a stony bee hive. He had not come so far. Not far enough yet.

And ahead—aye, he could just glimpse MacBeith's keep in the distance. A place upon which many a raid had been launched.

This ground between them, between him and Moira Mac-Beith, had seen much contention and much spilled blood. Mayhap she would not come after all. Likely she would send a troop of her men instead to attack him. To cut him down and end his life.

Was meeting her, was being with her, worth taking that chance?

Aye, och aye.

He no longer understood his own heart. What urged him to this? He'd always been a level-headed man. Had not Chief Camraith said many a time he was glad his wild-headed lad had such a steady companion?

How steady was he now? Walking out from safety to meet the enemy. Only she was not the enemy. Somehow, in a way he could not hope to explain, she was already inside him.

He discovered belatedly that he wore no weapons. Aye, right, he thought in confusion, they had taken his weapons from him at MacBeith before locking him up. So now he went to his fate as defenseless as a lamb to the slaughter.

He went to his fate. For better or worse. Did he want to live anyway if Moira MacBeith failed to see who he was? What he was?

Up ahead, he caught a flutter of movement. Light only, he told himself. The rising sun on the waters of the loch. But nay.

Och, nay, she came.

For an instant, he could not believe it. Then certainty hit him like a hard blow to the gut and he lost all his breath. His feet dragged to a halt.

A single figure walked toward him. Strong and slender she was, and the morning sun lit her hair in a bright nimbus.

He hurried then. He recovered his feet and half ran, the urgency inside him doubling. To meet her. To take her hands. To read the look in her eyes.

Was it his imagination or did she also quicken her step? He reached the water, which divided them. Her on one side and him on the other. The loch became more than mere water. It was a moral line they would have to cross.

In order to meet each other.

Well, if she refused to cross it first, he would.

Without hesitation, he waded into the water. It was not deep at first, but became so as he continued on. He lost his footing and began to swim.

The current pulled at him, and when he reached the deep water, he had to put all his muscle, all his heart into it. The wet weighted his clothing, dragged at his boots. He swam like an otter, the scent of the peaty water all around him. Whenever he lifted his cheek to look, he saw she waited.

Standing firm.

When he reached the far side and felt the loch bottom once more beneath his feet, he knew he stood on her ground. Awaiting her will.

He scrambled from the water soaking wet, and she reached out for him. He stood devoid of weapons with nothing to offer her, nothing save himself.

Like him, she wore no weapons, her leather scabbard empty at her side. Her hair and her eyes were both wild.

She looked torn, not precisely happy to see him. Yet she had waited for him, standing strong.

He stretched out his fingers to where she reached, and clasped her hand hard. She curled her fingers tight around his palm and hauled him to her, using all her strength.

He had made the crossing to her side.

A rattle at his cell door brought him from the dream. He stirred and cursed bitterly. He'd wanted to remain there on the bank, wanted to touch her, kiss her, question her.

Why did you come? What are we meant to be to one another?
Destiny.

He scrambled up even as the door opened and Moira stepped in. Aye, even half aroused from sleep, he had known it would be her.

She looked ill at ease and torn, just as she had on the shore. The cut on her cheek had once more scabbed over, but her eyes held a bleak expression, as if she did not want to be here.

Well God knew, neither did he.

"Mistress Moira," he rasped.

She cast one searing look at him before glancing everywhere else, all around the chilly chamber. She said, "I came to ask—have ye been fed this day?"

"Aye." She might have asked the guards that and not bothered to come in.

Still she did not look at him. "And your fever?"

"Gone."

"That is well. Has my sister been back to see ye?"

"The healer? Nay."

"Do ye need her to come?"

He considered on it as best he was able. All his nerves had come alive with Moira here in the room with him. He needed so badly to touch her. Anything to ease this awareness.

"Nay. I need—" He could not say it. He surely could not.

She tipped her head and her eyes did meet his at last.

He must wade across the water no matter how rough. He must go to her side.

"Mistress, I ha' been having strange dreams. Dreams about us."

Now she would scoff at him. She would show her disdain. He waited for derision to fill those blue eyes, waited for them to turn to ice.

Perhaps she would strike him. Bring in her monster of a right-hand man and reheat the irons. He did not care. At that moment, he did not. He held her gaze steadily, and at length—at length, she crumbled. A frown creased her forehead and she rubbed at it fitfully.

"I ken," she said far too softly for the guards to hear. "So have I. Wha's to be done?"

All the breath left Farlan in a rush. She'd been dreaming too.

Dreaming of him? What did it mean?

"I do no' ken," he admitted. "Will ye sit down wi' me?" He waved a hand at the floor in invitation. "Sit down and let us speak o' it."

She hesitated. Her gaze remained upon him, considering.

He cleared his throat and told her, "I mean ye no violence."

Her expression did not change. "Ye should. That is what bothers me."

Not waiting for his reply, she moved carefully, approached him and lowered herself to the floor, her sword rattling against the dirt. After a second's hesitation, he joined her. They regarded each other gravely.

"Why?" She tossed her bright head. "Why should ye dream o' me? I am naught to ye, save an enemy."

"True."

Something flickered in her eyes. "Do ye dream ill o' me? That I—that I lay on the irons again, mayhap?"

He shook his head.

"Then what?"

"That we meet one another. On level ground. As somewhat other than enemies."

He thought she would balk at that, get back to her feet and leave him to this bleak place.

Instead, she whispered, "Aye. It makes no sense. I should hate you like no other. I do hate ye." She made a helpless gesture with her hands. "Yet I do not."

"Tell me, Moira MacBeith." He engaged her eyes again. "Do ye believe in destiny?"

Chapter Twenty-Three

MOIRA NEEDED TO rise, get up off the floor of the cell and leave. Sitting here talking to this man was madness. This man who had killed her da.

Indeed, she must have been mad to come here. Losing Da had doubtless overset her mind. And yet—

And yet Saerla implied Da himself declared this man her destiny. And now Farlan MacLeod used the same word.

"I am not sure whether I believe in destiny or no. Especially as concerns yoursel', Farlan MacLeod. I deal in far more practical things. In sweat and blood and bone."

"Aye."

"Why should I pay attention to the ranting of a dream?"

"I do no' ken." He studied her gravely from those steady brown eyes. Fine eyes, they were, if she could be objective about it, trapped as they were between long, darker brown lashes. She could no longer be objective about it. He troubled her, did this man, on too many levels to contemplate.

She was the guardian of this place, doubly so with Da gone. What was she doing sitting here with him?

"Yet," he said softly as if in answer to her thoughts, "you are here."

"Aye. My sister, my younger sister Saerla, is the one wi' the prophetic dreams. She is fey withal. Not me."

"Nor me." He spread his hands on his knees. "I am the level-headed one who usually keeps Rory's feet to the ground."

Rory. Moira flinched inwardly at the sound of the name and hoped it did not show. She could give nothing away to this man, no matter how she felt about him.

How did she feel about him?

Torn.

"Do ye believe in destiny, Farlan MacLeod?"

He shrugged. "I never have in the past. Never wanted to. 'Twould mean, would it no', all the cruel things that happen to us in this world are meant?"

"What cruel things ha' happened to ye?" She waved a hand. "Besides this, I mean. Ye are best friends wi' the chief o' a powerful clan."

"I lost my own father when I was but eight. Taken in a battle against your folk, he was. My ma was never right after. She died a year later. I was fortunate that Chief Camraith took pity and raised me alongside Rory. So perhaps fate—or destiny—has two sides."

"I see."

"Because fortunate as that seems, I would rather have ha' my own da back. I loved him verra much. And I would rather have Ma back the way she used to be, happy and singing 'round the hearth."

"We ha' all lost much to this feud between us."

"'Tis difficult to believe such things come o' destiny. Or to accept a destiny that would force them."

"Aye."

"And yet," he said softly again, "ye are here."

Moira squirmed a bit inwardly.

"Saerla says—"

"Your fey sister."

"Aye, her. She says there may be several destinies laid out before us. Some lead to good outcomes and some to ill. How we choose makes for the result."

"Do ye believe that, Moira MacBeith?"

Moira shook her head helplessly. *She was here.*

"How are we to ken, when choosing, which leads to the good outcome and which to the ill?"

"That is the thing. We canna'. Saerla supposes that part rests on—well, faith."

"Saerla has a load o' wisdom."

"She does. Faith—they say it requires a kind o' leap. I like my feet solid to the earth."

Farlan MacLeod said nothing for a long moment. He seemed to contemplate her words, to measure them against some inner conviction, and she saw the thoughts move in his eyes.

Then he reached out, quite simply, and took Moira's hand. "Moira MacBeith, I am willin' to make the leap."

She stiffened. His fingers felt cold as the grip of death—the cell was horridly cold. She should react with offense. For him to touch her, this prisoner. A MacLeod.

The thing was, fast upon the heels of insipient outrage came another sensation, nay, a series of them. She could *feel* him. Not his hand just, nay, not the flesh or bone, but the man he was inside.

Warm and steady, a bulwark against the storm. At the same time quick and clever with rare laughter lurking within him. Och, she had hurt this man. She had held him captive, denied him comforts, and caused him deliberate pain.

He watched her contemplate all of it, his eyes never wavering from hers. She gazed back at him, breath caught in her throat. Saw him, spirit to spirit.

I am willin' to make the leap. Aye, so he had leaped. Was she able to leap with him?

Nay, certainly not. She had scores of reasons why this was impossible. A hundred responsibilities. A clan to protect.

A father's death to avenge.

And yet, and yet—

In the wake of his cold grip, warmth came stealing. It heated the flesh of her hand, her arm, and flared in his eyes. Comfort and the ease of belonging. A promise of passion.

She wanted to deny it. None of that was for her. She'd willingly passed the point of marriage. And anyway—

Not this man. Any other besides him.

She needed to pull away from him. To climb to her feet. To put an end to this mad, impossible interlude.

Instead, without conscious thought, she laid her free hand on his arm. The connection between them, the circle, became complete. It felt so strong, so right, she had to close her eyes for an instant against the sensation. When she reopened them, they were full of tears.

She whispered, "I do no' understand."

He shook his head, still holding her tight, as tightly as she held to him.

"I barely know ye. How—how can I feel this way?"

"Wha' would ye know, Moira MacBeith? I will tell ye all ye wish."

"'Tis no' so simple as that." He was the enemy. Part of the monster. Only, he wasn't.

It was some cruel trick, aye, of an evil fate.

"How can it be possible? I should hate ye. You should hate me."

"I do no' hate ye, Moira MacBeith."

"But I—" Her eyes strayed to his shoulder, where she'd inflicted pain.

"I do no' hate ye," he repeated, and his fingers tightened.

"Wha's to be done?" She could not imagine. Neither did she want to surrender this feeling. The road ahead seemed unimaginable.

"I do no' ken."

She stumbled to her feet, breaking the connection between them. This could not be. Just because she'd had a couple wild dreams involving this man, and because he claimed he had also, did not mean her feelings now, or these impulses, were genuine.

What of her fealty to her clan? The loyalty she owed her da?

He stumbled up after her and stood quietly. He did not reach for her again.

"I maun go. I ha' defenses to mount. I maun be ready when your chief attacks us again."

"Moira—"

"Nay." She called anger to her rescue. "Nay."

She left then, pounded on the door till the guards let her out. She fled. Not until she stood outside in the dark at a distance from his prison, drawing in great draughts of air, did she realize a spark of his warmth remained with her, burning bright as an ember inside.

She had not left all of him behind.

Chapter Twenty-Four

A LASDAIR FOUND MOIRA a short time later when she was giving orders for the prisoner's comfort. A pallet was to be carried in, some protection from the deadly cold of the floor. And a small brazier containing hot coals. Three good meals a day should be provided him.

She could feel Alasdair's disapproval the whole time she spoke to the guards, one of whom as Calan.

Before she finished, she pointed to that young man. "And I want ye, Calan, overseeing his care. 'Tis to be your main duty."

Alasdair barely waited till the men had moved off before lighting in to her. "Wha's the meaning o' this? D'ye want to treat him to a banquet also, and a feather bed?"

"Not that." Moira squared her shoulders and faced her war chief. This confrontation had been coming since the fight at the gate. Though she felt shattered and unequal to taking it on now, she had no choice.

Alasdair sneered. "Why no' just let him out o' there and send him on home wi' a pat on the haid?"

"He's a valuable prisoner. I do no' want him dyin' on us, that is all."

"I ha' told ye before, chop him up in pieces and send him back to his chief as a braw message."

"You ha' told me many things. Indeed, you tend to overstep

yoursel'."

He blinked at her. He looked as if a favorite pet hound had just bared its teeth at him.

"Now, lass—"

She lowered her voice to a growl. "I am no' a lass. I am chief of this clan. And ye, Alasdair, do no' make my decisions for me. Not when it comes to the care o' the prisoner, and not," she added with emphasis, "up on the battlements during a fight."

He reared back. "That is what has ruffled your feathers, is it? Ye did no' belong there—"

"Because I am a woman?"

"Because…" He too lowered his voice so they would not be overheard, and it came in a rumble. "We do no' need to lose another chief wi' the first barely in the ground." She began to speak and he swiftly forestalled her. "Moira, you may see it as your duty to lead even in battle. Your father, God bless him, allowed ye and Saerla to fight, ignoring the danger o' it. But,"— he drew himself up—"'tis my sworn duty to protect ye, and that I will do, to the death."

"I appreciate that, Alasdair. More than I can say. But ye canna be making my choices for me. And ye canna counter my orders in front o' the men. If ye do,"—she lifted her head—"I will ha' to ask ye to step down as war chief."

"Wha'?" No longer quiet, he roared the word at her. "Ye ha' no right."

"That is it, Alasdair, I do. Ye need to see, I hold every right."

"Now, lass, calm down. I understand this has been a difficult time. 'Tis still difficult keeping what we know under wraps, so to speak. But, lass, ye do no' wish to dismiss me."

He was right. In her heart, she did not. Alasdair was a bulwark, a rock upon which she'd come to lean even before Da's death. But he could not be allowed to openly differ with her, or take the leadership for his own.

"We mak' a fine team," he went on, oblivious to her inner turmoil. "I wi' the strength and ye wi' the smarts."

"We do," she had to admit.

"In fact—" He shifted from one foot to the other. Alasdair rarely looked less than confident, but he did so now. "I ha' been thinking. I meant to hold off on it till the word about your da was out and, indeed, this may no' be the proper time or place. But I thought we might join forces."

"Ha' we not already done so? Are we no' joined in our wishes to keep the clan whole and strong?"

"Aye. No' that. Lass, I'm talkin' o' marriage."

"What?" She gaped at him.

"Ye and me. To wed, lass. 'Tis a sensible solution to our difficulties."

That was as may be. But Moira did not want *sensible* when it came to marriage. She wanted the rush and tumble of emotion. She wanted love. That had never come to her, and she'd passed marriage by. Though she respected Alasdair and considered him her friend, she could not imagine anything more.

He hurried on in a rumble, "Ye maun understand, lass, my feelings for ye ha' grown beyond mere admiration for the daughter o' my chief."

"Nay, I did not understand that."

"Mayhap I hid it too well. Your father knew. He said ye maun mak' up your own mind."

"You never said." Moira felt as if someone had given her a hard push in the middle of her chest. This, on top of what had happened in the cell! She wanted to fall to the ground and cover her head.

"Nay, I suppose I was waiting for the right time. I ken fine this is no' it, wha' wi' everything goin' to pieces all around us. Mayhap there ne'er will be a right time."

He was correct in that. Life—her life at least—tended to plow from one difficult situation to another. That, as much as anything, was one of the reasons she'd given up on the very idea of love.

Her mind strayed back to the man in the cell, with his rugged face, tumbled hair, and steady brown eyes. He offered to meet her on a middle ground, if such a place existed.

"Alasdair, I admire ye far more than I can say."

"Aye, so."

"I value your service to my father and to this clan. Indeed, I do no' ken how I might go on wi'out ye."

"That is why—"

"Nay. I do no' think we should complicate things by changing our relationship."

"Now. Ye mean, now?"

Slowly and regretfully, she shook her head. "Not ever."

"Moira," he took a step toward her. "We would do well together. Ye ha' no idea—"

"Honestly, Alasdair, I need ye at my side as war chief and," she softened, "friend. I do believe anything more than that would be ill-advised."

Disappointment flooded his dark eyes. It made her reach out and touch his scarred hand.

"I need for ye to support me. My choices and my decisions."

He scowled. "Even if they be wrong-headed?"

"Even if you think they are. Can ye no' do that?"

"Moira, ye ken me for a loyal man."

"I do. None better."

"I was faithful always to your da, and will be the same to ye. If ye will no' accept my suit—well, that is one thing. Ye canna' expect me to keep strum when see somewhat I believe can harm us all."

No, she supposed she could not. "Very well, Alasdair, can I at least ask ye to discuss your objections wi' me privately? Not try to scold me like an errant child?"

"Aye, well, 'twould be difficult, that, in the middle o' a pitched battle."

Aye, so it would. "At least mak' an effort to avoid ordering me off until we find our feet."

His gaze measured her. "If ye mean to lead this clan, lass, ye will need a strong man at your side."

Again, her thoughts strayed to Farlan MacLeod. Impossible.

"I ha' one in ye, do I no'? Let us put all this talk o' courtship aside. We ha' important business at hand."

"Verra well. But remember I am here, lass, when you ha' need o' me."

She fled. In truth, there was no other proper word for it. She'd had far more than she could handle this day, and like a wounded animal, she sought the refuge of Da's chamber.

She hoped Rhian would be there. She might talk out some of her confusion, drop it in Rhian's sympathetic ear. Not her feelings toward Farlan MacLeod, to be sure. Even Rhian would be outraged by those.

Or maybe she'd find Saerla in Da's chamber instead. Saerla, who spoke of destiny.

She let herself into the room and looked eagerly to see which of her sisters awaited her. Rhian sat there, aye, on her usual seat beside the bed.

And in the middle of the floor stood Fiona, with a face like a thundercloud.

Chapter Twenty-Five

A HANDSOME WOMAN was Fiona MacBeith, and no delicate flower. She stood almost six feet tall, which meant she topped Moira by a good bit. She posed now with her arms crossed and her feet planted in a stance that declared her ready for battle.

Ah, no. This was the last thing Moira needed. She glanced at her sister, who made a face and shrugged helplessly. Before either of them could speak, Fiona lit in.

"Moira MacBeith, what is the meaning o' this? Where is your father? Wha' has happened to him?"

"Ye did no' tell her?" Moira looked at Rhian again. *Coward.*

"Nay, we waited for you."

"She told me you would explain, girl. Ha' ye taken him somewhere else for nursing? Ye maun let me tak' a hand. Ye ken fine what he means to me."

"I do." Moira sucked in a breath that hurt her lungs. Surely the woman could guess the truth from the empty bed. From the grief that showed so plain in Rhian's eyes. Fiona was anything but stupid.

Mayhap she did not want to guess.

Indeed, gazing into Fiona's warlike hazel eyes, Moira could see the knowledge there.

"Fiona, my dear, I am that sorry. He is gone."

"What?"

"He did no' survive that last battle."

"But—but." Everything within Fiona's body sagged. Denial flooded her face. "But ye brought him home!"

"We did."

"Rhian's been tending him here. She would no' let me in."

"Da did not mak' it all the way home. He died before we got here."

"Nay!"

"He is buried up on the rise."

"Och, nay. Nay!" Fiona fell to her knees. Rhian rushed to her and bent to embrace her with beautiful compassion. But Fiona pushed her off. "Ye lied to me, Rhian MacBeith. Ye said he did no' want to see me, or ha' me see him in his weakness."

Rhian's eyes flooded with tears. "I had to lie, Fiona. 'Twas for the good o' the clan."

"Do no' blame her," Moira told Fiona. "'Twas my scheme, mainly. Mine and Alasdair's."

"'Tis madness. Ye canna keep this fro' his folk! Ye maun tell everyone their chief is dead. My Iain is—dead."

She began to sob broken-heartedly, still kneeling there on the floor. Moira's own emotions rose in response, tears clogging her throat and closing it tight.

Rhian put her arms around Fiona. This time, the woman let her.

"Does young Saerla know?"

"Aye, she was there. We were fighting close to him when he took the wound. The five o' us swore to keep strum for the time, for we do no' want it to get back to Rory MacLeod."

"Then by all means, do no' tell that accursed blackguard. But ye maun tell our folk! Our chief's folk. Och, how will we go on?"

A question Moira had been asking herself for days.

She too knelt on the floor in front of Fiona.

"Fiona, listen to me. We did no' want to keep this from ye, or from the rest o' the clan. We dared no' let it get out that Iain

MacBeith was dead. If MacLeod found out, Rory would perceive us as weak. He would fall on us like an eagle on a hare."

"Ye did no' trust your own folk to keep the secret? Ye did no' trust me?" Fiona wailed the last words. "You think I could ever betray this clan when 'tis I knew what it meant to him? It meant everything."

"Aye, sure, I knew you would no' betray us by intention. But such a thing, such a secret, is hard to carry. Trust me, I know. All it would take is a word in the wrong ear."

Still kneeling, Fiona managed to draw herself up indignantly. "I know that I love to talk. I suppose ye think I can no' stay quiet when I must. Did I no' keep it quiet that your da had taken me into his bed?"

"Nay, Fiona. Everyone knew the very next day."

Da had laughed about it, his big booming laugh, and shrugged it off. "Wha' man does no' want his private business in everyone's ears?"

"Well so, but I would never betray this clan."

Moira got to her feet and pulled Fiona up with her. "This will be your opportunity to prove it. For we canna' tell anyone else yet."

"But, lass, 'tis a cruelty to keep it from his people. To let them think he will soon be hale and hearty, back among them."

"Da's spirit will always be here among his folk," put in Rhian, who had also climbed to her feet. "He is here. I can feel him in this chamber when 'tis quiet. And up on the rise, so Saerla says."

Fiona palmed her cheeks, which had gone blotchy with tears. "Aye, ye say Saerla knows. Who else?"

"Just Saerla, Rhian, me, Alasdair, and young Calan who was fighting alongside us when it happened—and yoursel'."

"And ye buried him? In secret? Wi'out the rest o' us there, or the honor he deserves?"

"We can have a grand ceremony later, once we are secure. Fiona, I fear if Rory MacLeod finds out about this, it will be no-holds-barred for him. He will lay siege and take all we have. Da would no' want that."

"Nay, he would no'. He often spoke o' how he and Camraith MacLeod both held their hands. They were enemies, aye, but there was respect between them. The running battles were little more than a game, even though in the end they cost Arran's life."

"Aye, but Rory MacLeod is in earnest. He plays at naught. My dear, will ye give us your promise to keep silent about this?"

Fiona bent her head and sobbed anew. Moira exchanged a look with Rhian and saw her own doubt reflected in her sister's face. If Fiona went out from the chamber in this condition, it would take mere moments for the truth to come out.

"I tell ye what, Fiona," Rhian said softly. "Ye can play an important part in this, just as Da would ha' wished. Ye can stay here as if ye ha' taken over the duties of nursing him from me. 'Twould be ever so helpful, since 'twill free me up to go out and see to others o' the wounded."

"Stay here? Wi'out him? In the very chamber where we—"

"Aye, well." Moira did not want to hear what Fiona and her father had done together in that bed. "We all maun find the strength now to do what's most difficult."

Fiona stared at her. "You—leading the clan. That is no' just temporary until he gets well."

"It is no."

"Ye mean to take that on in full? Aye, aye, if that bastard MacLeod gets wind o' it, he'll try to ride o'er ye as if our walls do no' exist."

Moira did not like thinking of it that way, but if it secured Fiona's cooperation, well enough. "Will ye keep the secret? Just for the time, till we find our feet. After that, I hope to form a temporary truce wi' Rory MacLeod."

"A truce! Wi' that monster?"

"One that will afford us some security. He wants the return of the prisoner we hold. I mean to bargain over that."

"Aye, but once ye hand the man over to him, once Rory MacLeod knows the truth, wha' is to keep him from destroying us then?"

What, indeed? Perhaps, Moira thought, she'd been looking at this the wrong way 'round.

Mayhap if she could not be stronger than Rory MacLeod, she would need to be smarter.

Chapter Twenty-Six

FARLAN DID NOT expect to see Moira MacBeith again so soon. Yet she was back at first light. He wondered if she'd slept at all. He hadn't, and had spent the night pacing the limited space of his cell with the blanket wrapped around him against the pervasive chill.

Wondering if he was going mad.

Again and again, he went over what had he told her when they sat together. That she meant far more to him than just the daughter of a rival chief. That he was willing to cross the gulf between them for a chance to be with her. Aye, he'd gone mad, clearly, for no such chance existed. No matter what he might feel toward her.

A thousand emotions there were, including respect, fascination, and strong desire. All inappropriate.

She came in accompanied by a number of others who brought all manner of goods. A pallet, a basket brimming with food and, by God, a flask. A small brazier that gave off lifesaving heat.

He did not know which he was happier to see: the brazier, the flask, or Moira herself. Moira, he decided, even though she brought a terrible load of complications.

The others left, having delivered their goods, and in order to give himself a measure of time for composure, Farlan went to the brazier and held out his hands.

"Mistress MacBeith?" He glanced at her over his shoulder. "Wha's all this then?"

She appeared tense, aye, but at the same time as if she'd made up her mind about something. Set and certain. She'd once more strapped her sword on over her gown.

Farlan still found that arousing.

"I wish to send a message to Rory MacLeod. I need ye to tell me the best way to go about it."

He turned from the brazier. "Ye expect me to help ye?"

She cocked her head and looked at him, an inspection that started at his feet and ended at his hair. He flushed with a heat that warmed him far better than the coals in the brazier.

"Wha' is all this then?" he pressed with a wave at the pallet. "A bribe?"

"Nay, more a show o' good faith."

"I see." Farlan was not sure he did.

"Tell me the best way to approach Rory MacLeod. I ha' no wish to send my men wi' a message only to have them slain."

"And what is this message to be?"

"I want a meeting wi' him. A negotiation."

"Over my release."

"Aye. I maun get what I can for ye. The best return."

She meant to trade him then. Despite all he'd said to her. Despite the dreams. The tangle of emotions inside him, an impossible morass of them, arose in a mighty wave.

She must indeed have come to a decision. She did not believe in destiny. And why, truly, should he? Did he not want to return home? Be free of this cell? Escape this madness? For a few comforts did not make this anything other than imprisonment.

But leaving her—ah, leaving her would be an agony.

She said, "Why would ye no' wish to help secure your release? Of course—of course 'twill no' be immediate."

"Eh?"

She shrugged, avoiding his eyes now and glancing around the

cell. When her gaze did return to his, it looked over bright. "I mean to hold ye hostage for a time. In better conditions than this, ye understand."

He gaped at her.

"'Tis quite often done, is it no'? An assurance of good will. Mostly 'tis a noble's son who is taken and held, but I do no' see but ye will do fine, since Rory MacLeod holds ye in favor."

A second wave of emotion arose. This one contained a measure of relief. She did not intend to send him away. Not right away.

"Tell me, Farlan MacLeod, will Rory be open to such an offer?"

"I do no' ken."

"If I lay his choices out before him—either I kill ye outright and send him the pieces, or I hold ye hostage as an assurance o' a truce between us—will he accept?"

If *she* laid the choices before Rory. Again, she did not mention her father who, were he at all able, would have a say in any such negotiation.

Iain MacBeith must be dead. She was not willing to admit it. She needed time to consolidate her power as chief.

Did she mean to lead the clan on her own? Or did she need the respite in order to find a husband, one who would lead at her side?

The mountainous Alasdair, perhaps.

But nay—nay. With every fiber of his being, Farlan knew that should not be.

"Well?" she prompted when he did not speak.

"'Tis a canny scheme. I can no' honestly predict how Rory may respond. I doubt he has ever heard such an offer. Or been faced wi' anyone like ye."

"He will no' want to see ye killed."

"He will no'." Farlan thought about it. "He may just reject the offer and continue an attack. Batter your gate and your walls till ye give in and hand me over."

"I will no' give in. If I send this message, I maun mak' it clear that should he attack us again, ye will be the first to die."

That made Farlan look at her with new attention. All the conflicting emotions inside him seemed to come together in one, with all his force behind it, the way an arrow looses from the bowstring.

"And could ye follow through on that, Moira MacBeith?" He approached her slowly, one step at a time. "Could ye kill me?"

She drew herself up, watching him approach. She stood tall by the time he reached her, and her eyes glowed like two jewels.

Gently, gently, he reached out and touched her chin. For an instant, she stiffened before easing into his touch, her lashes sweeping down and up again.

Still more gently, he leaned in. Closer and then closer till he could see the freckles on her skin. Smell the fragrance coming off her hair. He no longer navigated by wisdom or any star he knew. This was pure faith.

His lips brushed hers once. Twice. The third time they alit, and the arrow of his emotions found its mark. *Home.*

She made a small sound of protest that soon softened into something else, all her resistance melting in a surge of heat. He felt it go, and felt the surge of her desire. Her lips molded to his even as she stepped closer, as her fingers curled around his forearms. Their mouths quested for one another gently and tentatively, inquiring and finding answers.

The instant she drew away from him, he let her go. She did not retreat far, and her gaze clung to his.

"Impossible," she whispered.

"Aye, so." And yet it was. He could not deny this. He did not think she could either.

She stared into his eyes. "You are the last man, the very last I should desire." When he did not speak, she stumbled on, "I do no' need this complication. And ye, o' all men, the one who—"

She caught herself before she admitted it, that her father was dead. That he, Farlan, had struck the blow that killed him.

Impossible, aye.

Her eyes filled with tears. "I do no' want to kill ye, Farlan MacLeod, or see ye killed. But if I canna gain Rory's agreement, if he continues to attack us, I may have to."

"Once ye kill me, Moira, ye will ha' nothing wi' which to bargain."

"I ken."

"And Rory will be twice as angry."

"Help me." She reached out again and touched his arm. "Tell me how best to approach him."

Farlan turned away from her. He had his own loyalties to consider, and his friendship with Rory went deep. Yet he'd never felt toward anyone what he felt for this woman. He loved Rory like a brother. He cared deeply for his clan. And aye, he'd loved Ainsley for her sweetness and beauty.

All that faded before what he felt for Moira MacBeith. He did not understand it. Neither could he deny it.

"Ye said," she appealed to him desperately, "ye said ye would mak' the crossing to my side."

So he had.

He turned to the basket which contained the flask, one made of silver. Picking it up, he saw it bore the MacBeith crest. It must have belonged to her father.

When he unstopped it and took a drink, it felt symbolic. Symbolic and significant. The drink flowed down his throat like liquid fire and steadied him as he turned back to face her.

"Bring me ink and writing paper. Let me word the message mysel'."

Chapter Twenty-Seven

"**Y**OU WILL HA' to let me read it before 'tis sent." Moira spoke nervously and paced the limited space of the cell, which no longer looked very much like a prison.

A small desk and stool had been brought in. Parchment and ink. Farlan now sat there laboring over his words with painstaking care.

He glanced up at her. "Ye are able to read and write?"

"Aye." Da had insisted upon it, saying his daughters might need the skill someday, perhaps for a marriage contract. A woman should ken what's being written about her, and understand her fate.

She felt grateful now. She wanted every measure of control she could exert, because events seemed to be slipping away from her.

She'd asked herself over and over again whether she erred in extending to this man a measure of trust. In kissing him, by God. She condemned herself for it.

At the same time, she wanted—she truly wanted—to kiss him again.

She'd never experienced anything like to that kiss. Hadn't known anything like to it might exist. The heat of it had thawed something inside her, a hard frozen knot of emotions held seemingly forever in abeyance.

She hadn't suspected she'd been holding on to all that. But och, the joy of letting it go!

It caused the word *destiny* to echo in her head again. But och, why this man?

"There now," he murmured, and shoved the paper toward her on the desk top. "Read it."

Without thinking, eyes fixed on the sheet, she sank to her knees beside him. It placed her, aye, in a vulnerable position. But she did not think he'd hurt her.

As soon as he would hurt himself.

The message was not long. She puzzled over the words, and he waited, watching her quietly.

He told Rory he was being treated well, and was willing to remain at MacBeith as a hostage for the time being. His captors wished for a truce and a cessation of hostilities.

If ye attack again, I will be slain.

She looked up and found Farlan watching her, his gaze steady.

"Is that as ye wished?"

She nodded.

He tapped the paper. "It has the advantage o' Rory knowing my hand. We were educated together and he canna mistake my scrawl."

"Thank ye," she whispered. "I ken fine ye do no' ha' to do this—"

The corners of his mouth quirked. "Nay. I could just let ye— or more accurately, I suppose your ghillie, Alasdair—slit my throat."

Miserably, she nodded.

He caught her hands and drew her toward him, so she leaned halfway into his lap. "Do no' look so dejected, Moira. I want to stay."

"Do ye?"

"You are here, are ye no'?"

This time, the kiss lent a heat that scorched her. Even though she was prepared for it, it shook her to the core. Her hands crept up to his shoulders, fingers sliding over his bandages, and she let the glorious sensations overwhelm her.

She'd been kissed before, to be sure, by the young men of the clan. Some had attempted to be masterful. A few approaches had been fumbling and unsure.

Naught could be more certain than what she experienced now. And nay, Farlan MacLeod did not seek to overmaster her. They met on equal ground.

And och, by all that was holy, she could feel him, the strength that lay within the bone and muscle. The steadiness that so often reflected in his eyes. It summoned in her a measure of respect. With her father as a shining example, she did not admire many men.

She could respect and admire this one. Yet desiring him—him of all others—shook her badly. It made her pull away all too soon and regard him with somber attention.

"Whom do I send wi' the message? Who that will come back again? A party? Should I go mysel'?"

His hands came back out and cradled her shoulders. "Nay. No' you."

"You do think Rory will slaughter the messenger!"

"I hope not. But..." One hand cupped her cheek. "I would take no chances wi' ye."

He leaned forward and kissed the healing cut on her cheek. She turned her face so their lips met again, and went breathless.

"Send your giant o' a ghillie," he suggested then, his eyes gazing into hers.

"Alasdair?"

"Aye."

"I dare not. He is our war chief and I can no' afford to lose him."

She should have said her da, her chief, could not afford it. She was letting the lie slip away from her.

It was incredibly difficult to lie to this man.

"Is there someone else you trust?"

She scrambled to her feet. "Aye, scores o' men. None I care to lose."

"Rory might be quick to anger, though no' so much these days as when we were younger. He has learned a measure o' discipline. But he will no' kill the messenger if he thinks 'twill cost my life."

"Ye think not?"

Farlan nodded gravely.

"I can send Bean. He's smart and reliable." But och, she was fond of the man. And he was set to marry soon. The thing was, her men were not just warriors to her. They were individuals with lives of value.

Och, how had Da ever done this? Each choice she made could have consequences for someone.

She, and her own desires, must come last. That was, if she allowed herself any such desires.

She turned her gaze on Farlan MacLeod and admitted her desire for him had taken on a life of its own.

"I will speak wi' Bean, ask him if he is willing to go. Should he prove reluctant, I will ask for volunteers. Do I need to send more than one?"

"I would send a couple o' men at his back. No more than two, else Rory may see it as a threat."

Moira nodded. How odd, how strange to be taking council from the very man who had struck down her da.

"I maun go," she said hurriedly. Getting away from him and out of his influence should help her think more clearly. Mayhap not, though—because his presence now seemed to accompany her everywhere she went.

With the letter in hand, she hurried out past the guards, who shot her measuring glances. She should go to Da's room, supposedly to confer with him, or folk would grow suspicious. She should confer with both her sisters before she undertook this thing. What if it all went wrong? She would be wholly responsible.

She could not keep Farlan MacLeod here with her, however she might want to. She could not outfit for him a comfortable prison and hope they might—what? Have a legitimate relationship? A friendship? Something far more?

Eventually, she would have to send him back to MacLeod.

A shocking thought occurred to her: not before she had him. Had him in her bed.

She was twenty-four years old and had never lain with a man. As the eldest of MacBeith's daughters, she'd, aye, been courted back when she was a girl. After Arran died, she put all that away from her and concentrated on what must be done. On replacing for Da some of what he had lost.

Now—now Alasdair came to her proposing a marriage, one that would no doubt strengthen the clan. One she honestly could scarce imagine.

And here was she, wanting the enemy.

As if her thoughts had conjured him, she nearly ran into Alasdair. He wore his sword and his armor, along with a scowl, and looked like he'd just come down from the battlements.

Since he'd spoken to her of marriage, their relationship had been awkward. Now he raked her with a dark look and fastened on the sheet in her hand.

"Moira? Wha' is that?"

"I ha' prepared a message to send to Rory MacLeod, asking for a truce."

Alasdair backed up a step, precisely as if she'd struck him in the chest.

"A—what?"

"Just a temporary peace until we can tell our people—tell them the truth, and gain our feet."

"'Tis a show o' weakness." He did not shout the words as he likely wished, but groaned them at her.

"'Tis a show o' strength, Alasdair. We ha' the upper hand because we hold his favored companion."

"I told ye, we canna negotiate wi' that monster."

"Ye did tell me, aye." She gazed at him as steadily as she dared. "But 'tis I maun make the decision."

He swore, which shocked her a little. A woman who associated with warriors, who trained and fought beside them, heard her share of cursing. Sometimes the words slipped out of her own mouth. But Alasdair had always been careful not to use coarse speech around her.

Aye, they were all overwrought.

"Ye wrote thon monster a letter?"

To Moira's own consternation, she flushed. "I did no' write it."

Alasdair's expression turned thunderous. "He did? Thon beast who—"

"He is cooperating wi' me."

Alasdair snatched the paper from her and glowered at it. He could not read, but he looked angry enough to shred the paper.

"Ye canna trust him, lass. He is a MacLeod."

The thing was, she did trust Farlan MacLeod.

"I can use him," she told Alasdair. "That's what matters now. Please gi' that back to me."

He handed it over along with a dire pronouncement. "Ye be making a mistake, Moira MacBeith. I only hope it does no' cost ye dear."

Chapter Twenty-Eight

I N THE END, Moira did send Bean, backed by two of their most experienced warriors, both stout and steady men. All three had agreed to go, though that did not make it easier. She knew the girl to whom Bean was betrothed, named Ciara. She knew the families of the other two men.

She sent them off into danger, and then she waited.

Waiting, as she well understood, was a particular form of torture. This torture played out from the top of the walls where half the guard watched the progress of their small party across the glen.

She'd sent them in the morning of a clear day that allowed a good view. From the battlements, Moira could see the dark, distant building that was the MacLeod stronghold. She could see the light washing over the crouching hills from the east, and the glorious beauty of this place she loved.

What would she do if Rory MacLeod killed her messengers on sight? Farlan swore he would not, and she had to trust Farlan.

She had to trust Farlan. Oh, sweet heaven!

Alasdair stood on one side of her, watching the progress of their party. She could feel his disapproval, much the way she used to be able to feel Da's, though Da had never been sullen.

Saerla stood on her other side, and Moira did not much like the emotions coming off her either. Moira longed to ask her, *Have ye Seen something?* Perhaps, she told herself, Saerla was merely feeling tense like the rest of them.

It would take hours, perhaps the whole of the day, for their party to return. Longer, if Rory MacLeod took time to ponder his answer.

"I tell ye," Alasdair muttered, "this is a mistake and I do no' like it."

Aye, he had told her. And told her.

In an icy tone, she said, "Had we taken the prisoner's corpse to his chief's door, as ye wished, he would ha' killed the messengers for certain."

"I did no' say tak' the prisoner's corpse to his door. Merely slit his throat, dump him in a boat, and ferry him across. Then leave him on the other side for they MacLeod bastards to find."

"Rory would retaliate."

"Aye, so. Battle, I understand. These—these subterfuges, no' so much."

Nor did Moira, to be truthful. A straightforward woman, she preferred honesty. Yet just look at her now.

Saerla said, "Bean came to me this morning when I *sat* wi' Da, before they left. He asked me if he might ha' just a moment or two wi' his chief, in case he did no' make it back again. To swear his fealty once again."

Moira gasped in dismay.

"I had to tell him nay. Moira." She leaned close, her voice no more than a whisper. "When are we going to be able to tell—"

"Soon. Once we ha' this truce wi' MacLeod, I will make an announcement. We will ha' a chance to grieve."

Saerla captured Moira's gaze, her misty blue eyes tormented. "Ye promise it? I canna' go on this way."

Alasdair growled, "I say we get it all out in the open. Slit the prisoner's throat. Toss him out on the turf, and tell our folk why."

Slit the prisoner's throat. Moira could not let that happen. For whom was she fighting now? Could she protect everyone for whom she cared?

To Saerla, she said, "You ha' said your prayers up on the rise?"

"Sister, I have."

"And wha' says he—he who lies there? Does he approve or disapprove wha' I do?"

Again, Saerla looked at her, her gaze otherworldly. "He says he loves ye."

Aye well, Moira knew that. In her world, it had always been a certainty. Such love was a gift, and one, it seemed, that did not end in the grave.

When she could no longer stand keeping watch from the battlements, she went down, reminding herself she had a horde of tasks awaiting her. She could not possibly go to see the prisoner again. Talk would arise over the frequency of her visits. Already the guards looked askance when she turned up there.

Was she disloyal in giving her attention to the MacLeod? But she could not help—

"Moira!"

She came to herself to find Ciara standing in front of her. Ciara's older sister, Meghan, now long wed and with a crop of bairns, had been one of Moira's friends when they were younger.

Ciara, a pretty girl with fair hair, now looked half wild with distress.

"My Bean," she said in a rush. "Why did ye choose to send him? Why him, above all others? We are soon to wed."

"I ken, Ciara. I did no' like having to send him, or anyone."

"I asked Master Alasdair whether he or Chief Iain made the choice. He said you did!"

"Aye. Wi' my father laid up still—"

"Could ye no' ha' sent anyone else?"

"I chose Bean because I trust him, Ciara."

"I ken that. 'Tis what Bean said when I begged him not to go."

She'd begged him.

"He said, 'She trusts me, my heart. How can I refuse?'"

Och, what had she done? Sent brave, loyal men out perhaps to their deaths.

"Listen to me," she said, speaking as much to reassure herself as the frantic girl, "he will return. And wi' a truce that will gi' us some precious breathing space."

"You promise me that?"

She could not promise. Too many promises asked, and too many lies told.

"I do no' ken for certain what Rory MacLeod will do. I hope our men return safe and sound."

"Hope? Wha' is that? I hoped for a marriage wi' him and a house full o' bairns. Now ye ha' taken that from me."

Moira seized Ciara's hands. "I ha' not, lass. Ye maun ha' faith."

"Faith is a fine thing, aye. Just know, Moira MacBeith, if I lose my Bean, I will ne'er forgive ye."

The lass ran off crying. A wave of emotions rose within Moira's heart in response to Ciara's tears. If that happened, how would she ever forgive herself?

⋙⋘

HE'D PACED THE severely limited space of his prison, wondering what might be happening beyond its walls. Now that he regained some health, and with it some strength, the confinement and the isolation looked to drive him mad.

He thought too much, confined this way. He thought about Rory and what must be in his head. How would Rory react when he got Farlan's letter?

He would not like the prospect of leaving Farlan here as a hostage, or of any sort of truce with MacBeith. Farlan had watched Rory chaff when Camraith, refused to act, declaring his father might have crushed the MacBeiths at any time, taken their land, and been done with it.

"Sure," he'd ranted to Farlan, and to his cousin, Leith, all too often drawn into the discussions, "there might be uprisings here and there, a few men who think they could defy us. A small number o' men are soon put down."

Leith, though, had refused to condone it. "The MacBeiths are an ancient and proud people, son," he always told Rory. "They held this land even before our folk came o'er the water. No need to humiliate them."

Aye, and Camraith had not been the man to humiliate anyone for the sake of it. Farlan believed Camraith's words still echoed in Rory's head.

But the old chief was dead and Rory was more or less off the chain.

He would be shocked that Farlan had cooperated with their enemies and written such a letter. He would be angry. If only Farlan could sit down with him and explain the whole of it, he might coax him to reason. Attempt to explain something he himself did not completely understand. His feelings for Moira MacBeith.

Keeping his thoughts from her was hardest of all. More, far more than the waters of the loch divided them. Yet her face danced perpetually in his mind. Not a soft face, for a woman. Uncompromising, with eyes that could in an instant turn to ice. An uncommon beauty. One that, for him, eclipsed all others.

By the holy, sweet God, what had happened to him?

Distraught, he took a draught from the flask she'd left, which he'd very nearly drained. Being shut away here would drive him to madness.

A rattle at the door spun him to face it. Was it Moira? Had something already gone wrong with the plan?

She came in with a rush and a murmur of instruction for the guards. Almost before the door was closed once more, she flew across the floor, her boots clattering on the hard-packed dirt, and straight into Farlan's arms.

He wrapped those arms around her and drew her in tight.

Protecting, sheltering. As he did, something deep and powerful happened to his heart. This was not a woman to seek or accept refuge easily. Yet she came to him.

To him.

What had for days been an impossibility between them became a sudden truth. In that moment, naught else mattered. Not who she was, or who he was. Not what either of them had done in the past. The sense of belonging overshadowed all.

"Farlan." She spoke only his name. He could feel her trembling, feel her heart beat against his chest like the flutter of a wild bird. Such a fragile pulse in a woman so strong.

"There now," he crooned. He'd been tender with no one since Ainsley's death. There had been times he'd felt sure he would never again experience tenderness.

Now it swamped him. He bent his head to hers, breathed in her dizzying scent, and slid his lips across her cheek in a gesture of comfort. Across the wound that marked her skin, a symbol of her courage.

She burrowed closer, wrapped her arms around him, and grasped the back of his tunic, holding hard like a woman fearful of drowning. For several moments, she just clung to him and breathed before lifting her face to his.

He fell into her gaze and lost himself. It felt as if he swam through the stormy blue waters of her eyes, through the layers of her emotions. Fear, doubt, hope. Belief. Well enough. A strong swimmer, he was not afraid of the storm.

He should ask her what had brought her to him again so soon. He should speak words of encouragement.

He kissed her instead.

And aye, aye mayhap that was what she needed after all— mayhap 'twas for this she had come to him. Because her need came rushing at him, her yearning. Their lips met with a rush of wonder, and hers parted beneath his, inviting him in. Their tongues met and twined together. His Moira, it seemed, was a woman to kiss, and not just be kissed.

His Moira.

Surely she was that at this moment, here in his arms. Clinging to him and trembling with the heat rising to consume them both. But ah, it was more than just heat—lust, as he'd discovered in the past, was nothing more than a flash of flame. This was a claiming from which he might never escape.

Not even if she set him free right now. If she sent him back to MacLeod with his sword in his hand. He would never escape what he felt for this woman. He did not want to.

He broke the kiss and captured her face between his palms so he could gaze at her. He never wanted to look at another face for all his life.

"Wha' is it, Moira?" *Mo gradh*, my heart. He did not add the last two words. He felt them.

"Ne'er mind. Kiss me."

Rash, heedless, wonderful. What could he do but obey?

Chapter Twenty-Nine

"I FEAR THE party o' men I ha' sent to MacLeod will no' return. And then what shall I say to those who love them? Farlan, tell me again that Rory MacLeod will no' slay them all out o' hand."

They sat together on Farlan's pallet, side by side with their fingers linked. To be sure, Moira was not entirely sure she could leave go of him if she tried. Even though her mind told her she should not remain here, she did not know how to be anywhere else.

She needed the feel of the man, the steadiness that dwelt inside him, and the deep assurance that lay in his company. He answered a wanting she'd never dreamed might exist. It frightened her, but not so much as the prospect of trying to exist away from him.

And och, by God, she craved the taste of him. If she had her druthers, she'd strip him naked and use a month's worth of nights finding out if he felt as good as he tasted.

She glanced into his face, wondering—why him? Aye, he was pleasant to look upon, yet so were a good many men, and that could not explain these feelings. She liked watching the thoughts move in those eyes that lay trapped between long, fringed lashes. Even more, she liked the feeling of rightness he brought to her. Rightness, when it could not be more wrong.

His hands rested in hers, big and callused. His shoulder pressed against hers also, strength like the very rock of Glen Bronach. Perhaps, after all, it did not matter why her heart had fastened on him—only that they were together now, amid impossible circumstances.

"Surely 'tis not your responsibility alone, the fate o' those men? Ye maun ha' discussed it wi' your father the chief beforehand."

That should knock her right back on her heels—it should. Instead, she clutched his hands harder.

"My father—he is no' in a position to lend his opinion."

"Is he no'?" Farlan's brown eyes met hers. Did he guess the truth that she could not admit?

"Nay, so it all falls on me. Alasdair—Alasdair wanted to slit your throat and send ye back dead."

"That would no' go far to soothe Rory's anger."

"So I told him. Besides..." She turned again to him. "I do no' want ye dead."

She kissed him then because she could not help herself. His lips molded to hers. Would their flesh melt together in a similar fashion? Would it feel this natural, if he thrust inside her? Would they then truly be one?

She pushed him down beneath her on the pallet and stretched her body over his. "What good would ye be to me dead? I could no' do this." She kissed the angle of his jaw, covered by beard. "Or this." The side of his throat.

"Moira—"

"Hush. Gi' me this." She needed these few moments. She needed him so she could face the world.

"By God, woman."

Aye, she was a woman. She did not often play at it anymore. But he made her feel so, afire and ripe for plucking.

Her fingers, unexpectedly deft, worked open the front of his tunic. Warm hair and flesh lay beneath. Scars, and the shoulder she'd brought to torment. She dropped kisses on it all.

"Moira." He ran his fingers up into her hair, raised her face from his chest and gazed into her eyes. She lost her breath at what she saw there. "Lass, ye maun be careful. I care far less for mysel' than for ye."

"I ken."

"I believe—" He steeled himself visibly. "I believe ye should come here less often. Ye rest in a perilous position."

He had no idea. Once the news of her da's death was made public, and if word got out that this man had struck the blow to end his life, she would have all she could do to keep him safe.

"Aye," she agreed, and kissed him again. "But just now, I do no' care."

Dangerous ground. Yet she reveled in these few moments she stole. Lips bestowed caresses and fingers slid across warm flesh. She wished he would touch her as she touched him, slide his fingers inside the bodice of the plain gown she wore. He did not, though she could feel him hard beneath her, and could taste his desire.

When she cuddled close, burrowed into him for reassurance, he wrapped his arms around her just as if they'd been together this way a thousand times.

She whispered, "Wha' do ye think Rory will do?"

He considered on it before answering. She could hear the quiet breaths coming in and out of him, and his heart beating strong beneath her ear.

"He will be angry at first. But he will stop and think before acting out o' hand. If he agrees to the temporary peace—"

She lifted up and looked at him. "I will get ye out o' this cell then, for ye will be an honored guest o' sorts, will ye no'? I will find ye quarters and we may see one another more often while the agreement holds."

"Moira, Moira—" His hands caressed her back. "Wha' will your people say?"

"That I am mining ye for information, no doubt. That I am keeping the agreement I ha' made."

"Someone may well stick a dirk in my back."

"Do no' say that."

"'Tis true."

"Hostages ha' been held before, men of importance, which is wha' ye are."

He said nothing, and she protested what she saw in his eyes. "I tell ye, Farlan, 'tis our chance to be together." Their only chance. "We can consult by day." She pressed a kiss to his lips. "Be together by night, if we are careful."

Would he reject her? But nay. His lips clung to hers and his hands, at her back, bestowed caresses.

"Ye promise to stay wi' me, Farlan MacLeod?"

"Ha' I no' already sent the letter?"

"But—but ye will no' attempt to escape, should I afford ye a measure o' liberty?"

His gaze met hers, solemn. "I will no' leave ye, Moira MacBeith. But go fro' me now, else your guards will grow suspicious."

"Aye." It took another three kisses before she could pull away from him and scramble to her feet.

Not until she stood outside in the cool air did a measure of sanity return. Was her plan too wild, too dangerous? Could it possibly succeed? She had never before tried to scheme for anything she wanted.

Now she wanted two things with equal fervor. To guard the safety of her clan and to be with Farlan MacLeod.

She feared she could not have both, no matter how she schemed.

RORY WOULD BE furious when he received Farlan's message. No doubt of that, Farlan thought, pacing the floor of his cell after Moira left. He would suppose the letter had been written under duress. He would not easily believe Farlan cooperated voluntarily with his captors. He would never suspect he did so for the sake of a woman.

Rory knew him better, and knew how losing Ainsley had hurt him, how deep went the wound. Rory had suggested a score of times that Farlan look to fill the gaping hole in his life with another woman. Due to the ongoing troubles between MacLeod and MacBeith, there were plenty of young widows to be found, and not a few of them turned their eyes in Farlan's direction.

Farlan had steadfastly refused. For him, the physical release was not worth risking his heart again. He'd learned the lesson early, that what was loved could easily be lost. Best not to love at all.

Moira MacBeith had taken him unawares, overwhelmed him, and left him with no choices. He'd never dreamed desire of the spirit could be so much deeper than that of the flesh.

Not that he did not want her. The joining of their bodies would be a holy thing. One from which there would be no going back. But he could not go back from this anyway. He'd written the letter, had he not? He'd agreed to stay with her. He'd made the commitment.

Waiting, though, was hard, and as he'd told Moira, he could not be sure what Rory would do. The man could be hot-headed at times, though aye, since Camraith's death, he'd honed himself to focused determination. He wanted to achieve his goal, and would let nothing get in his way.

Except, perhaps, the life of his best friend.

Chapter Thirty

"THEY COME. THEY come!"

The cry sounded from the walk above the gate and caught Moira in mid stride. A day and a night had passed since the departure of the party to MacLeod, and in her heart she'd begun to doubt they would return at all. She had sent three of her good and trusted men to their deaths.

Everyone she met believed that—she could see the truth of it in their eyes when they stopped to talk with her, to worry and question. Was it true she had asked for a truce? With Rory MacLeod, the monster. He ate babies, you ken, for his breakfast.

She received a thousand suggestions. "If our men do no' return, ye should haul that prisoner up to the battlements and slay him there. Bathe in his blood."

Ah well, the days of them bathing in the blood of their enemies were long gone. Were they not?

Those she met also asked after her father in an uneasy manner that argued they wished he'd grow well enough to keep Moira from her wild schemes. When she encountered either of her sisters, they said folk asked them the same. So far, Fiona had kept strum. But they would have to tell the truth soon.

"Now she heard the call and her head turned even as her heart leaped in her breast. She was moving toward the gate without conscious thought, her feet stumbling on the stones.

153

For a day and a night, she'd kept away from the prisoner, even though she longed to see him. She kept away because she did not trust herself and because so many eyes rested upon her. But as she climbed the steps to the parapet, her thoughts flew to him.

Did their party return whole? And what answer did they bring? What would it mean for Farlan MacLeod?

If it came to the worst, if their men returned with an outright declaration of war from MacLeod, could she protect him? And where did she owe her allegiance? To her clan, or to the man she—

Moira would not allow herself to complete that thought.

Up on the ramparts, she met Alasdair, there ahead of her. The big man appeared distraught and shot Moira one burning look before returning his gaze to the distance.

A beautiful day it was, in Glen Bronach. Not yet noon, the sun arced high overhead, playing at ducking in and out from rafts of fair-weather clouds. The wind up here blew strong, and Moira planted both her palms on the top of the wall before leaning out to look.

"They ha' nearly reached the loch," said someone beside her. It was Eddis, an older member of the guards. "Ye can see, Mistress, they are three."

"Aye." A relieved breath whooshed from Moira. "I am going out to meet them."

"Nay." Alasdair's hand came up and clamped her arm. "'Tis no' safe. What if MacLeod sends a horde o' his men after them? It could be a trap."

"Then I shall don my leathers and my sword before I go." Their eyes met and she tossed her head. "Come wi' me, if ye will."

Everyone in the stronghold, which included many of those who had agreed to come in from the outlying farms, came pouring out in their wake. Moira saw Calan in passing and said to him, "Guard your prisoner well." If this went badly, God alone knew what would happen to Farlan.

Calan gave her an odd look. Since she'd assigned the prisoner's safety to him, he'd been much on duty, and he'd seen her go in and out of Farlan's cell. But he said nothing.

Outside, the wind seized Moira's hair and freed it from its moorings. Alasdair came at her back, glowering, along with three other men.

Not enough to keep her alive if Rory sent his army. They would have to fight.

But surely there would be cries from the battlements if a force appeared? She glanced back at the stronghold, and the crowd of people on the walls.

The place where she'd been born, and she loved each and every stone.

That love flooded through her as she marched out, filled her with every step upon the green turf. Whispered to her from the flying sky. How could love for any man compare with this braw duty she owed?

But what she felt for Farlan was not love. Not *just* love, she corrected. It was—

Och, she had no words.

The party of three rowed across the loch in the wee boat they'd left on the far side, and Moira's company met them as they disembarked. They appeared hale and hearty, but uneasy in their minds.

Moira turned to Bean. "Are ye well? Did yon MacLeod mistreat ye in any way?"

"Nay, Mistress. We were shut in a room overnight and guarded while himself made up his mind, but he let us out to meet wi' him this morning."

"Och, Ciara will be that glad."

A brief smile touched Bean's eyes.

"And the message?" Alasdair brayed, having no patience for such talk. "Wha' did the MacLeod ay?"

"Naught to us. He sent a letter." Bean dug inside his tunic and brought forth a sheet.

Alasdair made a sound of impatience, and their three guards gathered round. "Wha' does it say, lass?"

Moira accepted the sheet, which the wind promptly fluttered in her hand. "I canna' read it here. Let us go in."

In truth, she wanted nothing so much as to take the missive to Farlan, ask him to plumb its meaning. The last thing she could do.

Folk surged out through the gate to meet them, all asking questions. Ciara came forward and threw herself into Bean's arms. He embraced her fervently.

Wrapped in equal parts relief and anxiety, Moira pushed her way to the main hall, which stood cool and empty.

Saerla followed and Rhian came hurrying behind her. Only appropriate that MacBeith's three daughters should be together for this.

"Leave us, please," Moira appealed to the other faces that looked to push in, and shut the main doors. That left her, her sisters, Alasdair, and the two guards alone.

"Is thon a message fra' the MacLeod?" Rhian asked with dread in her eyes. "Pray read it!"

A beam of bright sunlight shone down from a high window, and Moira carried the letter there. No wind here to ruffle the sheet.

Rory MacLeod had a bold hand, unlike to Farlan's. The ink shone black and the force with which the letters had been made etched deep into the paper.

The sentiments, in contrast, were cold. Rory MacLeod greeted her with scant, icy courtesy. He denounced her actions in holding one Farlan MacLeod, but agreed to him serving as a hostage in order to enforce a truce.

Moira flooded with heat and her heart began to pound up in her ears. There was more.

The truce would endure for the span of thirty days and nights. On the morning of the thirty-first day, Farlan MacLeod would be returned. If MacBeith failed to return the prisoner at that time, or if Farlan MacLeod were harmed in any way, Rory MacLeod vowed to destroy their stronghold and all who dwelled there.

The blood drained from her head, and her heart thudded so she feared she'd fall down.

"What? Wha' is it?" Alasdair roared, and she looked up from the sheet.

"He has agreed to a thirty-day truce, at the end o' which Farlan MacLeod must be returned in good form."

"Thirty days?" Rhian's eyes had gone wide. Saerla said nothing.

It was what she'd asked—a brief respite during which they could find their feet, tell the clan the truth about Da, and find a way to move on without him.

At the end of that time she would have to give Farlan up, or engage in a war she could not win.

With hands that shook, she folded the sheet and glanced at the guards. "I maun tak' this at once to my father."

Why did she even keep up the ruse? But she must until she could decide the best way to tell the truth.

She met Alasdair's dark gaze for a moment. "I will go organize the guard," he said.

"Aye, ye do that." Anything to get him, with his glower, off her back for the time.

He gestured at the sheet in her hands. "Because this may be a trick. The MacLeod may think to pacify us so he can mount a sneak attack."

"So it may." Rory MacLeod owed her no truths. She looked at her sisters. "Will ye come wi' me? To—to Da's chamber."

"Aye, so," Rhian said briefly. She looked as worried as Moira felt.

Fiona would await them in Da's chamber. They would have little chance to speak. And they certainly could not do so on the way, amid the avid clansfolk.

Rhian said, "Surely ye maun mak' an announcement first? Everyone will be wondering."

"Aye." Moira bade Alasdair, "Open the doors."

When he did, she stepped out to meet all the waiting faces. She held the paper high in a gesture of victory.

"We ha' been granted a truce wi' MacLeod. It rests upon the welfare o' the prisoner we hold. We will, o' course, maintain a strict guard in case MacLeod betrays this truce, but I believe 'tis safe for those from the outlying farms to return home."

The word spread the way a boat bobs on water.

"At nightfall, we will all meet here again."

At night fall, she would have to tell them all the truth. And God help her.

Chapter Thirty-One

NIGHT FELL LATE at this time of year, and a soft, gray radiance still filled the air when Moira stepped up to face her people. All the high-flying clouds had cleared away, and the wind had died. Soon, she knew the stars would appear one by one, the jewels of this glen she loved.

Ah, how fortunate she was to have been born here, in this wild and beautiful place. The daughter of a man of valor and a woman of loving generosity. How blessed to have her two sisters standing beside her.

And how unfortunate to have to confess to their folk that she had lied. That the man who, for a score and a half years had defended them against all trouble, was dead.

She'd decided to move the meeting from the hall out here to the forecourt to accommodate everyone. Some few families had already left to travel back home to their farms. Word would soon reach them there.

The others watched her anxiously, their faces filled with doubt and hope.

Doubt and hope. Two emotions that seemed to dominate her days.

She must make this pronouncement, admit for better or worse what she had done. No use dodging it any longer.

Alasdair stood front and center, still glowering. She saw Calan there also, his expression guarded. Friends of Da's were here. People she had known all her life. She'd asked them to trust her. Now she must confess she'd deceived them.

Saerla, standing on one side of her, reached out and seized her hand. Even though she could not see this, Rhian, on the other side, did the same. Moira felt a flash of gratitude.

They stood united. MacBeith's daughters. And was Da's spirit here with them, dancing upon the cooling air? Might she feel him brush his fingers across her cheek? Aye, for where else would he be?

"My people," she called, and her voice carried on the soft air. "I ask ye here for my father's sake, and in my father's stead. I pray ye may listen." She swallowed hard. "Ye ha' all been told that Iain MacBeith was sore injured in the battle that followed MacLeod's last cattle raid, out there in the glen. 'Tis the truth, that. He was sore injured in that battle." She raised her voice higher. "Injured onto death."

Not a sound, beyond a few gasps, broke the ensuing silence. Faces stared up at Moira in her place on the steps, with both dread and incomprehension.

"I tell ye all now, my father, Iain MacBeith, your chief, died that very night. We brought him back fro' the battle, those o' us who fought close beside him. Only my sisters and those o' us defending him on the field knew the truth." She drew a breath. "We lied to ye! I lied to ye, to keep the MacLeods from knowing we had lost a vital part o' our defense. To protect us all till we could achieve this truce."

The paralysis that gripped her listeners broke. Folk cried out in dismay. In protest. In demand.

"But," a man bellowed, "ye've been looking after Himself. The three o' ye have."

"We deceived you in that also." Moira tipped up her chin. "The chief is buried up on the rise."

"Wi' no honor?" a woman screeched. "No' farewell?"

"We will ha' a ceremony for him, we will do that soon. Now

that the clan is safe for the time and we ha' Rory MacLeod's assurance—"

"The accursed MacLeods who killed him!"

It all broke lose then. The horror and dismay. The terrible grief.

Moira stood clutching her sisters' hands and let it break over her. She'd known this would be bad. So bad as this? Nay.

Women sobbed and some of the men also, tears running free down their faces. There were lamentations and questions, which Moira sought to answer as she could.

There were demands for the MacLeod prisoner to be hauled out and slaughtered in prompt retaliation.

"We canna do that," Moira stated, barely able to make herself heard over the clamor. "Listen to me."

"Tak' the bastard up to our chief's grave and wet tha' holy ground wi' his blood."

"Send his haid back to his chief. To hell wi' his truce!"

"We canna do that. We canna. Listen to me. Please!"

At last, Alasdair stepped up on the stair next to Moira and roared. "Silent! Listen to yer chief."

That sank in. Moira stood and watched—felt—it happen. Men glanced at one another. Women gaped.

Moira felt a rush of gratitude toward Alasdair. He meant to stand strong and back her, no matter what else he felt.

"Chief?" A woman wailed. "But she lied tae us!"

"I did no' want to. I did it to keep ye safe. I will do whatever I must to keep this clan whole and strong."

"That is Iain MacBeith talking," cried one of the older men.

Another protested, "A woman? As our chief?"

Rhian spoke. "Since our brother, Arran's death, Moira has stepped up to guard this holding, and us. She filled the place at our father's side. Who better?"

They muttered over that. Moira could not get a feel for whether or not they approved.

"Ye, Alasdair MacBeith, will ye stand at her side?"

Alasdair glanced at Moira and she saw the reflection of his marriage proposal in his eyes. He had been right. The clansfolk would accept her leadership more readily if it came backed by Alasdair's strong sword.

He said, "Where else would I be? I am to the death Iain Mac-Beith's man. And that means his daughter's after him."

"We want vengeance! We need to make war on MacLeod!"

Moira raised both her hands. "We ha' a treaty for the span o' thirty days and nights, one by which we maun abide. During that time, no harm can come to the prisoner, upon whose welfare that treaty rests."

More cries arose, ugly with hate.

"You expect us to stand meek and quiet when they ha' slain our chief? He we loved?"

Moira's eyes filled with tears. "It will give us time to prepare our weapons. Our defenses and our supplies. If war comes—"

"When war comes!" someone shouted.

"We will be ready. No' helpless and no' at a disadvantage."

"We want Rory MacLeod's head on a pike decorating these walls, in revenge."

"So do I," Alasdair returned. "But Mistress Moira is right. To accomplish that, we maun be strong."

"Tomorrow," Moira sang out, "will be a day o' mourning. We will go up on the rise and raise a cairn there. We will honor Iain MacBeith as he deserves."

She stepped away from her sisters then, down into the crowd among her folk, only vaguely aware that Alasdair remained at her back. She answered questions.

When, just, did the chief die?

Did he name ye his successor before he passed awa'?

"He did no." Her da had said nothing of the succession. In fact, remembering that nightmare journey home, she could remember him saying naught at all. She could not mark the moment he had died.

"There was no time," she said now, "for him to name me."

But whom else? She did not say that. Nor did she mention that it had been their prisoner's blow—that of Farlan MacLeod—that had cost the chief his life.

The truth of that might get out. The other four who knew might feel, with the restraints on their tongues now lifted, they should tell.

They would want revenge then, Iain MacBeith's people. How was she to protect Farlan and keep him in safety among them?

She spent over an hour answering questions and listening to threats and grievances. The warriors felt insulted by the truce she'd bargained. Did she no' think they could defend their own lands? She gave what answers she could and spread reassurance. To be sure, she did not doubt the strength of their swords, or their hearts.

At last, Rhian came and took her once more by the hand to lead her away.

"Come, sister. Before ye fall down."

Rhian carried enough authority, as the undisputed queen of the stronghold, that the others fell back. Even Alasdair, who'd stuck to Moira all the while, stepped away.

Only Fiona, her face streaming with tears, and a silent Saerla followed them back to Da's chamber.

This had become a place of privacy, a precious commodity, as well as of grieving. Fiona had been sleeping there.

Rhian now seated Moira on the convenient bench and commenced rubbing her hands. "Sister, be ye all right?"

"I do no' ken. I ha' been dreading telling them. I knew they would be upset, but 'twas worse than I feared."

"Aye, so." Rhian knelt in front of her. "What ye need is ease and some sleep. I will mix ye a draught."

"I want none o' that." What she needed was to see Farlan MacLeod. She'd had no chance yet to go to him. He must be half mad with wondering about Rory's answer to his letter.

"The worst o' it is done," Rhian went on. "Tomorrow, as ye say, we will honor him, and then try to go on."

Fiona wept harder. Rhian directed a fierce look at her. "Why do ye weep so? Ye already knew he was gone."

"This—wi' everybody else knowing—makes it real. I was putting the truth o' it awa' from me."

Perhaps they had all been doing that, Moira thought while they kept the terrible secret. Now she had nowhere to hide.

Chapter Thirty-Two

FARLAN COULD HEAR a limited amount through his door of sound and commotion. The general noise of the settlement, which came and went with the hours, dying away almost completely at night. The muted conversations of the guards and the rattle of bones when they diverted themselves with a game.

Sound also filtered in between the walls and the thatched roof. A while ago, he'd heard a great uproar—shouting and raised voices.

Had the party Moira sent to MacLeod returned? Had Rory rejected her offer? Did they prepare for attack?

He thought he'd go mad with wondering about it. He considered pounding on the door and asking the guards, but his pride would not bend so far. Besides, he did not think they would tell him.

And Moira did not come. 'Twas as if she'd forgotten him.

It entered his mind that she might just have been manipulating him in an attempt to gain his influence with Rory. Perhaps her talk of destiny was mere trickery. Mayhap those kisses meant nothing.

But, nay. He could not accept that. He could not be so deceived. What he felt for her was real and true.

When the guard—the young man who seemed to be so often on duty with him—brought his supper, Farlan fair fell upon him.

"Wha' is happening out there? Is it an attack?"

The youth shook his head. His dour expression did not change. "Nae attack."

"Have the messengers returned?"

The young man gave him a sharp look at that, perhaps wondering what he knew of it. "Aye."

Farlan could scarcely ask what word they'd brought, though he ached to.

Ignoring his supper, he paced as long as he could bear to. Until it grew quiet outside. Then he lay on his pallet with no hope of sleep.

Not until deep in the night, when everyone in the stronghold should be asleep, herself included, did she come. Farlan, who still lay awake, heard a very soft exchange with the guard and the bar lifted.

She stepped in quietly. He was on his feet by then and stood unmoving. So powerful were the feelings that came rushing, both doubt and certainty, they held him still.

She wore her night clothes with a dark gray cloak thrown over all. The soft fabric of her nightdress swirled around her feet, which were bare, and her glorious hair hung loose.

Seeing her so, a spear of pure love pierced him.

She should not come to him this way. It was highly improper. Perhaps she needed to tell him all had gone awry and his life was forfeit. Perhaps she'd never intended to save him.

For the span of two score heartbeats they stood so, regarding one another. Then Moira flew forward, straight into his arms.

"Moira, och, Moira." He drew her close, gathered her in, and the terrible tension inside him eased. He no longer cared what had happened out there, only that she was here with him.

She burrowed in hard. He felt the warmth of her through the nightdress and cloak, smelled the scent of her hair. If ever he deserved heaven, he wanted it to be this.

"I tried to get here sooner," she breathed into his neck. "I could no'."

"Rory—he sent his answer?"

"Aye. Gi' me a moment."

She held to him and he to her, and the terrible tension drained from her slowly. Before she left his arms, she lifted her face and slid her lips across his, and her eyes—her eyes told him all he needed to know.

"Here." She dug inside her cloak and dragged forth a paper. "He sent a letter in turn."

A single poor candle burned on the table, which had been left in place. Farlan went there and spread out the crumpled sheet.

Rory's hand. It caused him a jolt to see it there, bold and dark. Aye, the letters reflected the man.

He pushed his hair out of the way and read, his lips echoing the words.

"Thirty days." He looked up and his gaze met Moira's. "He demands my return then."

"Aye."

"We ha' only thirty days."

Agony that reflected his own invaded her eyes. "Aye."

"I canna—I canna even choose to stay. If I do, he will say ye kept me. If I send another letter, he will say 'tis coerced."

"Would ye? Would ye stay wi' me?"

He did not know. Would he, could he live his life here amid hatred for her sake?

Her eyes held his, and he saw agony there. In a rush, she said, "There is somewhat I must tell ye. My da, our chief, is dead. That blow ye struck on the field, it ended his life. We've been hiding the loss since that night so Rory MacLeod would no' find out before I had that reprieve." She nodded at the paper. "For our safety. We told the clan the truth this afternoon."

Farlan said nothing, and her eyes narrowed. "Ye do no' look surprised."

He made a helpless gesture. "I stuck that blow, Moira. I suspected he was gone, and ye keeping it secret. He died that night?"

"He was gone by the time we carried him home."

"I am that sorry, lass." How, how could she care for him, when he had struck the blow that ended her father's life?

She stepped up to him and took his hands. "I should hate ye for it. I canna."

"Your folk must be raving for my blood."

"We did no' tell them that ye are the one who struck the blow. But Calan knows, and Alasdair. It may well get out."

"I will be lucky to survive thirty days."

Grief flooded her eyes. "I hoped, Farlan—well, I hoped to keep ye still longer."

Farlan glanced at the paper again. "Rory means wha' he says. If I am no' handed over, he will come wi' destruction on his mind."

"So." She reached up and touched his hair, wove her fingers through it. "We ha' only a very short time together."

He put his arms around her and drew her close, but said, "Ye should no' be here, lass. Wha' will your guards say?"

"That I consult wi' ye."

"In the middle o' the night?"

"Better than the truth, that I canna keep away."

He kissed her hungrily, putting all the doubt and worry away from him. They had this one moment, and between them, moments had become precious things.

"I ha' assured your safety for the next thirty days," she told him when the kiss ended. "And your comfort. It seems only right that I should see to that."

➤➤➤◄◄◄

MOIRA UNPINNED THE clasp on her cloak and let the garment fall away. Beneath it she wore only a thin nightdress. Back in her room alone, she'd lain in her bed and imagined how it would feel if Farlan touched her. Ran his broad palms over the delicate fabric, spreading heat, and feeling her body beneath. She wanted his hands on her breasts and between her legs. She fair ached for it.

Now his gaze traveled everywhere she wanted his hands to be, and his expression revealed little.

She pressed up against him and experienced a surge of satisfaction. He might try to guard his reaction to her. The physical response, he could not hide. He wanted her as much as she wanted him.

Lifting her face to his and meeting his gaze full on, she begged, "Touch me."

"Moira." Her name sounded hoarse coming from him. He slid his hands up her back, a firm, gentle caress. Aye, she had known somehow that this man would be gentle with her until her control broke, and his followed. Then it would be wild, a storm of giving and taking.

Surely he could see how she wanted him, glimpse that in her eyes?

His hands continued to move from the plane of her back, around her sides till they cupped her breasts.

And oh, oh, it was far better even than she'd imagined. The heat of him came right through the thin fabric and melted the last vestiges of her restrictions. Her body responded helplessly to his touch. Aye, this was what it meant to be a woman. Despite the fact that she spent half her time in a warrior's leathers, she'd been born for this. *For him.*

"By God, you're so beautiful." His gaze broke with hers and followed the course of his hands. His thumbs found her nipples through the soft fabric and caressed them. They peaked in response.

She kissed him, knowing instinctively it was the only thing to make this moment sharper, keener, better. The taste of him engulfed her, and she nearly cried out in protest when he abandoned her lips, kissed the wound on her cheek, the corner of her mouth, her chin. Moved lower and lower.

His lips quested over her skin, spreading magic. He sank to

his knees, and she gasped. When his fingers fought the fabric of her bodice, she helped him and bared herself.

What followed changed her for life. No man had ever touched her breasts beyond a fleeting, clumsy grope. Certainly no man's lips had ever fastened to her, feasted this way and drawn up her soul by the roots. She'd never dreamed such pleasure might exist.

She buried her fingers in his rich brown hair and drew him closer. She arched her back and offered herself to him, one breast after the other. She wanted to weep at the intensity of the pleasure.

Who would have thought she'd be standing half-clothed within a prison, her damp skin pricking in the cool air, and wanting only—

"More," she implored him.

His mouth remained gentle on her, and yet demanding. She wanted the heat of it everywhere. On her belly, which she longed to bare to him. On her legs that trembled beneath her.

But he stopped and looked up at her, his eyes full of hesitance and regret. "Moira, lass, we canna."

"Eh?" Her breasts felt heavy and full of heat. Her nipples had swollen in his mouth and ached to be there again.

She drew him to his feet, reached under his kilt—a MacLeod tartan, by God—and cradled him in her hands. "I want—" It seemed she had the words for no more.

It seemed she did not need them.

Warmth flooded his eyes. "I ken. I want it too. But no' here, lass. By all that is holy, no' here."

Everything within her protested. The pallet lay right behind her, and she did not care where they lay together. She wanted to be naked beneath him, or straddled on top of him. She wanted him inside her.

"Please, Farlan."

"No' wi' your men listening outside. If it got out wha' we'd done, 'twould destroy ye."

"But—"

"I will not. I value ye too highly."

She gazed into his eyes and beheld the strength of his refusal. For her.

"Aye. Aye, you are right."

She drew the fabric of her nightdress back up over her breasts. Farlan picked up her cloak from the floor and placed it around her shoulders. He refastened the pin with careful fingers.

She gazed into his face, aching for him. "If no' now, then when?"

He shook his head, curled his fingers around her shoulders as if he could not keep from touching.

"Go now. Get some rest." His gaze fell on Rory's letter. "Take this." He leaned close, so his breath brushed her cheek. "Forget this happened."

That, she could never do.

Chapter Thirty-Three

"I WENT UP to the stones early and prayed it would no' rain. I may as well admit, I was keeping watch also for Rory MacLeod's men on the move. Several members o' the guard were there, no doubt for that same purpose."

Moira gave Saerla a sharp look. They'd met once more in Da's chamber, which seemed to have become a kind of meeting place, though neither Rhian nor Fiona was there now. Rhian had gone out to tend those recovering from battle wounds. Moira did not know where Fiona might be.

"Did ye see any? MacLeods on the move, I mean."

"Nay. It seems Rory MacLeod means to keep his word."

"Aye." Just as Farlan said he would. *Farlan.* After last night, Moira scarcely dared think of him. Even though she could do little else.

"And," Saerla rushed on, "'tis a glorious day. 'Twill be a grand send-off for Da."

Moira hoped so. She hoped the ceremony today would provide a measure of healing. God knew they needed it.

"Saerla, do ye think Da—his spirit—will abandon us once we ha' built his cairn? Go on to its eternal rest?" Moira should want that for her da who, heaven knew, had earned it. At the same time, she found knowing a part of him still lingered nearby enormously comforting.

"I do no' ken. I spoke to him while I was up there this morning. Told him how we mean to honor him."

And what would Da think of what had taken place between herself and Farlan last night? The very man who had struck him down.

The one man to whom Moira's heart wanted to fly.

Indeed, she ached to see him again, ached for far more than that, if the truth be told. Da, aye, had spoken of destiny. But did destiny include hot hands and a questing mouth?

Fiona came in the door, dressed in her best. "Folk are asking wha' time we are to go up the rise."

"As soon as the sun is up. I maun set the guard first."

"Alasdair has already done that and says he will stay behind to see to the defenses. I just spoke wi' him." Fiona reached out for Moira. "Lass, ye do no' look well."

"I got little sleep."

"Aye, so. This day will no' be an easy one."

"What of the prisoner?" Saerla asked.

"Wha' of him?"

Saerla gave Moira an unreadable look. "Ye had better strengthen his guard if ye mean to keep him whole. 'Twill be a good time for someone to tak' revenge, while we are all awa'."

Moira's heart leaped. "Why? Ha' ye Seen somewhat?"

Saerla shrugged. "Naught in particular. But 'tis a danger, is it no'?"

"He must be kept alive and well to uphold the agreement with MacLeod." One she hoped to extend. Even after the thirty days passed and Farlan was gone from her.

Gone from her.

"I must go and speak wi' Alasdair."

She found him, as she expected, on the walls, standing with his feet planted wide while staring into the distance.

Saerla was right. The morning fairly sang, golden light flowing in from the east to tinge a sky of clear blue. In the distance, the waters of the loch glittered and a herd of deer moved up the slope beyond.

The very picture of peace.

"Alasdair? Is all quiet?"

"Aye." He did not look at her, which she considered a bad sign. He wore all his weapons and his armor, along with a fierce expression.

"Alasdair, I think ye should attend the farewell today. Ye need to be there."

"Nay. I mean to stay behind and see to the defenses. 'Tis my place, is it no'?"

"Your place is up on the rise beside your chief."

"He would want me here, standing strong. Besides..." He did take a glance at her then. "Ye be my chief now."

"Then stand at my side. I will be up on the rise."

"Wha' o' the guard?"

"Ask for volunteers. On a day so clear as this, lookouts will be able to see if the MacLeods put a foot out from their keep."

He said nothing.

Moira touched his arm. "Alasdair, please. Ye need to be there."

"If ye bid it as my chief, I will come."

"I do so bid."

He turned to face her, a hard emotion she could not quite identify in his eyes. "And, lady chief, if ye might tell me somewhat? Why did ye go to the prisoner's cell in the middle o' the night? Clad in no more than yet nightdress?"

So the guards had spoken to him. Already. Moira should have known they would. It was far too interesting a nugget to hold back.

"'Tis no' proper, lass," he hissed before she could answer. "No' decent."

Moira tossed her head. "I wore my cloak over what I happened to be wearing at the time. I could no' sleep." Truth, that. "And I got to worrying about whether Rory MacLeod would keep to his side o' the bargain. I suppose I went for reassurance.

Farlan knows the man better than anyone else on MacBeith soil."

"Farlan," Alasdair sneered the word, "is a prisoner and should no' be relied upon for advice. Why did ye no' come to me?"

The very idea of approaching Alasdair in his quarters seemed unimaginable. "I am here now." She challenged him. "D'ye think the truce will hold?"

"If it does no'," he spat, "if yon MacLeod lifts one finger against us, I will tak' great personal pleasure in retaliating against the prisoner. He will no' die quick, I promise ye that."

Moira glanced along the battlements. All the guards stationed there watched them.

"Instruct the men, Alasdair, and then come along wi' the rest o' us. For a few hours, let us lay aside the hate."

As MOIRA DISCOVERED, however, when she climbed the rise in company with most of the clan members, the hate was impossible to leave behind. It accompanied them as they went up across the green turf and the rocky scree. It traveled in the hunched shoulders of the men and sounded in the muffled sobs of the women.

Grief, aye. But hate and anger too.

Moira had to remind herself none of them had known before yesterday that their chief was dead. They'd thought him laid up and mending, which had kept him present, his mighty strength still at their head.

She, her sisters, Calan, and Alasdair, had carried that burden longer, had time to begin growing accustomed to it. For the rest of them, the emotions were raw.

Including the hate.

But och, she wanted no part of it here in this glorious place, this holy ground where Da had gone to rest. She stood at the top of the rise beside his poor grave and inhaled that holiness, absorbed the light. He, aye, lay in a humble grave now, but they would make it a grand one. The love of his people would lie in every placed stone, and would remain here with him forever.

She spoke to their people as he might have done, of love and strength, and how one lay in the other. Saerla spoke after her, half singing a prayer, the beauty of which brought hot tears to Moira's throat. She then pressed Alasdair to speak even though he proved reluctant. The big man declared there had never been a chief to match Iain MacBeith, and never would again. A reflection upon Moira, mayhap? Ah, but Alasdair remained angry with her, and the big man's emotions ran deep.

After the speeches, they set to work gathering and placing the stones, of which there was no lack. Moira sent for food and drink to be brought up, and the mood lightened. Chatter and even some quiet laughter could be heard.

She caught Alasdair pausing often to look out over the glen, still on guard, and he was not the only one. Several of the men followed suit. She did herself. Under the bright sun, the glen lay innocent of danger.

If only it could remain so.

More than once, her thoughts turned to the man in the cell down below, and her heart worried for him. Was he safe? Calan was here with the others—she'd caught his eye once, and the look he gave her seemed accusatory.

Her imagination, surely.

At the end, when they were ready to go back down, she located Saerla.

"Well?" she asked her sister. "Is he still here? Da."

Saerla closed her eyes for a moment, hiding the veiled light that always seemed to hover there. "Aye. But he is wi' us also as we go about our lives."

"Good. I shall need that." Moira jerked her head at the clansfolk behind them. "What d'ye suppose they think o' me holding the place o' chief?"

Saerla gave a surprisingly undignified snort. "They will expect ye to wed. A strong man. I ha' heard Alasdair mentioned."

"Nay, not Alasdair." He was not the man who had claimed her heart.

Chapter Thirty-Four

"'TIS IMPOSSIBLE. ALL of it. I do no' ken what I am to do."

Impossible. It seemed as if Moira woke every morning with that word in her head, when she managed to snatch any sleep at all. Not a word she liked to entertain, but she did not know how to escape from it. Most of her existence, so it seemed, now chimed to that word.

She paced the floor of Farlan MacLeod's new quarters. It had been but one of the battles she'd had to fight since taking the place of chief in earnest—that he should be treated as a guest for the duration of his stay with them, and not as a prisoner.

The point had not gone over well. She'd argued it in private meetings with Alasdair and with the elder members of the clan, now a council, and before large gatherings. She'd tried to impress upon the dissenters that treating Farlan MacLeod well assured their safety.

They did not want safety. They wanted to wage war on their enemies across the loch, to destroy. They wanted revenge for the death of their chief.

Five days had passed since they'd built Da's cairn up on the rise. Five days that had flown by while Moira tried to reason with those whose minds were set.

Five days ticked off from her precious thirty.

She turned now and looked at the man with whom she

shared the space. He leaned against the hearth for, aye, his new quarters boasted such. Located at the rear of the hall, and not far from her own, the chamber had an outside entrance where guards could be posted—for his safety only since she did not expect him to try and escape. He had given her his word. She trusted him.

She worried night and day about his safety, that someone would storm this place or slip in at the dead of night and murder him.

Each time she came here, she feared she would step in only to find him lying in his own blood. Then the breath would freeze in her chest. For if somewhat happened to him, how could she go on?

Impossible.

Instead, she always found him looking as he did now, strong and healthy, recovered from his fever and his wounds with his eyes bright, his hair gleaming with vitality. A constant temptation to her fingers and her lips.

She would not touch him. She would not, for that would only make matters more difficult. If she once had him between her thighs where she ached for him, she would want that again, more than she did already.

Instead, it seemed she came here to rant at him, to pour out her trouble and doubt. It could not be a good experience for him, yet, like now, he always listened quietly, letting her pace the floor and rage.

"They ha' formed a council. A bunch o' the elder men who think they can approve or disapprove—at least hold up to criticism—every one of my decisions."

"Surely that is no' unusual."

"Nay, but Da never had to deal wi' such. These men did no' find it necessary when he was in charge. Och, he would meet wi' those he trusted, including Alasdair and me, and tak' advice from his contemporaries, but to be sure they never set themselves up to question him. And I canna help but think this would no' have happened had Arran taken over from Da instead o' me."

Farlan crossed his arms on his chest. The long cut down his left arm had healed badly, and left a scar that showed white against the tan skin.

"They do no' like the use ye are making o' me, or the treatment you afford me."

"Aye." She stopped pacing. "I ha' heard murmurings that Alasdair has come out and admitted he does no' approve o' it either." She frowned. "But I do no' believe he has told, yet."

"Told?"

She lowered her voice. "That you are the one who killed their chief. If that gets out—" She shook her head. "If that gets out, I despair to think how I can protect ye."

He stirred for the first time from his place at the fire. This used to be a fine guest chamber, afforded all the comforts. Aye, a source of resentment.

"You see why I say 'tis impossible," Moira told him bitterly. She held his gaze levelly. "*We* are impossible."

He grimaced and said softly, "We always were, lass."

"Aye." But she'd thought—hoped—if she got him out of his cell, treated him less like a prisoner and more like a guest, she would be able to see him more often. Perhaps have an opportunity to come to him here at night, and spend the dark hours in his arms.

She'd been a fool.

"Perhaps," he said slowly, "ye'd do better to send me back at once to MacLeod."

Nay. She did not speak the word aloud. Merely hearing the suggestion felt like a blow to the gut. Was that what he wanted?

"Then what o' the truce?"

"I might persuade Rory to hold to it, afford ye the rest o' the thirty days to get on your feet."

"Or he might attack immediately." She'd been frantically improving her defenses. Repairing the walls and the gate. Storing supplies. Organizing and increasing the number of weapons. The forge rang night and day.

She needed the time. *She needed him.*

Taking a step toward him, she asked aloud, "Is that what ye want?"

"Ye ken fine 'tis no'. But you might do better wi'out all this resentment my presence provokes. Especially as befits Alasdair."

Aye, and if it did get out that this man had slain Iain Mac-Beith—

Frustration and protest nearly strangled her. "We ha' only a score and five days left. I do no' want to lose ye before that." She did not want to lose him at all.

"Neither do I want ye to lose the good will o' your people by me being here. They see ye gi' me all this." He waved a hand. "They do no' understand why."

"I ha' told them and told them, your safety assures our own."

"Lass, they do no' care for my safety. Ye think they do no' heed ye. Me still standing here whole proves they do."

Aye, and it might explain why Calan and Alasdair had not spoken.

Even given all that, she did not want to send Farlan back early. The very thought had the panic rising.

"If Rory has no' attacked by now, Moira, he will keep to the treaty. But make no mistake, he too will be planning for what comes after, once he gets me back in his hands."

She drew a breath. "Then we maun make the most of the time we ha' left."

Slowly, she approached him. She should not touch. She had promised herself she would not. Surely she was not so weak as to give in.

Half an arm's reach from him, she paused. He did not stir, but watched her with emotions burning in his eyes.

Her chin jerked up. "I want ye before ye go from me, Farlan MacLeod. I want ye at least once."

"Impossible." The word now came from his lips. "The guard would ken. Everyone would."

And he'd sent her from him once before, when she would have stayed. Deep in the night, when she'd bared her breasts for him.

It had been a long while since she'd wanted anything for herself. Since before Arran had died and she'd put aside all hope of achieving ordinary desires.

She wanted this, by God.

A step closer and she could feel his heat. She could smell him, a fragrance that haunted her in her sleep.

"Moira, 'twould be unwise. 'Twould open the door to a whole new crop o' complications."

"Are ye saying ye do no' want me?"

Light flared in his eyes. "I am no' saying that. I am saying I care for ye far too much to have ye."

"But—"

"Moira, think on it."

"I think on little else."

His hands came out and grasped her shoulders. To pull her closer, or push her away? "Wha' if I give ye my bairn, eh? Where would ye be then?"

The chief of a clan carrying her enemy's child. The offspring of a MacLeod. Yet he was not her enemy. He was her breath. Her life.

His eyes darkened. "I will nay do that, Moira. I once before gave a woman I loved my child. It killed her."

A woman he loved. As he loved her? Moira heard little else but that. The word had not yet been spoken between them.

Her mind fumbled over it. Belatedly, she grasped his words.

"Ye loved before? Were ye wed?"

"Aye, we were, as little more than children."

"She died?"

"And the bairn. It taught me there are consequences o' such love."

He lifted his fingers to her hair, stroked the curls that had escaped the plait she wore. "Moira, I would do naught e'er to cause ye hurt or harm."

Ah, and here was a man with a heart. Be he MacLeod or otherwise, that heart beat strongly and fairly. For her?

She closed her eyes an instant, fighting the sensation of his fingers in her hair, and the desire to have them everywhere else. Without opening her eyes, she leaned in to him. Her mouth found his by pure instinct and she whispered, "I canna help mysel'."

His resistance broke as their lips and then their tongues met. His fingers cradled her head as he drew her closer, angled his mouth, and consumed her.

No doubt then about where his desire lay.

Yet it did not take long before he tore his mouth from hers. "Go fro' me, Moira MacBeith. Do no' come here again. Let me serve out my thirty days wi'out this temptation."

"Why?" She stared into his eyes. "Why maun I be denied this one thing?"

He still held her close in defiance of his words. She saw the agony in his eyes, as real as her own.

"Because 'tis deep and dark and dangerous, and could cost ye dear." He removed his hands from her. "Go. Do' no' return here for any reason."

Go. The word echoed in her head even as she gathered herself and turned to do just that. Even as she paused at the door and looked back at him.

It was not fair and it was not just. She'd guarded this place she loved and forgotten to guard her heart.

Chapter Thirty-Five

A LONG TIME had passed since Farlan MacLeod uttered any prayer. Once, as a lad, the words had come easily enough to his lips. He'd spoken prayers before he went to training, that he would succeed at arms. He'd prayed his ma would stop grieving so hard and grow well after his da died. Later, he'd prayed Ainsley would look his way.

He'd prayed, deep in one terrible night, that the midwife might staunch the blood that flowed from his young wife when their wee son was born too soon.

Earnest prayers and frivolous ones. He'd learned that, all too often, they went unanswered, and some time ago he'd left off beseeching an Almighty who did not seem to listen.

He had no business praying now. Yet after Moira left him, he found himself doing just that, sitting on the floor near the fire with his legs drawn up and his head pressed against his knees.

He prayed for strength. Strength enough. For he'd never wanted anything the way he wanted Moira MacBeith.

It should be easy to put the wanting away from him. Desire was just desire and readily overmastered. He'd been denying those impulses since Ainsley died. A man of reason, him. One who thought things through. No victim to his impulses.

Yet Moira shook him. Something about her reached right inside him and yanked on his emotions. He already felt connected to her in spirit. Only imagine if they connected as well in the flesh.

The splendor of that prospect fair undid him. He could almost feel it all. The healing strength of being inside her. The heat and the rightness.

He pressed his head harder against his knees. There was no rightness in any of this. In her keeping him here, a supposed hostage instead of a prisoner. In him cooperating with her, quite likely to Rory's detriment.

His loyalty should be to his friend, not to Moira MacBeith.

Instead, he thought of her—naught but her—all day long. And all night. Worried for her wellbeing. Longed for her conversation and her kisses.

'Twas like an illness.

Was this love? If so, 'twas unlike to any love he'd experienced before. He'd loved Ainsley, aye, and the wee bairn they had made together. Ainsley had been all brightness and pleasure, and his affection for her had been an innocent emotion.

This for Moira was deep and dangerous, just as he'd told her. Inexplicable. Impossible, as she'd said. Could that be considered mere love?

And yet—he meant what he'd told her, that he was willing to cross the gulf between them to be with her. In writing the letter to Rory, he had already breached that gulf.

He owed her that truth. Perhaps he also owed her the words that went along with the emotion, that he loved her. For aye, he could label what he felt as naught else.

It did not mean he could stay with her, did it? They balanced on a precipice. She had given him this comfortable chamber, yet the door remained guarded on the outside. She told him he was at liberty to go out and about the settlement when he wished. She trusted he would not try and escape. Yet if he did venture out, he had no doubt the guards would follow.

He was naught but a prisoner in a finer prison.

He needed to sever these connections between them. To

prevent her from coming to him carrying that look in her eyes, keep her from offering her lips to him, from offering much more. He did not know if he could.

"Please," he beseeched aloud. "Gi' me strength."

She said she wanted him at least once before he went back home. Came out clear and stated it like the honest woman she was. Mayhap they had that in common, that they were both honest.

He could have her in his bed, right here in this room. He had only to capitulate to the desire.

He knew already how she'd taste. He'd feasted on her breasts and damn near lost his mind. And how would she taste down below? Would she throw her legs wide for him, and let him feast there also?

He knew fine and well he could provide her that pleasure without risk of giving her his bairn. He could provide them both untold pleasure.

And as he'd told her, there would be no going back from it. If he thought it would be hard leaving her at the end of the thirty days, having her in his bed first would make it—

Impossible.

He prayed fervently with his fists clenched against the desire and his head pressed to his knees. It brought no relief from his agony.

MOIRA FOUND ALASDAIR on the wall above the gate when she went up there to clear her head after leaving Farlan. The big man, fully armed, leaned on the parapet, gazing into the distance.

Soft the air felt, promising wet. The days moved swiftly into the height of summer, a time when rashes of storms blew in from the sea. They would have rain before nightfall.

"D'ye see anything out there?" she asked Alasdair.

He shook his head. "It seems MacLeod intends to keep his word."

He would not come out and admit that she'd done the right thing, forging a truce with Rory MacLeod. He hated the entire idea of it, and of them holding Farlan hostage.

Farlan. When his name sounded in her head, she could taste him. Desire threatened to swamp her.

"How go the armaments?"

"Well enough. I ha' sent your message to all the outlying places that any young men o' fighting age are welcome to come in and train."

"And the reinforcements to the walls?"

"In hand." Alasdair grunted. "Your father was always careful to keep up wi' that. There was no' much to be done."

"If he comes, Rory MacLeod, he will attack the main gate directly just like before. It needs to be strong."

"'Tis a matter o' *when*, not *if*. He is just waiting to get his man back. I say gi' him back, aye, on the thirtieth day. We did no' say he'd be handed back alive."

"We did. We implied it. 'Tis what's guarding this peace."

"Rory MacLeod will attack us either way, whether his man goes back to him alive or no'. And there is such a thing as justice."

"Justice?"

Alasdair lowered his voice to a rumble. "Ha' ye forgotten Farlan MacLeod killed your da?"

"I have not."

Alasdair raked her with a look. "At times it seems ye must have. Spending a lot o' time, so I hear, wi' our *guest*."

"I seek information from him."

"The way to get that is no' a soft bed and a warm fire. Gi' him into my hands. I'll soon ha' all the details o' Rory MacLeod's defenses."

Moira said nothing.

"In fact, I ha' been thinking," Alasdair went on. "When we return him to his chief, it should be at the head o' our army. Why should we sit and wait to be attacked? We should tak' the fight to him."

There spoke the war chief and no mistake. Quite likely, for the benefit of the clan, Alasdair was what she needed at her side.

"We are no' ready, Alasdair, to carry the fight."

"We will be, by the end o' the thirty days." He turned to face her with a hint of challenge. "If ye hand it over to me."

It. He meant Farlan MacLeod.

"I ha' given my word for his safety."

"I will no' kill him. Yet."

But ultimately, Alasdair wanted Farlan MacLeod dead. How many others among the men did also?

"There is honor involved, Alasdair."

He spat over the wall.

"Always there existed a measure of honor between my father and Camraith MacLeod."

"Camraith is gone, as is your good father. And Rory is a different man entirely."

"He must still possess a measure of honor. He's keeping the truce."

"That will no' prevent me from sharpening our swords."

"No." It should not. "But, Alasdair, is no' peace always better than dying? If we attack, and even if we defend, we will lose warriors. Our men will die."

"Die, aye, for a cause, a braw one. Ye think I am afraid?"

"I do not."

"Moira—" He grasped her arm. "Ye speak o' making use o' the hostage. Why no' make use o' me?" His eyes burned fierce and dark. "I may be your best weapon. Reconsider and wed wi' me, if only for the sake o' the clan."

She should be willing to do that, to sacrifice herself. It had been what she intended to do when Da died—give herself over to MacBeith. She had not wanted Farlan MacLeod then.

In just over a score of days, Farlan would return to MacLeod, and she would be left with nothing.

She nodded. "Let me think on it before I say aye or nay."

"Ye do that, lass, and then tell me wha' the future should be."

Chapter Thirty-Six

THE WIND ON the height blew strongly, and the rain Moira had seen hanging to the west while up on the wall with Alasdair no longer threatened but blew in with a will. She could not see the stones behind her for the gathered clouds. She could spy little of the glen below.

She stood beside her father's cairn and wished with all her being he were here to help her. What would she not give for a few moments conversation with him?

Farlan's life. She would not give Farlan's life.

What was her future life to be? She'd never given much thought to that before. Now, she wanted time that would stretch on into infinity. She wanted to keep Farlan with her. She wanted to pass the years with him.

That could not be.

She was the keeper of their defenses, the chief of this place, not just a woman. She could not choose for herself. She must think always what was best for the clan.

Perhaps she should wed with Alasdair. Send Farlan back where he belonged, acknowledge that her feelings for the man had been no more than fancy. Alasdair would be the strength at her back. She could do that, could she not, for the sake of all she loved?

Aye. Maybe. Maybe she could. But she wanted Farlan Mac-

Leod first.

If she had to go to Alasdair, it would no' be as an unbroken maiden. Farlan would be the first. If she must sacrifice herself, at least she would have that memory to hold for the rest of her life.

As a woman, surely she had the right to choose that?

The wind blew harder against her, rocking her on her feet, and a few drops of rain dashed into her face. She planted her palm on one of the stones that made up Da's cairn. It still felt warm.

"Da? Would that be so wrong? I will gi' the rest o' my life to MacBeith, but I want this one thing for me."

Something stirred behind her. Not the wind. She turned and felt rather than saw the mist that cloaked the holy stones swirl. Someone stood there.

"Da?"

She would not disbelieve it now if she saw him walk out to meet her, his tall, familiar, rangy form, the hair of gray. The great love that always looked at her from his eyes.

And aye, a figure stepped out from the mist. Moira's breath caught in her throat. But nay, that was not Da.

It was her sister, Saerla.

"Moira? What are ye doing up here? 'Tis getting ready to storm. This no place to be."

"What are ye doing here then?"

"I was at my prayers. Come." Saerla caught Moira's arm. "Let us go down."

"No' yet. I need an answer, Saerla. I canna' go yet."

Saerla looked at her. Moira could see raindrops on her sister's face and the memory of magic in her eyes. "Can ye no' feel the fury coming?"

She could. *She could.*

"Let us go down while we can."

"I thought Da would be here."

"He is here, Moira. I ha' told ye—"

"I need him to tell me what to do."

"I ken 'tis a torment trying to go on wi'out him. But, sister, I believe ye possess the strength to hold his place."

It was well one of them believed it.

Moira grasped Saerla's arms. "I do no' ken wha' to do. I love him, Saerla."

"Da? Of course ye do. And he—"

"Farlan MacLeod. I am in love wi' Farlan MacLeod." There, she had said it, if only to her fey sister.

Saerla went dead quiet for an instant, her eyes wide.

"Da said it was destiny, did he no'? He allowed for destiny. I want—I need him to come forth from this pile o' stones and tell me I need not deny what's in my heart."

Saerla still did not speak.

Moira clung to her sister's hands. "Alasdair wants me to wed wi' him, and aye, 'twould be the best thing for the clan. But—"

The storm hit them then, unleashing a fury that stole the rest of her words. They held to one another while thunder boomed overhead and lightning crackled, reaching for the stones behind them.

Was this Moira's answer? Did Da, or God, display fury at the very prospect of what she wanted?

"We maun find shelter."

Saerla pulled Moira away from the edge of the rise and in among the stones. Dubious protection that, since Moira had just seen the lightning strike here.

They huddled beneath a trio of stones that formed a kind of doorway and Saerla put her arms around Moira as if she was the one doing the protecting.

The storm passed. It took its time about it and lashed the height right well before moving down into the glen. A steady rain followed, drumming hard on the ground and the ancient stones.

Not until it began to ease and they could hear each other speak did Saerla catch Moira's face between her hands.

"What did ye say? Alasdair wants to marry ye?"

Moira nodded miserably. Wet to the skin and shivering, she only now realized what else she had confessed.

"Well." Saerla bit her lip. "I knew he was in love wi' ye—"

"What? Alasdair in love wi' me?"

"Och, aye. Could ye no' tell? 'Tis in the way he looks at ye, always. Besides," Saerla added delicately, "I could feel it coming off him."

Moira had no cause to doubt her sister's sensitivities. "I never knew."

"Ye pay no heed to men of any kind, do ye? Except it seems the MacLeod hostage." Saerla's blue eyes questioned Moira. "Ye tell me ye love him."

"I should no' have said so."

"Sister, ye can at least be honest wi' me. Ye carry a heavy burden for silence."

"Ye ha' no idea."

"I do, sister, I do. I can feel that also. But ye no be a woman who turns easily to others for help. Nor do ye let others in very often."

"He has got inside me, Farlan MacLeod. I am no' sure how."

"Ye did say, when we spoke here before, as how ye had feelings for him. I thought it mainly attraction. But, love?"

"Ye told me Da spoke o' destiny. I came up here in the hope o' hearing it from him. But I ha' not your ability."

"Nor I yours. Sister, your courage astounds me. Da is so proud."

"Truly? Proud o' me? Even though I ha' given my heart to the very man who ended his life?"

Saerla wrapped her arms around Moira and drew her close. Despite the rain that continued to pelt them, peace came of that embrace, peace that whispered of magic. The magic spread around them, flowing to and from the stones.

For the first time in days, Moira quieted.

"Tell me so I can understand," Saerla bade then. "Why d'ye love him?"

"I ha' been asking myself that over and over. Why him, of all men? He is handsome and steady. There's a quiet strength in him that does no' need to boast or brag. He is patient and willing to meet me on my ground. Willing to sacrifice also for my sake. Saerla, though I ken fine 'tis hard to warrant of a MacLeod, he is a good man."

"Aye well, I suppose they can be found everywhere, even among the MacLeods."

"No' many MacBeiths would acknowledge it."

"Ha' ye spoken to him o' your feelings?"

"No' as such." But he must know.

"Has he spoken o' his for ye?"

"Nay."

"And be ye certain 'tis not just—well, desire o' the flesh? For you are right, he is no' ill-favored."

"That is part o' it, Saerla. I ache to be wi' him."

"That may well addle a woman's wits."

It might, and Moira was living proof. "But 'tis no' just that. What draws me to him is deep and wide, and has taken hold inside me. What am I to do?"

Saerla smoothed Moira's wet hair without answering.

"In just over a score o' days, I maun send him back to Mac-Leod. I fear when I do, my life—any chance for happiness, will end."

"One thing is certain. Ye canna take Alasdair for husband feeling the way ye do for another man, any other man. 'Twould no' be fair to him. Alasdair too is a good man."

"Aye."

"And some things go beyond what may be asked, in sacrifice."

"Do they though, Saerla? Is there aught too much to ask for the sake o' my clan? 'Tis that I came here to ask Da."

"He canna answer ye, but I can. Ye be worth more than heartache." Saerla mopped at Moira's face, though how she could tell tears from rain, Moira could not guess. "Let us mak' our way down and get dry."

They got to their feet, Moira still clutching her sister's hands.

"Saerla, ye will no' tell anyone? Ye will keep my secret?"

"Aye, to be sure. Will ye promise then to go carefully? To do naught rash?"

"Och, aye." Even as she gave the promise, Moira wondered if she could keep it.

Chapter Thirty-Seven

FARLAN LAY SLEEPING, but lightly, when the door rattled him awake. The guards, so he assumed, remained outside, though he pitied them their places in this downpour. Due to his supposed change in status, the bar was now on the inside of that door. He was expected to lock himself in, and the guards were for his protection.

He'd only just dropped off after the worst of the thunder and lightning passed. Rain still drummed down so hard he barely heard his visitor.

Ah, but he knew who it was even before he scrambled from the bed and padded there on bare feet. Knew who *she* was.

He could feel her there.

"Moira." Her name was on his lips even as he dragged the door open. "Ye should no' be here at this hour. The guards—"

"No guards." She slipped in past him, soaking wet and shivering. Naught lit his chamber except the dying fire, but he could see her as well as feel her. Face stark white and glistening with the rain. Hair a sodden mass down her back. Eyes desperate.

"Wha' has happened?"

"Lock the door. Bar it again."

He did so, while wondering over her alarm. A horde must be on the way to slaughter him. What else could make her look so?

"Ye be wet and cold. Come to the fire." He towed her there

and chaffed her icy hands. First things first. "Get warm. Then tell me."

"I was up on the rise. Hoping for answers." Her eyes met his. "Answers about us."

Oh. A tangle of now-familiar emotions arose in him, including frustration and desire. Fear for her. "Ye should no' be here. Ye'll be seen—"

"By whom? 'Tis what I am trying to tell ye, the guards ha' gone. Taking shelter somewhere, no doubt. I met my sister, Saerla, on the rise. In the storm. We spoke together and then came down. I was on my way to my own quarters to change my clothing when I saw your chamber stood unguarded."

He watched her quietly. He doubted her path would ordinarily have taken her past his door. She'd wanted to come. Well, he could not argue with that. He wanted to see her every hour of the day and night.

"The guards," she reiterated, "were no' there. They ha' abandoned their post."

"Aye. They will be back when the rain lets up." And her, here with him.

He turned to the fire and stirred the embers, added some wood. "Aye well, you get warm—"

"I will."

"—before ye slip awa' again."

"I am going nowhere."

When he turned back from the fire, she was already working the ties at the front of her gown, struggling with the wet fabric. "Here, help me. My fingers are too stiff and wet."

"Moira—" A breathless protest.

"I canna get warm wearing these soaking things, can I?"

She could not. And he wanted to protest further, but his tongue stuck to the roof of his mouth.

He went to her. Replaced her fingers with his own. He used to do this for Ainsley, long ago. He did not want to think of Ainsley, not now when Moira looked at him this way, with heat burning in her eyes.

She was beautiful, so beautiful he saw when the garments came away. High, full breasts—aye, well, those he'd already seen and tasted. The very thought had him hard. Square shoulders gleaming wet in the firelight, which flared up as if to bless the sight. A strong, narrow back and slim waist. Long, long legs with a nest of curls between them.

She watched him admire her and lifted her chin with a hint of pride. "I hope ye do no' mean to continue wi' sending me away."

"I do no' think I ha' the strength."

"Good. Because I am staying."

"The guards—"

"By the time they return, I'll ha' had ye, and ye will have had me."

At least once. The way he felt, he might need to take her over and over again.

But he did not want her to regret this. Anything but that.

"Are ye certain?"

Stark naked as she was, her skin slick with rain, she pressed against him. She did not have far to move. They remained only a step apart.

"I am."

The kiss was pure fire. It exploded from some place deep inside her and caught him in its conflagration. Having been in bed, he wore very little, his sark half undone, his leggings tight, and now doubly so. He could feel every bit of her as she could no doubt feel him. Glorious.

Her tongue tussled with his and invited him in. He swept her mouth, plunging into her precisely the way he wanted to, below. His hands roamed down her back, cupped her buttocks and spread them, fitting her more snugly against him.

He would not get out of this alive, not without taking her. It might be worth the dying.

It would be worth it.

She tore her mouth from his and tugged at the fabric of his

sark. "Off."

"Aye."

"Let us go to the bed."

Not a command a man could deny. She stood and watched him as he shed his clothes, with pure honest admiration in her eyes.

"Will ye mak' love to me?"

When a goddess stood naked in the firelight and asked such a question, when she held out her hand, all sense and sanity flew away.

He laid her gently on her back on the sheets he'd just vacated. Despite his impatience, he wanted to be gentle with her.

She turned her head slightly on his pillow and smiled. "It smells o' ye. The best scent ever."

He stretched above her, every muscle aquiver. Resting on his elbows, he looked into her face. She must be able to see—and feel—his condition, that he was up and hard for her. Aye, she must have seen that. The raw need inside him reached for her also, aching to connect in spirit.

"There is no going back from this, Moira MacBeith."

"I do no' want to go back."

"Ha' ye e'er been wi' a man?"

She shook her head. "That is why—I want it to be ye. Only ye."

He lowered himself and kissed her, big deep sweeps of his tongue that lavished desire. She opened to him, spread her legs so his weight settled between her thighs, just where he needed to be.

Ah, no, it would no' be as quick as that.

He broke the kiss and ran his tongue down her neck, across her collarbone and to one breast. Already her nipples had swollen with her desire. He latched to one of them and feasted, feeling her desire spike.

"Och, God. Farlan. Och, God, do no' stop."

He had no intention of stopping. He wanted her to feel what he felt for her. He wanted to claim her soul as well as her flesh.

He wanted her alive with desire for him, teetering on the edge so that she exploded when he plunged inside.

"So beautiful, Moira. Ye be so, so beautiful." Raising from her breast, he gazed into her eyes—blue eyes wild with demand and supplication, damp hair spread across the pillow, breasts rising and falling with her desperate breaths.

She reached one hand to caress his face, touched his hair. The tenderness of the gesture pierced him.

"I love ye, Farlan MacLeod. I love ye right well."

The last thing he expected her to say. Aye, the words had hung between them for days. But for her to speak them out—

It claimed him. It held him fast.

"As I do love ye, Moira MacBeith."

She wrapped her legs around his hips and drew him to her. He went in like a sword sliding to its sheath, and the moment when he did, when he felt her all around him, was so pure and glorious he never paused to wonder whether he caused her pain.

Her face revealed none. Only pure need, a desire as desperate as his own. This went beyond lust to completion.

He wanted to remain gentle with her, even as their pace quickened. She might never have lain with a man before, but her body knew what to do. She tossed her head back and arched herself to him so he could plunge deeper. Her body and spirit both clung to his, so he felt it the instant she came apart in his hands.

The wonder of it seduced him into spilling his seed.

She still had her legs wrapped around him. They lay linked together while their hearts pounded in time and emotions that he could not name tore through him.

"Moira." He buried his face in her wet hair. She kissed the beard that covered his cheek, her tenderness palpable.

"I should no' ha' done that," he whispered when his breath calmed.

"Should no' ha' made love to me? How can ye say so?"

"I should no' ha' given ye my seed." He raised up to look at her. "I did no' mean to."

"I want every part o' ye. Every bit o' yet."

"The only thing that could mak' our situation worse, Moira, is me giving ye my bairn. I will ha' to leave—"

"Hush. Do no' speak o' it now." She bestowed kisses all over his face, the corners of his mouth, his jaw. "Allow me a measure o' peace."

Peace. Aye, it was that, after desiring her for so long. Surely they both deserved a few moments to bask in this feeling of pure belonging.

"Verra well." He shifted to her side and gathered her in, arms strong around her. They lay so while the firelight danced across the chamber and the rain tapped on the roof.

He held her close and gloried in the fact that, for an instant at least, he had everything he desired in his arms.

Chapter Thirty-Eight

H E'D TOLD HER he loved her. Farlan MacLeod had. Granted, she'd spoken the words first, confessed what had near overtaken her heart. But she had no reason to disbelieve him when he'd followed the words by making love to her so sweetly, with such a sure tenderness—

That, no woman could doubt.

Instinctively, she'd known there would be tenderness. He was not a cruel or a hurtful man. Indeed, she was the one who had hurt him, pressing the hot iron to his torn flesh.

With grace, he had forgiven her that. Just as she'd forgiven him for having struck the blow that ended her da's life.

Had she not?

She closed her eyes and pressed closer against his shoulder. Two men had she adored in her life, only two. And the one had deprived her of the other. How strange fate could be.

When Arran was still alive, he had treated her, the eldest of his three sisters, with kindly amusement. But he had turned to her also, for advice. Since his death, everyone tended to turn to her. Folks relied upon her, but very few stopped to wonder if she might in turn require support.

Or cherishing.

So this, lying in Farlan's arms, felt like a moment out of time, and the smallest details impressed themselves upon her being.

The drumming of the rain overhead. The soft crackle of the fire as it died down. The beat of Farlan's heart.

The bed smelled of him, and now of their lovemaking. Warmth came off him along with a marvelous sense of belonging. He lay naked beside her, hers to touch.

She ran her palm across his shoulder, the one she had tormented, and down his arm. Strong he was, this man of hers. Strong enough that he could be quiet with it.

She needed this in her life.

Her hand moved of its own accord, and she raked her fingers through the hair on his chest. How different they were, he and she. How exquisitely they fit together.

"Moira."

"Tell me again how ye love me."

"I am no poet, lass. I am but an ordinary man, and no' certain I ha' pretty words to tell ye the way I feel."

"I do no' want pretty words."

"I ha' never known anyone to match ye, Moira. So determined. So beautiful inside and out. Ye might ha' been born for me, made out o' all the wishes I never knew I had."

And he said he was no poet.

"Aye?" She moved her mouth a hair's-breadth from his, the better to catch the words.

"I might ask nae more in life than to be wi' ye. Like this." He slid his hand across her hip. "Like this." He kissed her.

He might claim he had no fancy words, though she liked fine what he said. His kiss spoke far more. It pierced her clear through and strengthened the bonds lovemaking had formed between them, reached right inside her and claimed her heart.

She could lie here like this forever and kiss him.

His hands crept up and plunged into her hair, soothed down her back, lighting fire as they went. Delighting in the friction, she raked her fingers through that warm mat on his chest and lower, wrapped around him and had the thrilling experience of feeling him grow into her touch.

She had the power to do that. To this man. *Her man.*

"Moira, Moira," he kissed her every time he spoke her name. "I do love ye."

"And I you. I swear it."

He paused long enough to gaze into her face, brown eyes intent. "Let me show ye."

Surely he had already done? But Moira had no concept, no inkling of what followed. For his mouth left hers to move lower, shedding kisses as he went. Across her breasts where she wished he'd linger. Onto her belly. Lower still.

When he parted her thighs with gentle hands, she stiffened. "What—"

"Trust me, lass."

Trust him, of all men. Aye, of all men.

She spread herself at his urging, felt his breath whisper across her most private of places an instant before his mouth landed there.

Oh, Holy Mother! She should not allow this. Such an act, such intimacy. But och, the way it felt—

She lay not daring to breathe while he plundered her with his lips and tongue, invaded her and stole from her every last shred of resistance. Never before had she surrendered thus to anything. But she tossed back her head, arched her hips, and gave herself to him with abandon.

Even when the ripples of pleasure broke over her, he did not quit. He drank of her as if he could not get enough. She fought to keep from crying out.

Someone might hear.

"Inside. Me." She gasped then.

The sensation when he drove into her, and her so utterly open to him, sent the ripples through her again.

This time, though, he did not leave his seed inside her. He withdrew before she wanted him to and scattered it across her belly.

She held to him, still quivering. "By God. By God—" He

kissed her, the flavor wild and sweet. She gasped. "Ye did no' ask me to repeat how I love ye, Farlan."

Tenderly, he caressed her hair. "There is no need. I ken it fine, Moira MacBeith."

"I am yours. Whatever happens in the future and whatever comes between us—"

"Hush. Naught can come between us."

"Hold me."

He wrapped her in his arms, tight. She wondered desperately how she could ever live without this.

The rain on the roof lessened. The guards would soon return.

"I maun go," she whispered.

"Aye."

She arose, used the hem of her dress to clean her skin before dressing again. Naked as he was—beautiful in the last glow of the firelight—he arose and wrapped her in her cloak, fastened the garment, still wet.

"I will come again," she told him then. "When the guards abandon their duty." She should chastise them for it. She would not.

"When it rains?"

"Aye, perhaps."

A smile crooked one corner of his mouth. "A fine thing 'tis Scotland, and rains every other day."

Every other day. Her head swam.

"I will be back," she repeated. "Ye know that for certain, for I canna live wi'out ye." She kissed him once more before turning to the door. Lifting the bar, she peered out into soaking dark.

She did not want to go. Yet she slipped out into the wet, grateful to find no one there to see her, and heard him drop the bar across the door behind her.

A thickness of oak between them. But nay, 'twas as he said—naught could ever come between them. Not ever again.

➤➤➤❧❧❧

ALL THE NEXT day, she did not succeed in banishing it from her mind, no matter how she tried. As she went about her duties, as she trained with the men, and met with various others of the clansfolk.

She and Farlan MacLeod had been as intimate together as a man and a woman could be. She wanted him again. Somehow, she must keep that desire hidden.

She had no hope of having him; at least, she suspected, not before it rained once more. Maddeningly, the sun staked its claim in the sky above the glen, and day after fair day rolled by.

Her sisters, so she feared, were at risk of challenging her with the truth. Rhian struck first, clothing her curiosity in concern.

"Sister, are ye sickening for somewhat?" she asked when they met in passing.

"Nay, why should ye think so?"

Rhian narrowed discerning blue eyes at her. "Ye do no' look aright."

"I have my courses, that is all." And right glad she was about it. At least Farlan need not worry about having left her his bairn. She longed to go and tell him.

She wanted to be with him.

"I ha' told ye before, ye should no' go to the training field when you're bleeding. The men are too rough."

"Mayhap ye be right, Rhian."

"Why d'ye no' sit for a time and put your feet up?"

"I ha' tasks to complete."

Her exchange with Saerla proved still more dangerous. Saerla knew the truth, that Moira was in love with Farlan MacLeod, and anyway, Saerla observed the world with far more than her eyes.

She came searching Moira out and found her in Da's chamber, which had now quite disturbingly become Moira's own.

"Sister, a word if ye ha' a moment."

"Only a moment," Moira replied, sorting through Da's clothing. She had no idea what to do with his belongings. Some—like his weapons—she would surely keep. She could think of no fit place for the rest.

Saerla stepped into the room and shut the door behind her. She flicked her gaze over Moira before she said, "Wha' ha' ye done?"

Moira froze. "I ha' done many things, Saerla. Practiced at arms with the men, met wi' the guards—"

"Ye ken fine I do no' mean that. Ye ha'—ha' been wi' him, have ye no'? Farlan MacLeod."

In a flash, Moira experienced it all over again. His hands sliding over her skin. His mouth between her legs. She turned and faced her sister.

"I do not understand why ye should suppose so."

"I can see it on ye. Do no' try and deny."

"Fine. I will no' deny it."

Compassion flooded Saerla's eyes. "Sister, I ken ye've said ye love him. But d'ye ha' any grasp o' how dangerous it is?"

"I do, aye. But Saerla, I canna help myself. Ye would no' understand."

"I ha' never yet been in love wi' a man, nay, at least no' the way ye are with the MacLeod."

The MacLeod. As if she needed reminding.

"Did ye go to his chamber? Wha' if someone saw?"

"No one did. By any road, I would ha' made up some reason I sought Farlan out in his chamber, say that I asked for information about his chief."

"Folk will grow suspicious."

"I know it."

"Promise me ye will be careful, that ye will no' go to him again."

"I will be careful, aye. I canna promise the other."

"Moira—"

"I need him, Saerla, as I never imagined I could need anything. No' just his touch, though God knows that is a powerful attraction, but his strength and his warmth."

"My heart grieves for ye, Moira. For he will have to be sent back to his chief. Believe me, since ye confessed the truth up among the stones, I ha' wracked my mind trying to think o' a way for ye. I can see none."

"I know that too."

"He will ha' to go back." Saerla repeated it. "If he lives that long. I ha' heard rumbles. Some o' the men still want to extract a price for Da's death, and he is the only target they see."

Ah, nay! Moira should increase the guard. But if she did, how would she ever slip in to see him again?

Surely, protecting Farlan's life was more important than her own feelings. Her own needs.

"Thank ye, Saerla, for that warning."

Saerla laid her hand on Moira's arm. "My heart goes out to ye, as I say. But ye walk a treacherous ground."

More treacherous, indeed, than she'd ever imagined she might have beneath her feet.

Chapter Thirty-Nine

I AIN MACBEITH HAD kept always an open door and an open heart to his people. None of them, so he'd declared, should ever feel reluctant to approach him. None should fear speaking their minds.

It had bred an atmosphere that encouraged men and women to freely express their opinions. A fine thing, and as Moira had discovered since his death, at the same time a terrible one. He had in truth been a father to his clan. Moira supposed there were fathers, and fathers—some feared by their children. Some much loved.

Iain MacBeith had been both adored and respected. Some of that liking had been transferred to Moira in his stead. The respect seemed sorely lacking. Either way, they had no hesitation in bringing her their objections.

They stopped her whenever they saw her, regardless of whatever task she might have in hand. They expressed troubles great or small. They clearly struggled with their loss and grief. Many of them complained about the truce with MacLeod.

Some were polite about it. *We ken fine, Mistress, ye think 'twill protect us and allow us time to prepare our defenses. But 'twill make us look weak in the eyes o' our opponents.*

Some were downright rude. *'Tis a poor way to deal wi' an enemy. Rory MacLeod will think he has us already under his thumb. I say slaughter the prisoner and so put an end to this madness!*

Having been warned by Saerla, Moira was now alive to the prevailing sentiment against Farlan. The clansfolk did not see him as an asset or a means to assure their safety. Their hearts cried out for revenge.

And by God, they did not even know the truth. That their beloved chief had died by Farlan's blade. Or that she, Moira, had laid down with him.

She did not go to see Farlan MacLeod again, neither by day nor by night. She avoided walking past his door when she could, but spent much effort on ascertaining the strength and reliability of his guard.

The days slipped by like water through her fingers. She did not forget. Whenever she encountered someone who spoke against Farlan, fear fluttered wildly in her gut. She wondered how she could continue assuring the safety of her people and of him also.

One bright morning when she arrived in the hall, a group of elders awaited her. These men were Da's contemporaries and friends, men beside whom he had fought in days gone by. Most of them were members of the council that had formed without her permission. Did they trust her and her judgment so little they felt they had to follow after her?

Seeing them now brought a stirring of dread. This could not be good.

The interior of the hall seemed dim after the bright sunlight outside. She'd been up with the dawn and had walked to the cairn on the height, seeking a measure of peace. Seeking her da.

How she wished he were here with her now.

"Good morn," she greeted the men. There were five of them, all wearing dour expressions.

"Mistress. We hoped we might speak wi' ye." That was Ewan, who'd been very close to her father. Her best memory was of him and Da laughing together over a dram.

He was not laughing now.

She steeled herself and faced him. "If this is about the truce—"

"It is."

"There can be no altering that now. We need to prepare ourselves as best we can and let the time run out."

"I disagree," Ewan said. And gestured to his companions. "*We* disagree. Surely, we as senior clan members have some say? Your father always allowed us that."

"My father lies up on the rise."

"Aye, so." A second man, Keithan, scowled at Moira. "Did he no', we would not be here."

"Aye ye saying…" She faced him. "Da would not ha' sought a peace with clan MacLeod for the benefit o' his own people? Why, he had a tacit truce wi' Camraith MacLeod, more or less, that kept the full might of clan MacLeod from falling upon us, for years and years."

"We do no' believe that would ha' held had his own father and chief been struck down."

"It held through the death o' his son. Because it was to our advantage."

A shadow blocked the sunlight streaming in through the door, a large one. Alasdair hovered there.

"My apologies for being late," he rumbled, and came in.

Alasdair? Had these men enlisted him to stand against her?

He wore his sword and looked ready for battle. He cast one look at Moira before focusing on the men. He walked up and stood partway between them and Moira, as if refusing to choose a side.

But aye, she knew where his heart lay.

"We ha' heard complaints far and wide about the treatment o' the prisoner," Ewan resumed.

"He is no' a prisoner but a hostage. There is a difference. As a hostage, he assures the treaty stands, and so maun be treated well."

"The men, young and old alike, do no' hold wi' that."

Alasdair, still not looking at Moira, agreed. "I ha' heard the same."

"The men, our warriors, say we are ready for the fight. We ha' the weapons. We very nearly ha' the supplies gathered in case o' siege."

"Ye want to send Farlan MacLeod back? Early?" Moira's stomach fluttered again.

Ewan shook his head. "We want his blood. We want to haul him out o' that grand chamber ye ha' lent him and slaughter him for all to see."

"I canna do that. I ha' given my word. Assured his safety."

"Aye, but a point maun be made. The way we see it, war will come as soon as Rory MacLeod gets his man back. Be it in ten days or tomorrow. Let us show the bastard we are no' afraid o' him. That we are strong."

"Wha' o' my word that I ha' given? Is that to mean nothing?"

"Aye so, Mistress. We respect your word. But 'tis outweighed by the hunger we ha' to avenge the death o' our chief."

Moira looked at Alasdair. He alone of these men knew the truth, that Farlan had struck the blow that had ended their chief's life. Would he say so now?

He met her gaze at last, his dark eyes burning. Moira could see so much there. Anger and grief, and hurt. He hurt because she'd rejected his suit. Would that make him speak out and break faith with her?

"Alasdair?" she challenged. "What do ye think?"

He cleared his throat. "'Tis gey difficult to think at all wi' the grief o' losing our chief upon us. There is much to be said for easing that grief wi' battle. 'Tis a lot to ask our men to hold their swords when they want to avenge Iain MacBeith. There is also much to be said for keeping our word. And ye, Mistress, ha' given that word."

As had he. The five of them had promised not to tell what had happened in that battle.

"So," Ewan pressed, "ye are saying, Alasdair, we should hold to this truce?"

Alasdair shrugged. "The younger men want war."

Moira said quickly, "The younger men do no' ken what full on war would entail. My da was always careful to shield us from that."

"Should we trade our consciences for safety?" Keithan snapped. "Wha' sort o' men would that make of us?"

"Alasdair, tell us truly." Ewan swung toward the big man. "D'ye back Moira, or d'ye no'?"

"Of course I back her. She is my chief."

Relief swept through Moira. She nearly sagged where she stood.

"But," Alasdair added directly to Moira, "that does no' mean I do not think ye be wrong."

She gasped.

"'Tis a matter o' loyalty," Alasdair concluded, "and the fealty I owe ye."

The elders did not know what to make of that, no more than Moira. With Alasdair's backing, they were willing to accept her decisions. Yet his backing was not unequivocal.

Aye, but she would take whatever support Alasdair offered, for in the end, it might well save Farlan's life.

Chapter Forty

FARLAN SUSPECTED HE might be going mad. What, with the confinement and the isolation, the constant wondering what might be happening beyond the walls of his chamber. The wanting of Moira MacBeith.

That last, it rode him hard. Raw and hungry, it roused him from the miserly sleep he managed to snatch, for he did not expend himself enough physically to be tired. He relived a hundred times all they'd done together that one night. The sensation of his palm sliding up, and up her leg. The way she'd opened herself to him.

Even more than that, desire for her presence haunted him. The way she had looked at him. The connection he felt to her, deep inside. He would have wagered his life she felt all that too.

Yet, she did not return to him. Following the night she'd walked away from his chamber, out into the rain, he'd had not so much as a glimpse of her. The days crawled by, their number dwindling till there were more of the temporary truce passed than yet to come.

He ached to see her for a thousand reasons, he did. A patient man for the most part, he told himself he should wait. That he should trust in her. There must be reasons she did not come to him. She—living in the thick of their situation—knew best.

His mind, though, refused to quiet. Reason with himself as he was a man in love. Deep in love. He needed to lay eyes migfa, to know she remained well and in good spirits.

On the morning of the tenth day, and with only a score more .ays remaining, he lifted the bar on his door and hauled it open. The three guards stationed there stared at him in surprise.

By now, they were all familiar to him. They'd passed him his food many times. Accepted his odious slop bucket. Brought fuel for his fire. One, an older man, now narrowed his eyes and frowned. One of the younger gaped. The third young man seemed always to be on duty. Farlan had heard the others call him Calan.

He placed his hand on the hilt of his sword. "Wha' d'ye want, MacLeod?"

The *MacLeod* did not sound friendly. "'Tis a braw morning. I thought I would take the air."

They exchanged incredulous glances. None of them said anything.

Farlan raked the young man who gripped the sword with a glance. "It is Calan, is it no'?"

The man nodded.

"Calan, I understand I am no' a prisoner and might walk out whenever I wish."

"Aye," said the older man. "If ye wish to ha' yer head lopped off."

Farlan peered past them and into the morning. Early as it was, not many people were afoot.

How long had it been since he'd gazed out across the glen? Inhaled free air?

"Ye may follow me, if ye wish, with your great swords."

Calan spoke again. "I maun advise ye stay inside. For yer own protection."

"So ye ha' done."

He stepped out and they backed away from him as if he carried a contagion. He supposed he did. The only dreaded MacLeod for miles.

Calan said to the other young man, "Go fetch Mistress Moira."

Aye, do. 'Twas she Farlan wanted to see.

He'd had very little chance since arriving at MacBeith's stronghold to appreciate the place. To admire the view and the perspective, so different from that at home.

Now he filled his lungs with the sweet air and let his eyes roam. What folk were early at their business stared at him in shock that gradually changed to loathing. The two guards came after him. To defend, or strike him down? His back pricked.

MacBeith's stronghold, as he saw, was set on higher ground than MacLeod's across the way. The green turf rolled softly down from it like the folds of a woman's gown all the way to the loch, which, at this hour, dreamed beneath a thin mist. Shadows still cloaked the far side of the glen where Rory kept his word, and his peace.

Suddenly, with unexpected ferocity, Farlan wanted to go home. He wanted the comfort and ease of it, the company of his friends, especially Rory and Rory's cousin, Leith, who never failed to make him laugh. The blessed familiarity.

Yet—Moira was here. And had he not vowed to her he'd cross the distance between them?

As he ventured to do now.

He did not know if his appearance walking out among his enemies would spoil her plans. He did not know quite why she'd kept away from him. He wanted to see her, nothing more.

He walked out in front of the hall, for his quarters were located to the rear of that building, and stood admiring the view. Beautiful, this place was, even though soaked with the blood of both his and Moira's ancestors. A pity to war over it.

He tore his gaze from the glen and realized a crowd had come drifting up. Warriors for the most part, some hastily-clad. They formed a half ring around him. Och, was he going to die right here, on this glorious morning?

For the love of a woman. He supposed there were worse

reasons to die.

Someone shouted at him to turn back. "Get to yer quarters, monster!"

The two remaining guards behind him gave no response, did not draw their weapons or flank him in any show of protection.

A woman who held a basket took something from it and threw it at him. An apple. He wanted to laugh, except for her glare of hate. The apple was followed far less humorously by a rock thrown from the other side, which nearly took him in the ear.

A commotion broke through those gathered. Moira appeared, and a jolt shot through Farlan, straight to his groin.

She wore the garb she had that night she'd come to him and he'd sent her away again, at a great expenditure of will. A nightdress with her sword strapped on over it, and the cloak flying behind.

Her eyes widened when she saw him, and her lips parted. She drew the sword just as a second stone came sailing and thumped his shoulder.

"Wha' is all this?"

"I told ye, Mistress." The young guard who'd been sent to fetch her came puffing up. "He was bent on walking out."

"On our ground!" a man in the crowd shouted angrily. "We will no' have it."

Moira raked Farlan with one unreadable look before stationing herself in front of him, an unmistakable gesture of protection. "I ha' given my word no harm will come to this man. Which o' ye will break that word?"

They stirred and muttered, but none of them spoke outright.

"Be gone about your business. Allow me to deal wi' the Mac-Leod."

They scowled at her. So did Calan and the three guards who still had not drawn their weapons, making their feelings clear. They would not act against their own people to protect a MacLeod.

As, apparently, Moira would. For she stood now facing them all down with a naked blade in her hand.

Ah, he'd been a fool to leave his quarters to come out here. It might now cost her dear.

Those gathered dispersed slowly and with many an evil look. Only the three guards remained.

Moira spun toward Farlan. "Come wi' me."

"Mistress," Calan spoke. "D'ye want us to accompany ye?"

"Aye. We will speak in the hall. Ye three wait outside. Make sure no one comes in."

They went in silence, the clan members still staring. Moira had put her sword away and shoved open the doors of the hall, using all her weight.

Inside the space lay shadowed, cool and empty. She pushed the door shut again, leaving the guards outside, and led Farlan across the floor before turning to him.

"Ha' ye lost yer mind?" Her eyes had once again gone wide and accusing.

"Aye, I'm thinking I have. I had to see ye." He reached for her, gripped her shoulders before plunging his fingers into the wealth of her hair. He kissed her, shedding upon her all his pent-up frustration and need.

For a breathless moment, she failed to respond. Then something inside her broke and she kissed him back fervently, her lips saying what words could not. For several long moments, they spent their desire on one another before she broke away and studied him.

"Are ye hurt?" Her hands groped across his chest. "That stone took ye in the wounded shoulder."

"No harm done. Moira, I would tak' far more than a blow to be wi' ye."

She huffed a breath. "Ye be the one who sent me awa' from ye. Who told me no' to return to your chamber. That 'twas dangerous."

He caressed her cheek, brushing his thumb over the wound

there, which had faded to a pink line, and smiled sadly. "That was before."

"Before?"

"Before we lay together and ye became a part o' me. I ha' no' seen ye since that night. I needed—I needed to know ye were all right." To know that she still cared for him, though he would not admit that.

The expression in her eyes changed, grew hot and misty. She ran her lips over his again, a fleeting blessing. "I wanted to come. Believe me, I ha' been putting out small fires and trying to convince the elders they might place their faith in me."

"And I ha' just made things harder for ye."

"No matter. Seeing ye was worth it."

Aye, so it was, but he wanted more. To cup her breasts and capture their warmth in his hands. To taste her wildness. But aye, all he had done was cause her trouble. "Moira, love—" But he could not say all the things he wished to. "I will go back to my chamber."

"Let me accompany ye. And I will ha' another word wi' Calan, who is in charge o' your safety."

Calan—the young man who looked at him with such doubt and loathing.

If that was his safety, then aye, he rested in perilous hands indeed.

Chapter Forty-One

"MISTRESS MOIRA? MISTRESS Moira, ye ha' better come. They are attacking the prisoner! Dragging him fro' his chamber."

Moira, who occupied her father's bed, came awake with a sickening jolt. Someone pounded on the door, calling out for her. It sounded like one of the younger guards.

Surely, this must be a dream. She could not have been asleep long, and dreams often took one so. She slept very little these days and suffered from exhaustion of both body and spirit.

She sat up, her heart pounding in her throat, and thrust her bare feet over the side of the bed. "What?"

She must have spoken the word aloud, for the man on the other side of the door responded, "They are goin' to kill him."

She stumbled across the floor and hauled open the door. The young guard there, Orthan, had been often assigned to guard Farlan. He looked frantic now.

"What has happened? Tell me. Quickly."

"They cam' in a crowd no' long ago. Cryin' for his blood."

"Who?"

"A group o' they warriors. Our warriors."

"Where's Calan?"

Orthan's face went blank. "There, Mistress."

"Defending the hostage?"

The lad shook his head.

Oh, holy mother of God! This was deep and bad and dangerous.

She buckled on her sword with fingers that fumbled, but did not pause for her cloak or her shoes. "Come."

Three days had passed since Farlan had gone out walking. During that time, she had not been to see him. She'd wanted to, had wanted to spend another night in his arms with a need that fair frightened her.

What was a woman to do with such need?

But she'd been able to feel the ill wind blowing toward him. Whispers and complaints. Frustrated anger. Their people still needed a target for their grief.

It seemed they'd found one.

She ran, and young Orthan panted behind her. Moira could hear the commotion now, and see a flare of light out behind the hall where Farlan had his quarters.

They would no' be so mad as to burn the place down, would they? Ah, they could lose everything.

She could. Had she not lost enough? Her ma. Arran. Da. If she lost Farlan, would that be the thing to finish her? Aye, she was strong. And she had devoted herself to defending this place. But—

Unexpectedly, Orthan grabbed her arm, making her stumble. "Mistress, ye should know—Calan says the MacLeod is the one who struck our chief down. In that battle. They want revenge."

Of course they did. Calan, who was angry, had broken his promise. That was the trouble with a secret.

All the breath left her in a whoosh. She did not waste time speaking but gasped and pelted on toward that flare of light.

The light came from a number of torches. They'd arrived, these attackers, prepared to do harm, a crowd over a score strong, all armed and with their weapons drawn.

The guards, including Calan, stood aside, not participating in the horror but not intervening either. All but this loyal lad at her back.

They had already dragged Farlan outside. They must have broken in the door to do so, for he would have had it barred on the inside. Moira could not see very much of him—just a tumble of brown hair and a splash of MacLeod tartan.

The badge that would likely cost his life.

Aye, most of them had their weapons drawn, but they did not employ them yet. Instead, they had Farlan down and, like a pack of wolves, attacked him with their fists and feet from all sides. A blow here. The thud of a kick here. They howled and chirped and accused in garbled, muddled phrases.

Eventually, one of them would reach down, seize him by the hair, and employ a dirk to slit his throat. She could feel it coming.

She leaped forward, hollering to make herself heard above their howling. "Stop. Stop!"

They did not seem to see her and certainly did not heed her. A kick landed on her shin, breaking the skin as she took a position over Farlan. A blow landed on her back before Calan realized the truth and sang out.

"It is Mistress Moira!"

The anger did not abate and the attackers did not fall back, but they did hesitate and stare at Moira, as if seeking to grasp the reason for her presence.

"Stop!" she bellowed again. "Wha' is the meaning o' this? I—we—ha' guaranteed this man's safety."

"Young Calan here says he is the one! This MacLeod blackguard struck the blow that killed our chief. We can no' let him live!"

Moira met Calan's pale blue gaze. He still stood with his back pressed against the wall beside Farlan's doorway, his sword in its scabbard, looking both stricken and defiant.

Ye did no' keep your word. She did not speak the words aloud. No time for it, for Farlan lay motionless at her feet, a patch of red spreading at the back of his head.

Dead? Fatally injured?

"Calan says," shouted an older man, "ye were there when it

happened, fighting close by. Ye knew the truth, Mistress, and still ye protected this MacLeod bastard."

"I defended this clan as I always have. As I always will," Moira shouted, not quite truthfully. "This man's safety guaranteed our own. If ye ha' harmed him, Rory MacLeod will bring war."

"Let him!" shouted a younger man called Rab. "We are no' afraid o' war. We are ready. But first we will tak' our revenge."

They pressed in again and Moira shot a desperate look at Calan. Why did he not act? Could she hold all these wolves back on her own? She wished Alasdair would arrive. Or her sisters.

"Chief Iain was your own father, and loved ye right well," shouted Ewan from the back of the crowd. "How can ye defend his killer?"

"I defend our honor, and the truth o' our word as MacBeiths. I will no' stand for this. Clear off and we will hold a meeting come morning."

She turned to Orthan. "Help me move them out."

He jerked to life. "Ye ha' heard the chief. Go home. She will sort it all out in the morning."

Moira looked at the man sprawled beneath her feet. He still had not moved. He lay face down, one hand splayed against the ground, the knuckles raw. He had attempted to defend himself. What other wounds would she uncover when she turned him over?

He might already be gone. She could be defending a dead man.

The attackers began to move off. Calan unpropped himself from the wall and helped Orthan hurry them. Moira reached out and snagged Cathan's arm. "I will want words wi' ye."

His expression turned defiant. "I only did wha' was right."

He pulled away from her and she let him go. Suddenly, Saerla was there beside her, dressed also in her nightclothes but with a sword in her hand.

"Help me," Moira begged her sister, and knelt down beside Farlan.

"Is he dead?"

"I do no' ken." Moira fought back a sob. She could not let those remaining nearby see her weeping over a MacLeod.

Saerla stooped down next to her. "Let us turn him over."

They did and gasped in unison.

"He breathes," Saerla said.

For how long?

"Run and get Rhian, sister," Moira begged. "Go swiftly, please.

Chapter Forty-Two

"**Y**E SHOULD NO' be here," Rhian said in a low voice. "It does no' look right."

"As if I care for that," Moira returned tersely.

Rhian shot her an intent blue stare. "Ye should. Folk are unhappy. Unhappy enough to do this." She gestured at the man who lay beneath her hands. "The last thing they need is to see ye taking sides."

Moira looked at Farlan. They had carried him into the hall before Rhian arrived. To her surprise, Alasdair, who had turned up once most of the crowd cleared, had helped. They could not take Farlan back into his own quarters, since the door had been ripped from its moorings.

Someone had brought torches into the hall—some of the same that had been taken to Farlan's door. He lay sprawled, arms out and head turned to one side. Like a dead man.

Alasdair stood at the door. Keeping folk out, or keeping Farlan in, Moira could not tell which. Farlan was not likely to go anywhere on his own, not very soon, if at all.

Rhian touched Farlan with her healing hands, feeling the back of his head, his jaw, and his cheekbones. She folded his hands across his midriff, examining the abrasions there.

"He fought back. I think he hit his head when they finally took him down. And he is badly beaten."

"Is he going to die?" Tears slipped unchecked down Moira's face. If she had cost Farlan his life by keeping him here just so she had the chance of seeing him, of touching him—

Rhian blinked at her. Her lips parted and she hissed, "Sister? Be ye in love wi' this man?"

Moira could not answer. "Is he going to die?"

"Look at me." Rhian seized Moira's arm. She lowered her voice so Alasdair, at the door, would not hear. "Are ye? In love wi' him?"

"Does it matter?"

"Aye, I think it does. Moira, he is the one—the man—who killed Da. Is he no'?"

"And now everyone knows it. 'Tis what has brought all this down upon him. Me and my schemes." Moira swiped at her cheeks. "Thinking 'twas a good idea to force a truce wi' Rory MacLeod. Thinking I could keep Farlan safe."

Rhian stared at her.

Saerla came pushing into the hall, paused to speak with Alasdair, and joined her sisters. "How bad is it?"

"Bad," Rhian pronounced.

"Sister," Moira turned to Rhian, "ye maun save him. Use your healing magic."

"'Tis no' magic."

"It is. Da used to say—"

"I could no' save Ma, and I could no' save Arran. Nor Da."

"'Twas too late for Da."

"I will no' withhold care from him, or from anyone, because he is a MacLeod. Hatred is a weapon I refuse to wield."

Moira breathed out a sigh.

Rhian turned to Saerla. "Did ye ken?"

"Eh?"

"That Moira has fallen in love wi' the man."

Saerla bent her head. Rhian gave an exasperated sigh. "So this is why ye refused Alasdair, as good a man as can be found."

"Hush."

"Can ye save him?" Saerla asked.

Rhian shrugged. "I do no' ken. If his head be too badly broken, he may no' survive till morning."

"Ye maun save him, Rhian. Do ye ken what Rory MacLeod will do if we fail to send his friend back to him living?"

Rhian got slowly to her feet. "It seems we are fated for war either way. 'Tis but a question of when."

Destiny, Moira thought, gazing in desperation at the man on the floor.

"I will help ye care for him, Rhian. I will do whatever ye ask—"

"Then go speak to your people. Try to explain this breach o' faith and the way ye protected this man."

"I need to stay here."

"Absolutely not. Saerla may stay and aid me."

"Saerla." Moira turned to her younger sister. "Will ye pray for him? Ask mercy. Please."

Saerla bit her lip and nodded.

"Leave us," Rhian ordered Moira again.

Moira stumbled out blindly and nearly ran into Alasdair, who turned and glared at her.

"Ye and I need to speak together, lass."

"Aye." She supposed they did.

He fixed her with a dark stare. "Ye drew a weapon on your own people."

"They would ha' killed him." She wasn't sure, but they might still succeed.

"They wanted justice for the death o' their chief."

She fixed her gaze on him. "Is that what ye want also?"

"I wish to serve ye the way I did yer father, as ghillie and war chief." He gestured at the door. "Am I no' standing here?"

"Yet you want Farlan dead."

"O' course I want him dead." He narrowed his eyes at her. "For more than one reason. I heard wha' yer sister said before she thought to lower her voice."

"What—" Moira pressed her lips together in consternation and her face grew hot. "Alasdair, I did no' mean for it to happen."

"I am certain ye did no'. Him, o' all men."

"We canna help how we feel."

He thrust his sword into its scabbard. "That we canna."

"He may yet die."

"Aye well, if he does 'twill be a form o' justice."

"And we will be for war."

"I am ready."

"I must go speak with Calan. He did no' keep his promise. 'Twas he who told—"

"The truth? Ye canna blame the lad for telling the truth. He is grieving for his chief, as are we all."

"Still, he broke a promise."

"Ye will, or so it seems, do as ye will."

Moira glanced behind her where Rhian bent over Farlan's sprawled form, with Saerla kneeling beside her. She turned back to Alasdair. "Ye will stay here? Make certain he is no' attacked again?"

He swallowed down some emotion before he said, "I will, lass. Leave it wi' me."

She was not being fair to Alasdair, so she acknowledged as she went out. Calling upon a loyalty she perhaps had no right to demand under the circumstances. Not if he had honest feelings for her beyond that loyalty.

Perhaps she was not being fair to anyone. Rhian, for example. She'd just placed the man who'd killed Da in Rhian's hands. And the clansfolk grieving.

She went out in search of Calan, only to be stopped by people with questions and fears to express.

From most of the women, she got fear. *Will he be coming for us now, Rory MacLeod? Will he kill us all? My daughter lives out down the glen. Will she be massacred?*

From the men it was edgy anger. *Is he dead, the man who took down our chief? And, why did ye defend him?*

The hard-eyed looks were nothing like what she usually received from these people.

She told them she'd defended Farlan MacLeod in order to uphold the truce, but she felt guilty about it. By God, she felt guilty withal.

She eventually found Calan up on the battlements. When she approached him, he took one look at her and turned to walk away. She hurried after him and snagged his arm.

"A word, Calan, please."

He spun back to face her angrily. "Mistress? Wha' is it ye want?"

She released his arm and took a moment to discipline her emotions. Anger would not do her any good, nor accusation. How would Da ha' handled it? With unflinching strength, the same kind of strength she saw in Farlan MacLeod.

She experienced a rush of grief, which let the accusation slip out. "Ye made a promise the night our chief died. Ye ha' broken it."

"Aye, well." He tossed his head. "Mayhap 'tis a promise I never should ha' made. I am fed up wi' seeing the MacLeod pampered and afforded comfort while our chief lies cold up on the rise. And Mistress, I am fed up to my back teeth wi' the way ye go creepin' in to see him. Our folk needed to know the truth."

Moira staggered back a step as if struck.

"And then," Calan sneered, "for ye to draw on us and defend him—"

"He lies under our protection. *Our protection.* All I ha' ever done is try to guard the safety o' this clan."

"Keep tellin' yoursel' that, Mistress Moira. But take heed o' one thing. That will no' be the last time he's attacked. He killed our chief and he owes his life in return."

Chapter Forty-Three

MOIRA SAT BESIDE the pallet where Farlan MacLeod lay, with her hands folded and her head bent, trying to pray. Rhian had insisted her patient be carried to an area often used as an infirmary, where she'd finished tending his wounds. Until a short time ago, Saerla had also been with them. But both Rhian and Saerla had now gone, Rhian home to her bed and Saerla heaven knew where. A number of guards remained outside, men chosen by Alasdair whom Moira hoped she could trust.

The man lying in the bed did not stir and did not make a sound.

Rhian had told her they'd know by morning whether or not he would live. Morning light now grayed the doorway. Moira knew nothing more than she had hours ago.

"Farlan?" She took one of his hands into both her own. The skin there was scraped raw, all the knuckles split open. She whispered a thumb over it, but he gave no response.

His eyes remained closed, the lashes casting long shadows on his cheeks. A bonny man and no mistake, but it was not that—it was not that which anchored her to him.

Was she weak or strong for loving him this way? She could not tell. She had her faults, stubborn at times, so Da had said of her. Too sure her way was the right way. But what she'd said to Calan held true. For as long as she could remember, and especially since her brother's death, she'd thought only of standing with her da, and defending this place she loved.

If she was a defender, should she not also defend this man who had all unexpectedly claimed her heart? Was her love for him so much different from her love for her clan?

"Farlan, please come awake."

If she had killed him with her lies and her scheming, how could she ever forgive herself? And how could she go on without his steady light? Warming her, supporting her.

Her fault. All her fault.

She bent her head once more over his fingers, hurting so badly even tears would not come.

A movement at the door caught her eye. The panel creaked open. Alasdair stood there, peering in.

When she turned her head and looked at him, he ducked away and once more shut the door. Did the man never sleep? Thank God for it, because she trusted Alasdair. Whatever he felt, she believed he would stand between her and harm.

In the bed, Farlan breathed deeply and regularly, his broad chest rising and falling. He seemed to be at peace. If he slipped away now—

But nay, she could not endure it.

"Farlan, I want ye to hear how I love ye. Aye, I ken I told ye so before, but I am no' entirely sure ye understand the strength and the breadth o' it. I am no' sure I understand that mysel'. 'Tis so wide, this feeling, and so deep I do no' ha' words for it. Ye ha' taken root in my soul, and if ye were to go from me—" She stopped there, unable to force out any more words. The magnitude of the looming grief terrified her. How could he mean so very much? Him, of all men.

A radiance danced around her. Just a glimmer from the gray light filtering in, she told herself. Yet a sparkle caught her attention and made her look up from Farlan's fingers. Someone was there on Farlan's other side, though no one was.

"Da?" It would be just like him to come, with his great, forgiving heart to comfort her now, even though Farlan had caused his death. Or perhaps he came to lead Farlan away. Though when the dancing radiance took form, it was not male.

A young girl stood there, on the other side of the pallet where Farlan lay. Incorporeal and glittering, she had long fair hair hanging loose down her back and a sweet, youthful face. She held a tiny infant in her arms.

Moira gasped.

The spirit reached out and caressed Farlan's brow. Rhian had been forced to cut away some of his rich brown hair in order to treat the gash on his skull. The spirit laid her hand on the place.

She blessed it.

Then she looked at Moira. Her lips moved and the words followed an instant later, sounding only in Moira's mind.

Love him. In the end, 'tis all about love.

The spirit bent and kissed Farlan's brow before breaking up into separate, tiny bits of radiance, which disappeared into the strengthening morning light.

HE DREAMED OF Ainsley. Not as she'd looked when she died, awash in a welter of blood, but the way she'd looked back in the days when they'd played at the game of love together, and later, run the hills looking for a place they could be alone.

"Ainsley's for ye," Leith had often said with a smile, for Ainsley had been the younger of his two sisters. "She will look at no one else."

So, aye, he had not looked elsewhere either, and there had been no one else.

She'd been sixteen and he seventeen when they wed, joining in the old way with a knot tied around their clasped hands. He'd gotten her with child soon after, so soon. She'd been scarcely grown.

That's what the midwife had said. Ainsley was too tiny, and

birthing the babe had come on too soon. His son. Farlan had looked at the bairn, covered in blood and perfectly made with a shock of fair hair like his mother's. He had died before Farlan's eyes, and his mother had followed him with the dawn.

It happened, so everyone told him. Not every woman survived childbed. He would move on and love again.

He'd not believed that.

Now Ainsley came to him and she looked well, her gray eyes unclouded by pain and not a speck of blood on her. She held the child and he moved in her arms, kicking his wee feet. She bent low over Farlan where he lay and kissed his brow.

Love her, Farlan. Love her well. In the end, 'tis all about the love.

He felt that love, felt the warmth of it come flowing into him from Ainsley's kiss, and from the child in her arms. It warmed him throughout, traveled down his arm and into the fingers of the woman who clutched his hand.

It gave him the strength to open his eyes and look at her. Ah, such grief lay in the features of this woman who so often displayed only unflinching determination. Except when she looked at him. When she looked at him, he could see the—

Love.

He wanted to speak her name but could not. He wanted to tell her how he loved her. It seemed important to voice it, but he could not do that either. Instead, he wiggled his fingers, and even that took all his strength.

Her eyes flew to his. A fierce joy transformed her, lit her from within and banished the sadness.

"Farlan?"

"Moira." He forced the word through his dry throat. He spoke to her with his eyes even before words. "I love ye."

"And I ye. I ye!" She began to weep. He could feel her tears, taste them when she bent her head and kissed him on the lips. "Och, Farlan, I do love ye so."

She clung to him, and he felt the strength that lay within her still. It came to him in a rush, that strength did, right along with her love.

She caressed his cheeks with frantic, cherishing fingers, wiping her own tears away. "I thought I would lose ye," she told him brokenly. "And 'twould have been my fault."

"Nay," he whispered. No fault in loving. He sought to take stock of himself. "My head hurts. My hands."

She still clutched one of them. He held the other up before his eyes and marked the scrapes and abrasions. It returned to him dimly. He'd been in a fight.

"Aye. Ye were attacked there in your quarters. Word got out—word got out 'twas ye struck the blow that killed my father."

"Ah." He thought about it. "Justice then."

"Nay, Farlan."

"We maun all pay for our deeds. 'Tis only right."

"Nay. I will protect ye. I will, Farlan, any way I can."

He wanted to shake his head, but it hurt too badly. Beholding the fierce fire in her eyes, he knew there would be no use anyway. She was so different, his Moira, from the first girl he had loved. Gentle Ainsley who now bade him to go on living. To go on breathing, and loving.

A warrior, his Moira. One with a flaming sword that burned within her. For him.

Ah, he was blessed. Lying here broken and battered and aching, he knew that for truth.

"Is there water?" he begged, and she sat him up and held him there while he drank greedily. Water from the depths of Glen Bronach, this place they both loved. It went down like another blessing.

"Now rest." She pushed him back down with disconcerting ease. "I'll no' leave ye. On that ye may rely."

Chapter Forty-Four

"**I** KEN FINE wha' I must do." Moira stood beside Saerla up on the rise above the glen, having finally been persuaded to take a break from Farlan's bedside.

Rhian was with him now and had ordered Moira away. "Ye need to take the air, sister. Besides, folk are talking of how ye refuse to leave the MacLeod's side."

Three days had passed since the attack, another three gone from Moira's precious store. She supposed Rhian was right. The folk she'd met on her way up here had looked at her with either outrage or suspicion. But och, it made her uneasy being away from Farlan and not on guard for him.

Saerla glanced at her. Moira had found her sister already up on the height among the holy stones when she arrived.

"What is it ye must do?"

Moira puffed out a breath. It hurt her to say it. And following through on it would be like plunging a dirk into her own heart. "I maun send him back."

Saerla's attention quickened. Her misty blue eyes narrowed on Moira's face. "Farlan?"

"Aye."

"But 'tis no' yet time. There is—how long left?"

"Just under a half score o' days."

Saerla said nothing. Moira could feel her thoughts racing.

"I canna keep him here, Saerla. 'Tis no' safe for him. Folk ha' been biding their time to see if he will live or die. Once 'tis known he will live, he will come under attack once again. Calan told me as much."

"Calan—he is hurting. Da was his hero."

"We are all hurting."

"But, Moira, ye canna send Farlan back the way he is. Rory will see he's been battered. He will be afire to retaliate."

Moira shrugged. "He means to attack us either way, and from what our warriors say to me, they are ready for battle."

Saerla snorted. "No one is ever ready for battle. They say that out o' anger, and boasting."

"I canna keep him here, Saerla. They may well kill him next time. How could I live wi' mysel'?"

"Ye love him so much as that?"

"Enough to send him away. It will kill me, but I must."

The wind blew strongly up the slope and swayed them where they stood. Overhead, two eagles rode the updraft, and beneath them, the glen lay peaceful, deceptively so.

"Have ye told him yet, that ye mean to send him home?"

"Nay." Moira shook her head. "I keep thinking, give it another day for him to grow stronger. For me to keep him in my sight. But he is able to make the journey now. I just have to find the courage."

"Moira," Saerla whispered. "I am that sorry. I ha' never been in love the way ye be. In truth, I can scarce imagine it." She shook her head. "The spirits speak to me, but I canna seem to listen to the words o' men."

"Perhaps that is to your benefit," Moira told her sadly. "It hurts. It hurts to love like this."

"When will ye tell him?"

"Today. He's been getting up on his feet in the afternoons. Growing restless, which means his strength returns. I wish," Moira spoke not to her sister now but to the sacred air, "he could make love to me one last time before he goes."

"Unwise. If folk were to find out—"

Moira looked at her sister. "I ken 'tis unwise. But this need in me is such, it will no' answer to reason."

Saerla touched Moira's shoulder. "I ache for ye, Moira. But once he is gone, like a song on the wind, ye will still ha' a future ahead o' ye. We need ye here, with us."

"Aye." A song on the wind. A pretty fancy, but Moira wanted far more.

❯❯❯❯❮❮❮❮

HE WAS UP out of the bed when she got there, pacing awkwardly across the floor. He still wore a bandage on his head and looked edgy enough to cut leather.

Rhian had kept him situated in a room behind the infirmary, reasoning folk would not defy her by intruding here with violence. A guard remained always outside. Not Calan any longer, but men Alasdair assigned, and often Alasdair himself. But when Moira went out about the settlement, she still heard ugly rumblings.

Some of the agony fled Farlan's eyes when he saw Moira. "There ye be. I wondered where ye had gone."

Did the same craving plague him that rode her so hard? The desire always to be in his company? That assurance of peace?

"I ken fine I canna tak' up all your time," he acknowledged grudgingly.

"I went up on the rise searching for some clarity."

"Did ye find it?"

"Aye, I think so. Farlan, ye are no' safe here."

"Do ye think I care?" He came to her swiftly, caught her shoulders in his hands, and kissed her. All his need spilled through that kiss, and it called up Moira's own, wild and sweet.

She needed to push him away. She needed to tell him—

But the hunger rose through her like a beast held back too

long.

With a sigh, she leaned into him and kissed him back. The words she'd fought to order in her head flew away, lost in the rightness and sheer pleasure of it.

Och, how could she deny herself this? How ever send him away?

They kissed till she went breathless when he rested his forehead against hers and gazed into her eyes. The bruises that marked his face had just turned from black to purple and green. One eye still had swelling around it, but his gaze remained steady and strong.

"Beautiful lass. I thought I'd go mad wi'out seeing ye. 'Tis like somewhat pulling at me all the time. Ye ha' staked a claim in my heart."

"I ken," Moira whispered back.

He tangled his fingers in her hair and kissed her until her bones turned to water. Summoning all her strength, she drew away from him.

"Lass?"

"Gi' me a moment."

She turned away from him and faced the door. If this was to be their last time together, the moments upon which she would have to live for the rest of her life, she would make them worth remembering.

When she settled the bar across the inside of the door, he stiffened. "Wha' are ye thinking? Your sister will soon be back—"

"She will no' be able to get in, will she? Nor will anyone else." She faced him once more.

"Nay, lass." Reading the longing in her eyes, he held up his hands. "'Tis too risky. The backlash on ye, should anyone find out—"

She'd come here to tell him she meant to send him away from her. She would not have the courage for it unless she touched him, tasted him again.

"Hush," she told him. "Someone may hear."

"Moira, I need your company. And your kisses. But I would protect ye from the consequences o' anything more."

He sought to protect her, did he? But nothing could keep her heart from the pain to come.

"Hush," she repeated, and began to undress him. He stood stock still while she peeled off his shirt. Bruises bloomed into view, a garden of colors spread across his chest and ribs. They'd given him a good kicking once they got him down.

"Lass," he said, breathless now, "I am no' sure I'm fit."

"Ye need do naught besides lie back. 'Tis I will make love to ye this time."

He made no further protest while she finished stripping him of his clothing, or when she pushed him down on the bed.

Chapter Forty-Five

FARLAN SENSED SOMETHING new in Moira's touch as she stripped him of his clothing and ran her hands over his skin. The desire, aye, remained—enough to set his flesh afire. It came accompanied by a rare tenderness—respect, likely, for his healing injuries—and even more, a deep solemnity. He saw the latter in her eyes when she leaned into him, and felt it in her fingertips.

"Lass—" He made one last attempt at protest. "We canna do this here." Her sister might arrive. Someone else, looking for Rhian, or for a remedy. 'Twould be suspect if they tried the door only to find it barred, and Moira in here with him.

She made no answer to that, merely set about removing her own clothing, a process that made him catch his breath, before bending down and kissing him again. He raised his hands involuntarily to cup her naked breasts. Ah, who cared what happened tomorrow or an hour from now?

When she broke the kiss to trail her mouth down over his body, he was lost.

"Moira." It sounded hoarse to his own ears.

"Farlan, let me ha' this. Let me heal you."

She set about kissing every one of his bruises, bestowing comfort and arousal all in one. Across his ribs and over his belly. He lay barely breathing while she worked a glorious pattern upon him.

Did she mean to arouse, and then ride him? His battered ribs protested the notion. The rest of him responded with unbridled enthusiasm.

Moira, straddling him with her head thrown back and her bright hair spilling around her shoulders. To hell with his pain.

"Moira, I dare no' gi' ye my seed." They'd been lucky last time. He could not count on being so again.

"Do no' fret over it, my love. Ye just lie back." A hand planted on his chest kept him down. Her other hand moved between his legs to cup him.

Her mouth followed.

He became certain then he was going to die. If he died thus, with Moira MacBeith's supple body bent between his knees and her mouth enfolding him, he could ask for no more. He buried his hands in her hair as the licked and laved him, enfolded him again in her mouth, and took him ever deeper.

"Moira, lass—" He was not sure he said the words aloud.

He must have, because she withdrew her lips from him long enough to say, "I want ye, Farlan. All o' ye."

He could feel her strength and, aye, her demand. What could he do but succumb?

It was, he decided as he filled her mouth once more and she accepted him, taking him still deeper, as intimate an act as being inside her. It was all about intimacy with this woman. An exchange both spiritual and physical. He rode the crest of both, and found heaven.

She came burrowing up into his arms and he held her tight. *Tight.*

She purred into his ear, "I did no' hurt ye, nor harm ye, did I, Farlan?"

"Ye did no'."

"Sometimes a woman maun have what a woman maun have."

He palmed her breasts. "I hope ye do no' suppose we are done."

"Eh?" Her blue eyes, wide and hiding nothing from him, gazed into his. She was beautiful, his Moira MacBeith, and wild, and so, so clever with her tongue.

"Spread your legs for me."

"Eh?" she chirped again. "But—"

He whispered in her ear, "Sometimes a man maun give what a woman should ha'."

Obediently, she opened to him. She felt wet to his touch, aroused by what had just passed between them. When he thrust one finger inside her, she inhaled sharply. A second finger had her arching against him. Ah, she felt tight. Hot and arousing.

"'Tis the task of a man," he whispered just before he kissed her lips, "to bring as much pleasure to his woman as she brings to him."

Their mouths were joined, tongues touching, when she convulsed around his fingers. So close were they, so connected, he experienced the ripples of pleasure along with her. After, she clung to him, riding the aftershocks. The tangy, primitive scent of her engulfed him.

"Farlan. I did no' expect—"

"I love ye, Moira. I love ye wi'out reservation."

"And I you. That is why—" She stopped speaking abruptly.

He studied her, their foreheads nearly touching. "That is why—?"

She sat up, all that glorious hair tumbling around her. She swept her gaze over him where he lay, marking the healing injuries, the new abrasions, the old scars.

"That is why I maun send ye away."

"What?" He tried to sit up also, but she kept him where he was with the flat of her hand on his chest. Protest rose inside him. "Nay, Moira. *Nay.*"

She wagged her head slowly and tragedy invaded her eyes. "It is no' safe for ye here, Farlan."

"I do no' care."

"'Tis only a matter o' time before ye will once more come

under attack. Next time, they may well kill ye."

"I do no' care!"

"I do." She touched his face. She kissed him softly. "I do."

"The time is no' up. The treaty—"

"I mean to send ye back early. Ye can take another letter to Rory telling him 'tis for your safety I send ye ahead o' the terms of our truce."

"Moira, Moira." He threaded his fingers through the curls at her cheek. "I maun be near ye. I maun be able to see ye. Even if we can no longer be together like this."

"This was farewell." She scrambled up off the cot. "Thank ye for making it such a fine one."

Farlan understood then what it meant for a man's heart to break. His had cracked in two when he lost Ainsley and his wee son. Now he felt it shatter, and his spirit along with it. It came apart in distinct pieces, sharp shards that wounded as they exploded outward.

"Moira, listen to me. I do no' care what it costs me to stay wi' ye. Let them beat me on a daily basis. 'Twill kill me to leave ye."

She scrambled away, began gathering up the clothing she'd shed for him and climbing into it. Then she picked up his things, held them out to him.

"Farlan, do no' ask me to watch ye fall beneath the sword o' vengeance."

He did not know what to say, how to reason with her. How to persuade her. "I want to marry ye, Moira. To live wi' ye the rest o' my life."

"That canna happen." Her hands trembled violently as she fastened the front of her gown.

"We are meant to be together. It is destiny."

She froze for an instant before she picked up her head and looked at him. "I am meant to love ye for the rest o' my life. Longing for ye, loving ye, I will no' endanger ye." She added when he did not move, "Now get dressed. I maun unbar the door."

He did so numbly, no longer feeling his bruises or the battered ribs. Perhaps he should have, but he'd not seen this coming. Of all the madness that had occurred since he'd been taken prisoner on the field that night, the night Iain MacBeith had died, he'd been sure of one thing.

She would fight to keep him with her.

Now she gave him the kind of sendoff that might melt a man's bones, and destroyed him with the next word.

He was still only half-clad when she turned to face him. "I maun go write the letter and choose the men to accompany ye. The rest o' it will be public. This must be our goodbye."

He got to his feet, hurting, hurting. He went to her and drew her into his arms. "I canna say goodbye to ye, Moira MacBeith. Do not ask it o' me."

Her eyes filled with tears. "Then we will no' say it. Not now. Not ever."

So, was he to live his life—bleak life without her—on one side of the glen and she on the other? Separated more by anger and old ambitions than aught else?

Did he want that life?

He kissed her, putting all his love and longing into it. All his devotion. For an instant, she clung to him before breaking away.

"I love ye, Moira MacBeith."

"I do this because I love ye, Farlan MacLeod."

She unbarred the door and ran.

Chapter Forty-Six

MOIRA COULD STILL taste Farlan on her lips when she rushed out from the infirmary. How, how could a woman handle such a range of emotions, from the height of bliss to crashing despair in such a short while?

She never should have touched him, or let him touch her. She'd gone to the chamber meaning to tell him she must send him away. Better to have done just that. And yet—

And yet she would not sacrifice what had just passed between them for worlds. Now she had something to hold to her, after he was gone.

Gone.

Steady, she ordered herself. *You are the leader of your clan, of your father's people, and his father's before that. So be a leader. Able to make hard decisions. Do what has to be done without carping or moaning about it.*

But could she live without Farlan MacLeod?

Certainly. She had lived without him before they met and she would again. He was just a man.

One who'd gotten inside her. Deep inside.

She nearly ran straight into Alasdair on her way to her chamber to write the letter. The big man's hands came out to steady her, and his dark eyes narrowed on her face.

"Moira? Wha' is it?"

"Naught. Leave me go."

He released her but stood like a rock, blocking her way. His gaze flicked up and down in a swift examination. Had she fastened her clothing wrong? Or could he smell Farlan on her?

"Alasdair, I need ye to do somewhat for me."

"What is it?"

"I intend to send the hostage back to MacLeod. I wish for you to accompany him there, and assure his safety."

"Wha'?" He backed up a step.

"Choose a party. Men ye can trust. See him o'er the water and deliver him to his chief. I will send a letter also. I must go now and write it."

"But—the time is no' up."

"And it is no' safe for him here. If he remains, I fear it will cost his life."

Alasdair took another step back, eyeing her with acute suspicion. "What of the treaty? D'ye care more for his life than for upholding yer word?"

Aye, she did. But she could not say so, especially to Alasdair. "By sending him back, I will be upholding my word to keep him whole."

"And if Rory MacLeod takes offense at us breaking the agreement and decides to attack?"

"Ye ha' been telling me ye're ready for war."

"Aye, so." He did not look happy about it.

"Anyway, Rory should be glad to have his man back. I will ask, in my letter, that he might respect the length o' the treaty nonetheless."

Alasdair snorted.

A prick of anger and despair speared Moira. "If ye do no' want the assignment, Alasdair, I will take him back mysel'."

"I did no' say that." He gazed past her to the door of the infirmary. "Does he know ye mean to send him back early?"

"I just came from there."

"Aye." Alasdair could see. He could see Farlan's mouth on

her, his hands in her hair. He could doubtless see the great sorrow in her eyes. "I will tak' him. When?"

"Today. As soon as I can prepare the letter." If she did not send him today, she might not be able to carry through with it.

"I will go and choose the men."

Alasdair stalked off and Moira fought back her tears. A chief did not succumb to her emotions. The clan chief, no matter how she felt, did not stand out in the open and weep.

RHIAN CAME TO Moira, shocked and breathless, before the letter was half written.

"Wha' is this I hear, sister? Ye be sending the hostage back? Back to MacLeod?"

"Where did ye hear that?"

"Alasdair."

Moira hoped he was not telling everyone.

"Sister," Rhian joined Moira at the small table where she sat. "I am no' sure he is ready to travel. Farlan, I mean."

"He is able."

"His ribs need more time to heal. As does his head. It may be dangerous for him to move so far."

"'Tis more dangerous for him to stay." Moira raised her eyes to meet Rhian's troubled ones. "They may kill him next time."

"Ah. So that is it." Rhian glanced at the paper. "Wha' is this?"

"I am explaining to Rory MacLeod why I am breaking the terms o' the treaty I requested by returning the hostage. He will doubtless think me a madwoman."

"D'ye think he'll attack at once?"

"The treaty, and a desire for Farlan's safety, are the only things staying his hand. Still, in exchange for Farlan's life, he may prove merciful."

Rhian snorted. "By all accounts, the man has very little mercy in him."

"Then we are for war."

"You're certain about this course o' action?"

"Aye. If Farlan should be attacked and killed, if he canna be returned whole at the end of the thirty days, Rory will come wi' vengeance."

"That is no' what I meant. Sister, ye say ye love the man. This must be—"

Moira looked into her sister's eyes. "After losing Da, I did no' think my heart could break any further. I was wrong."

"I will go and prepare him for the journey as best I can."

Rhian slipped out and Moira glanced at the paper, which blurred before her eyes. A woman made sacrifices for those she loved.

The letter did not turn out as neatly written as the one Farlan had scribed, nor doubtless as coherent. Full of blots it was, and scribbles. Rory MacLeod would struggle to read it. Moira tried to imagine it resting in his hands, those of her mortal enemy. Failed to imagine his reaction.

She changed her clothing before she went out. Shed the gown that had so lately lain on the floor of the infirmary, washed herself and donned her leathers. She buckled on her sword with hands that had become steady.

This was who she was. A protector, a defender. The keeper of the gate. It was her destiny.

She found Alasdair standing outside the door of the infirmary with two of the older men, both of whom looked clear-eyed and grim. All stood heavily armed.

Saerla was with them. She turned to Moira with sympathy in her mist-blue eyes, enough to threaten Moira's hard-held composure.

"Sister? Are ye accompanying them?"

"Nay. I will keep watch above the gate." While her heart traveled from her body and across the glen.

"I will stand wi' ye."

Moira nodded and faced the men. "Go swiftly, but do no' press the pace beyond what the hostage can endure. Here is the letter." She thrust it at Alasdair. "Place that directly in Rory MacLeod's hands."

One of the other men spoke. "Mistress, ye are no' announcing to our folk that this is taking place?"

"I am no'."

He looked like he wanted to protest, but after a glance at Alasdair, held his peace.

"We'll gather some notice," Alasdair said, "setting out. The guards on the ramparts will mark our departure."

"Aye. Let me deal wi' that."

Farlan emerged from the infirmary accompanied by Rhian. Moira wanted to look anywhere but at him. Her eyes went nowhere else.

Grim and steady he looked, if vastly unhappy. Aye well, the steadiness was one of the things she loved best in him.

Though she loved it all.

No time for further farewells. No time to touch him or kiss him one last time.

Rhian spoke. "I am still no' certain this is wise."

"He is ready to go." Moira flicked a look into Farlan's eyes. "Are ye no'?"

"Aye."

They were the last words he spoke to her, or she to him. Farlan pulled the hood of his cloak up over his hair. Alasdair handed him a sword. Farlan's own sword it was, that had been taken from him the night he'd been captured.

The blade that had killed her da.

She should be glad to see this man go from MacBeith soil. *She should.*

She was not.

She and Saerla climbed to the walkway above the main gate and watched as the party set out. Just as Alasdair had predicted, they gathered immediate notice, first from the guards stationed at the front battlements. Then from the others on the walls. The clansfolk in the forecourt collected in groups to stare. A small train of them followed the departing party out onto the green turf.

One of the guards, spying Moira in her place, hollered up at her. "Mistress, wha' passes here? That be the hostage!"

"I am sending him back ahead o' the treaty."

"Why?"

"I am done wi' such agreements for the time."

They liked that answer, these men who spent so much of their time staring out toward MacLeod's fortress. Some of them might even have been among those who attacked Farlan.

"Let them go," she called down. "Wi'out interference."

"Good riddance!" cried one man, and a couple guards went to call away those who trailed the party.

Relief assailed Moira. And grief. He would get safe away. Once they reached the other side of the loch, he would be back on MacLeod land. She had only to stand and watch.

It seemed to take an age. The party went at a slow if steady pace, creeping across the great green distance. None of them looked back.

At length, Saerla put her arm around Moira. "Let us go back inside."

"Nay. I maun pay witness."

"Moira, there is sacrifice, and then there is torment."

Moira looked at her. "Pray do no' be kind to me, Saerla, or I will come apart at the seams."

"I understand."

Moira wondered if she did.

Chapter Forty-Seven

FARLAN HURT. HE ached from head to foot. Every step he took across the green turf—and he took an uncounted number of them—jarred his healing skull. His ribs set up a throbbing that kept time with his every breath. His heart—well, his heart had gone numb at the outset when he stood watching Moira send him away. He'd thought, when it came to it, she might change her mind.

Too strong for that. The woman he loved was all strength.

His heart had shed its protective numbness the moment he walked away from her. Now it bled inside his chest like a bird wounded unto death.

No good that he told himself it had been doomed from the start, any sort of relationship between him and Moira MacBeith. No good he told himself she acted out of a desire to protect him. He had pinned too much hope on destiny and could scarce believe it now failed them.

His party did not speak, at least not much. Alasdair led them, setting a pace he no doubt assumed Farlan could manage. A time or two, he sent Farlan a glance, measuring his physical condition.

Good thing the man could not see the condition of his heart.

They did not pause, not before they reached the loch, and the pain steadily increased, pounding through Farlan. He should be glad to go home. To see Rory and Leith, and others of his friends.

He would have to try and reason with Rory if he could. Argue him out of an immediate response. Give Moira some time to prepare for any onslaught.

He wondered what she'd written in the letter she'd handed to Alasdair. Had she announced that her father was dead? Should he, Farlan, share that information with his friend?

His chief.

Either he told Rory the truth or he'd have to lie in an attempt to shield Moira and face the consequences later.

He should have asked Moira about it. Found out what she wanted him to do. He'd been too busy lying beneath the ministrations of her mouth, and after that, bringing her a similar, scorching pleasure.

A small, sturdy boat lay above the waterline at the side of the loch. His guards put him aboard and two of them rowed across. The familiar scent of the water rose into Farlan's nostrils.

When he was young, his ma used to tell him that a serpent lived here, a dread *each uisghe* that could consume a lad in a single gulp. All the mothers and nurses had told the lads that, Rory's included.

It had been a tale meant to keep them safe from intruding upon the detested MacBeiths on the far side. Though so far as Farlan knew, none of them had ever been so dastardly as to harm a child.

Stories and exaggerations, the means to whip up anger and ill feeling. Were the MacLeods and the MacBeiths really so different?

Moira was a woman. His woman. And he was her man to the death.

They reached the far side of the loch and beached the boat. Alasdair, much to Farlan's chagrin, had to help him disembark. He muffled a groan.

Rory's guards would pick them up soon. In fact, quite likely they already had and now followed every movement. If he knew Rory, he would send out an armed party to intercept them.

Alasdair must be thinking the same. "Be ready, lads," he told the three guards. The big man tensed visibly, his eyes everywhere.

It did not take long to spy movement on the walls of the stronghold up ahead. The distant gates opened and a crowd of men poured forth. If Farlan was not mistaken, the man at their head was Rory himself.

No one else moved like Rory, head back, sword winking in the afternoon sun.

Farlan grunted to his companions. "Better put me out front." When Alasdair glared at him, clearly offended, he added, "Unless ye care to die."

"Treacherous MacLeod bastards," growled one of the guards.

"If they want a fight," Alasdair bellowed, "I will gi' them one."

"Do no' be a fool. You be no use to Moira slain."

"That is Mistress Moira to ye." Alasdair raked Farlan up and down with a glare. "I am no' certain ye're fit to walk at our head. Can ye mak' the distance?"

"Aye." If willpower could carry him.

The MacLeods came at a run, a full score of them. Their leader checked when he saw Farlan's tartan.

"Wait here," Farlan told his companions, and held up his hand.

"Farlan!" Rory bellowed it at him as he pelted up, his eyes performing a swift examination before moving to the armed MacBeith warriors behind him. "Wha's this?"

"Stay your weapons, all o' ye. The truce still holds. I'm merely returning to ye early."

"Aye, and look at the state o' ye." Rory, predictably, flared with anger and offense, his green eyes sharp and glittering in his handsome face. "Did they do this to ye, man?"

"There was an altercation. Mistress MacBeith sent me back ahead o' the agreed day, to keep me from harm, ye ken."

"Mistress MacBeith? Who is that? Wha' about Iain, the chief?"

"He was injured in the fight."

"The fight at the gate?"

"Nay, the one before that, when I was taken."

"He is dead." Alasdair, unbending and uncompromising, stepped forward. "His daughter leads us, the now."

Rory swore beneath his breath and swept Farlan with an incredulous glare. "Is it so?"

"Aye. There is a letter for ye," he repeated, in case his words had not penetrated Rory's agitation. "The truce still holds."

"Wha' letter?"

Alasdair dug it out from inside his jerkin. Rory accepted the paper and scowled at it. "Another damned letter. Wha' is this, scribe's folly?"

"Be glad to ha' yer man back," Alasdair grumped. "He might just as well be dead."

The warriors behind Rory pressed forward, weapons drawn. Rory held up his hand to stay them. He glared into Farlan's eyes. "I am glad to get ye back. These men may go in safety." He spat at Alasdair. "But the next time, the very next time I catch a glimpse o' MacBeith tartan, we will no' hold our hands."

Alasdair spat on the ground before he and the MacBeith guards turned to go.

As soon as their backs were turned, Rory gave Farlan a speaking look. Farlan shook his head in reply.

He stood there, stood and watched the men make their way back to the loch and thence to MacBeith land. The very place he could not follow.

⟫⟫⟩⟨⟨⟨

"TELL ME," RORY said. He had taken Farlan inside to his lair in the back of the hall, dismissing the men and other clansfolk, all in an uproar. Leith hurried out to meet them, his broad face wreathed with concern and his tongue, for once, silent.

The clansfolk would talk of this for days. Everyone there had marked Farlan's battered condition. They would talk of vengeance and of war, endlessly.

Rory could hold them if he chose. It would be Farlan's task to convince Rory not to unleash the violence.

"We feared ye dead, man!" Leith roared as soon as they were inside. He embraced Farlan heartily, causing him to wince.

"Aye, we did." Rory snagged a flask from the table and slopped liquor into three glasses. "And ye look to be halfway there." Once again, his green eyes swept over Farlan, measuring the damages.

"There's a story in it," Leith declared.

"There is."

"Drink this." Rory thrust a cup into Farlan's hand. The familiarity of the gesture, and the comfort of being in the company of these two good friends, assailed Farlan, making him glad to be home. Almost glad . . .

"Sit," Rory added, toeing out a heavy chair. "I am that glad to see ye, man. To be sure, we had the letter. The last letter." He frowned. "But we were taking bets as to whether or no' they forced ye to write that—for to be sure I ken your hand—and then slit yer throat."

Farlan wondered how best to explain all that had befallen him. Could he, should he tell these two of his feelings for Moira MacBeith? Would they understand?

Rory, focused on his ambitions, had never yet fallen in love with any woman. Indeed, Farlan found it difficult to imagine the sort of woman who might succeed in snagging his attention. Of course, he'd once thought that of himself, that he would never love again.

Leith—well, women loved Leith, and he liked them right back. Many of them. He spread his charm and his smiles far and wide, but so far as Farlan could tell, took none of it seriously. In fact, Leith's ma—Rory's aunt—the only one of their mothers still alive, despaired that he would never wed.

Were there two worse men to whom Farlan might try and

explain what he felt? When even he did not fully understand it?

Rory sprawled in the chair opposite Farlan's. "Tell me about the old chief, Iain."

"'Tis true what his man told ye; he lies dead. He perished the very night o' that cattle raid, the one that went so wrong. Ye remember the fight there at the end? Ye and me, Rory, were fighting near each other."

"Aye."

"I struck the old man a blow, a right fierce one. He was aiming for ye, though I do no' think ye saw it."

"I did no'. As so often, ye were there to guard my life."

"Iain fell back but did no' go down, and I doubted mysel', thought that blow to the neck must ha' glanced off his armor after all. Those fighting close to him closed in. The battle turned then and ye fell back. That is when they seized me."

Rory's eyes went grave, his expression bitter. "Ye canna imagine how I felt when I realized they'd taken ye."

In truth, Farlan could. He'd spent the last agonizing days imagining it. More brothers than friends, their bonds went deep.

"The group o' them hauled their chief, and me, back to their stronghold. I was locked up in a cattle pen. I did no' find out for some time that the chief succumbed to the wound I gave him."

"So," Leith rumbled, his gray-blue eyes wide, "ye killed him. And they had ye there in their hands, ripe for revenge. 'Tis a pure miracle, man, ye remain alive."

"Only because Moira MacBeith decided to mak' a hostage o' me."

"Moira MacBeith, old Iain's daughter."

"The new chief o' the clan."

Chapter Forty-Eight

"**I** TOLD YON Rory MacLeod the truth, Mistress," Alasdair announced, head back and shoulders straight. "That our chief is dead. If he wants to come and attack us, let him. I would no' ha' the bastard think we are afraid o' him."

Moira did not know how to respond. She'd been sick with worry the whole time Alasdair and the others were gone. Relief half staggered her, seeing them safely returned. And aye, the truth about Da would have come out eventually. She supposed she could not blame Alasdair for choosing defiance in the face of their enemy.

But this damned ache inside her just would not ease.

"And the hostage? Did he arrive in good form?"

Alasdair grimaced. "He was hurting by the time we got there, and no mistake. Those who thrashed him made a fair job o' it."

Bruises—acquired from punishing feet—spread across Farlan's ribs and aquiver beneath her lips. The taste of him as she'd moved ever lower on his body. How could she live without—

"But aye, he arrived in one piece."

"Good." Somehow, she forced the word through her throat. "Good."

"MacLeod looked surprised to see him."

"And he accepted the letter? Did he say whether he'd keep wha' is left o' the truce?"

"He did not, but I would no' take any bets on it. I wager he'll seek vengeance as soon as he can muster up his men. I go now to ready ours, with armor and weapons."

"Alasdair—" Moira reached out and touched his arm. "Take some time to rest first. It has been a gey difficult time."

"I need no rest."

"Ye do. God knows we all do."

His dark gaze moved from her hand on his arm to her face. "I ha' no cause to rest. My chief lies dead. I ha' just announced it to his enemies. And I will defend the woman who has taken his place to the death."

"Och, Alasdair." Moira's eyes filled with tears.

"Do no' weep, Moira. If yon MacLeod thinks we will be easily conquered, he is verra much mistaken. I am here between him and ye."

She should follow her own advice, Moira thought after Alasdair went out, leaving her alone in the hall next to the dying fire. Get a measure of rest. Only her mind and her heart remained too full.

What had Rory MacLeod made of the letter she'd sent? The one begging him to keep the balance of the truce. Alasdair had come away without getting a reply.

In returning Farlan, she'd lost her sole assurance of Rory's restraint. And she'd quite likely saved Farlan's life.

She palmed the tears from her cheeks, angry at herself for weeping. Surely she was stronger than that. As a woman leading this clan, she would have to be stronger still. Stronger than she had ever been.

She could not allow herself to sit and weep for a man.

FARLAN SLEPT. HE slept deep and long, his damaged body seeking solace and healing. All the while he'd been at MacBeith's

LAURA STRICKLAND

stronghold, he had not slept so.

He awoke in his own quarters—even better, in his own bed—his head muzzy. He should be glad to be here. Part of him was. The other part—

The other part ached for what it could not have.

He needed to pull himself together, get hold of his emotions. Get up out of this bed. He needed to sort out his mind and his heart if he could, and go talk to Rory. Try to discover the man's intentions. Reason with him, if possible.

He'd always been good at reasoning with Rory, talking him down, sometimes out of crazed notions. As boys, when Rory did not heed Farlan, he'd often ended up in trouble with Camraith.

Leith had been of little assistance in keeping Rory out of that trouble, him more often than not being amused by their exploits. Leith took few things seriously.

Two good friends. Could their company do aught to fill the gaping hole inside Farlan?

He struggled out of the bed, groaning and cursing. Every part of him hurt.

He found Rory and Leith together in the room off the main hall that used to be Camraith's study. That, only after running the gauntlet of scores of clansfolk who met him on the way, and who expressed their gladness at having him back and their previous conviction that he'd been dead.

Or as good as.

When he entered the study, Leith greeted him with a wide smile. "Here he be then! Both alive and awake. Man, we thought ye dead after all, the way ye were sleeping."

"I checked on ye three times," Rory put in, "and sent in the healer as many. He said the sleep would do ye naught but good. D'ye feel better for it?"

Farlan did not, but shrugged and nodded. He'd still not determined the best way to approach the matters he must with Rory, and sought to measure his mood. Edgy—well, that was normal for the man. Rory spent his days either planning great

258

KEEPER OF THE GATE

things, or going after them.

The truth was, Farlan did not think Rory had gotten over the death of his father yet. That, in part, spurred him in his actions. Rory wanted to accomplish what his father had not and failed to see that Camraith had his reasons for sometimes staying his hand.

Farlan had respected Camraith, had loved him like a second father. He believed there'd been things Camraith considered more important than conquest.

How could Farlan convince Rory to embrace a similar wisdom? Was it even possible?

His friend swept him now with a cool green glance. "Yon healer says they busted ye up well and good. Ribs. Head."

"Aye." Both hurt.

"They questioned ye, was that it? About our numbers and our intentions?"

"There was some o' that at the start." Farlan refused to think about Moira pressing the white-hot metal to his flesh. The glimpse of horror, even then, he'd spied in her eyes. "I took this beating when word got out that I was the one who'd struck Iain MacBeith down."

"Aye well, we will pay them back for it, blow for blow, and kick for kick."

Farlan glanced at Leith who sat half-sprawled beside the table. Could he count on him as an ally?

He lowered himself onto a bench, trying not to groan. "Wha' was in the letter Moira MacBeith sent ye?"

Rory's sharp gaze turned to him again. "She said she sent ye back early out o' concern for your safety. That she hoped, in light o' that, I would hold to the terms o' the truce for the balance o' the thirty days we set. She did no' mention that her father is dead, and they wi'out a leader, since his son has been dead this long while."

"They are no' wi'out a leader. She is in charge there at Mac-Beith."

Rory snorted. "A lass."

"Rory, she is no' just a lass. She is a strong woman who has stepped into her brother's place, since there is no one else ready to hand."

Leith raised his eyebrows. "Ye seem to ken an awful lot about it."

Ignoring him, Farlan pressed, "Ye will no' roll over her, Rory."

"We shall see about that."

Farlan narrowed his eyes. "D'ye intend to do as she asks and keep the rest o' the truce?"

"By God, nay. Why should I gi' up an advantage such as she presents to my hand?"

Horrified dismay speared through Farlan. "Because she has acted in good faith in sending me back. 'Tis a matter o' honor, and answering that in kind, is it no'?"

Rory got to his feet. Indeed, it seemed a wonder he'd remained still for as long as he had. "Acts o' good faith are for fools."

"Ah, so your father was a fool then? He believed in acting fairly, even to his enemies." If any argument could sway Rory, Farlan believed it was that one.

"Aye, perhaps he was a fool at times," Rory retorted, making even Leith stare. "Where did all his fair dealing get him? A lifetime o' petty battles and naught to show for it beyond some stolen cattle. We could ha' gained control o' all this glen years ago, had he acted wi' just a wee bit o' ruthlessness."

The criticism did not hit Farlan well, and he saw similar protest fill Leith's eyes.

"Your father was a good man, one o' the best I have ever known," Farlan declared.

Rory directed a glare at him. "I am no' saying different."

"And I do no' believe showing forbearance and keeping from destroying an entire clan o' people can be considered a weakness."

"Well, well." Rory turned to face him and scowled. "Look

who is come home wi' an opinion."

"I always had opinions. Your father half raised me. Ye canna' be surprised if I agree wi' the way he led this clan."

Rory stalked around the bench where Farlan sat, moving like a wild cat. "Wha' did they do to ye there at MacBeith, Farlan, to draw on your sympathies? Was it the beating? Torture? Did they douse ye wi' poison?"

"A magic spell mayhap," Leith suggested, and for an instant, his eyes met Farlan's.

Rory missed the exchange and ranted on. "I would ha' to be a fool indeed if I fail to seize a chance like this one. To turn down an opportunity to end years and years o' strife. Their chief dead. Led by some slip o' a lass. One who writes pleas to me for mercy." Rory bared his teeth in a grimace. "The thing to do is strike at once before they are ready for us. This—" he waved one hand, "could all be over by autumn."

"They are no' unready for ye, Rory. They prepare even now for attack. Do no' underestimate them."

"Then why did she plead for more time?"

"Who would no'? She was counting on that time. Ye maun consider, she could ha' just held me there, and let the truce run out. She acted only to my benefit, to get me out o' harm's way. I think she deserves a measure o' benefit in return."

"Ye do, do'ye?" Rory paused in his pacing and glared full into Farlan's face. "I do no'. And if she expects such regard from me, then more fool she."

Frustration seized Farlan by the throat. "List to me. That big man who brought me back, Alasdair, he is her war chief. And more than prepared wi' his defenses."

"She is fortunate I let him return to her then. She has had her share o' mercy from me. Tell me, Farlan, when it comes down to a fight, will it be her I'm battling? Or this Alasdair?"

"Her." His best friend, ranged against the woman he loved. "But Alasdair will be staunch at her side."

"Well enough then. Ye will ha' information for me, Farlan,

and right valuable information at that. Ye can tell me all about their fortifications and the numbers o' their men."

Farlan closed his eyes in pain.

"It appears, cousin," Leith told Rory, "our Farlan needs a bit more time to recover before he begins wi' giving ye any information."

"Aye, so," Rory snapped. "But do no' take too long, Farlan. I am eager as a man can be for the attack, and for the conquest."

Chapter Forty-Nine

"TELL ME MORE about this Moira MacBeith," Leith requested. "She seems an unusual sort o' woman, withal."

Rory had gone out, declaring he meant to begin organizing the men, and leaving Farlan alone with Leith. The big, fair-haired man still sat beside the table, his limbs deceptively calm, his gaze fastened on Farlan's face.

"Aye, so she is. From what I was able to gather while there, she has stepped into her brother's place wi' a fierce heart."

"No weakling then, as Rory would ha' it?"

"Not at all. She was there on the field when I struck her father. Battling right beside him, against us."

That caused Leith's brows to fly upward. "I saw nay woman on the field."

"That is because she dresses hersel' as a man, and wields a sword like one also."

Leith cursed softly.

"They are three sisters, old Iain's daughters. Two o' them ha' trained as warriors, and fight like the same."

"And the other sister?"

"A healer." Absently, Farlan rubbed at the long scar on his arm. "Likely saved my life not long after I was captured when I took a fever."

"Well so. Rory is right. Ye likely can provide us some valuable information. Capture these sisters, it seems to me, and most of the conquest will then be done."

Farlan stared at Leith in consternation. "'Twill no' be so easy as that."

"Nay? I do no' ken whether or not I agree. This seems like the very opportunity Rory has been awaiting. I tell ye, if he did no' love ye so well, he would already ha' his feet o'er there under Iain MacBeith's table."

"He tried it no' long after they took me, only to be beaten back from their gates. Did he no'?"

"Aye, but we would ha' been back at that gate wi' a vengeance had we no' received your letter. Tell me," Leith cocked his head, "wha' made ye write that? Rory insisted it had to be forced fro' yer hand. Torture, maybe."

"Nay."

"Nay," Leith repeated it thoughtfully. "Now that I see ye, and listen to ye, I think there's a far different cause behind your cooperation wi' our rivals across the glen." Again, Leith's gaze met Farlan's. "Me, I think it might be the influence o' this woman."

Farlan froze where he sat. How could he have forgotten? Leith so often acted the light-hearted layabout, with such innocence of spirit; it was easy to overlook a lightning-quick mind lurking beneath the casual demeanor.

Was there any use trying to deny his feelings to Leith?

"In fact," Leith pressed it, "I think it possible ye ha' grown feelings for her." He tapped the table with his thumb. "What puzzles me is, just how does one go about fallin' in love wi' one's jailer?"

Farlan puffed out a breath. "Leith, she's an extraordinary woman. Like no one I've ever known. Strong. Valiant—"

"Beautiful?"

"Och, aye. Wi' a rare kind o' beauty."

"Aye well, 'tis unlike ye, this. So far as I can tell, ye've barely looked at a woman since Ainsley died."

"I had no cause to look."

"A man always has cause." Leith, born charmer that he was, might well say so. "Women are one o' life's greatest pleasures."

"And," Farlan added, "one o' its greatest risks."

"Aye." Leith's voice softened. "Ye learned that lesson early, did ye no'? 'Twas not surprising ye chose to keep from mating up a second time. This is surprising, though."

"This?"

"Ye returning home from imprisonment wi'out your heart. Does she know? Did ye tell this new chief o' clan MacBeith how ye feel for her?"

Despite the aches in every limb, Farlan pushed to his feet. "I did."

"And she did no' laugh at ye? Scoff?"

"Nay."

"Do no' tell me she returns your feelings!"

Farlan glanced at his friend. "I suppose that is surprising, aye. I am no' much to look at, and even less o' a prize. No rank, no prospects."

"I would no' say that, Farlan. And by any road, there's no accounting for why a woman takes a fancy to something. I am just trying to stretch my wits and explain how it happened. Ye being her prisoner and having slaughtered her father and all. How did she come to look wi' such favor on ye?"

Following in Rory's footsteps, Farlan took a turn around the chamber. "I am no' sure I can explain it either." He looked Leith directly in the eye. "D'ye believe in destiny?"

"Well now, I do no' ken whether or not I do."

"Nor did I before I met Moira MacBeith."

"Ah." For once, and though it did not happen often, Leith seemed robbed of further words.

"I must persuade Rory to keep from attacking her."

"Good luck wi' that, lad. Ye'd as well save your breath. He's been champing at the bit for this since he was fourteen, though he for certain would no' cross his da or defy his wishes. And now he has what he sees as this grand opportunity—"

"I ken. Still, I maun try and persuade him."

"Why?"

"Eh?" Farlan stared at him.

"Say we attack MacBeith and say we overthrow them."

"At great cost o' life."

"Agreed, aye, but likely your lady will survive, being a person o' some importance."

"And given she does no' perish in the fighting."

"Rory will no' kill every member o' that tribe. They will be conquered, so, living under our rule. Ye can marry your woman then."

"As if she'd have me under those circumstances!"

"If 'tis destiny, she will."

"Nay. Nay." A broken, defeated Moira MacBeith was not what Farlan wanted. He needed her alive in his arms, heart-whole.

"It may be your only chance." Leith got to his feet. "Farlan, it has been a long time coming, this conflict. Generations. Let it happen, let things settle out afterward, and see what happens then."

As if he could hope to survive that long without Moira.

"One piece o' advice," Leith added.

"Wha' is it?"

Leith turned to face Farlan, no hint of humor left in his eyes. "Do no' tell him."

"Eh?"

"Do no' tell Rory how ye feel for this woman. He will see that, aye, as another advantage and will try and use it, as well as despise ye for what he'll call your weakness."

Aye.

"Ye ken fine what he is."

Farlan did. The three of them—him, Rory, and Leith—so different from one another. Such fast friends. Would Rory truly

KEEPER OF THE GATE

turn on him?

Farlan made a rueful face. "He may well guess, just as you did."

"Och well, he is all tied up in his intentions and so is no' as perceptive as me." Leith gave Farlan a brief smile. "Just go carefully, man."

"I want to help her, Leith."

"I understand that ye must. But doing so, lad, will mark ye a traitor in Rory's eyes."

Despair flooded Farlan's heart. "Ye may be right. But I do no' ken how I will live without her."

"As bad as that, is it? Well, ye maun ha' faith then. If 'tis in truth your destiny, then naught at all can stand in the way o' ye finding yer way back to her."

Chapter Fifty

MOIRA ENCOUNTERED ALASDAIR just before nightfall when she went up to walk the battlements. The sun had shrugged its way over the shoulders of the mountains to the west, and long shadows stretched the length of the glen. Deep shadows they were, that might hide all manner of dangers.

She'd climbed up here because she did not want her supper, and if she went to the hall where it was laid Rhian would pester her to eat. In the nicest possible way, of course. Rhian was worried about her—Moira could see that in her sister's dark blue eyes. God knew, Moira was worried about herself.

She dared not go early to bed either. She would just lie there while her mind ran in circles. It had been days since she had snatched more than a few winks. Tired enough to drop, she nevertheless began regarding the nights as torturous.

She could feel herself coming to pieces. No fool, she'd known that sending Farlan away would be hard and had done it anyway, for his sake. She'd never imagined she might suffer so terribly, so...fundamentally.

He'd taken part of her away with him, ripped a measure of her soul up by the roots and carried it off. She could not function, could not think aright. She stumbled both mentally and emotionally over small things and had trouble making up her mind.

The troubles they now faced as a clan were not small, but

very big indeed. Four days had passed since she sent Farlan home. Home. MacLeod was his home. Not here with her.

It would not take long for Rory MacLeod to launch an attack. He had made no reply to the letter she'd sent, and she had no idea if he meant to allow the requested reprieve. At any moment, she expected him to storm their walls, especially since Alasdair had announced to him that Da was dead.

She walked to the wall above the main gate and gazed out at the gathering darkness. This, to her, was a sacred place, one she'd set herself to defend. Maybe being here would lend her some much-needed heart.

She recognized Alasdair's step even before she turned and saw him approaching. No doubt, the big man spent most of his time on duty.

"Moira." He leaned on the wall beside her and fell silent. She imagined his eyes probed the shadows, just like her own, looking for movement. For danger. For signs the attack was imminent.

She wished he would speak, alleviate the tension that existed between them. Discuss the numbers of their warriors, perhaps, or the messages he'd sent to the outlying clansfolk.

Instead, when at last he broke the silence, he rumbled, "Yer sister—she is worried about ye."

"Which sister?"

"A fair question. I should say the both o' them, but 'twas Saerla who came to me."

That did surprise Moira. Rhian could be a right mother hen. Saerla most times kept her own council.

"Saerla? She came to ye?"

"Aye, so. Seems to think that you and I be friends."

"So we are. Friends." Moira hoped, still.

"And that I care about ye."

She cocked an eye at him.

"She is no' wrong there. Moira, I ken fine a number o' things ha' lately come between us."

"Aye. It's been a—a difficult time."

"Are ye angry because I told yon pillock, Rory MacLeod, yer father is dead?"

"No, Alasdair. He had to find out eventually. Are ye angry I sent Farlan back to him?"

"Well now, no' that ye sent him back, nay. He had to go anyway, in less than a fortnight." He took another moment of silence. They were alone save for the guards patrolling the wall on the far side, and the shadowy land below.

"The reason ye sent him back. Now, I may be a wee bit perturbed about that."

"The reason?"

"Aye. Ye see, I do no' believe ye sent him for our sake, so much as his own."

Moira's heart thudded. "'Tis one and the same. Keeping the hostage safe assured our safety in turn."

"Wi' all due respect, Moira, leave off wi' the shite."

"Eh?"

"I understand your love for this clan and for your folk. 'Tis your heart, as it was for your father before ye. But you and I both ken there be more to it, as concerns yon Farlan MacLeod."

Moira's mind raced. Aye, Alasdair knew how she felt for Farlan. He'd overheard Saerla speaking of it, and had charged Moira with the truth. Yet speaking with him about it made her vastly uncomfortable. It seemed all too much like facing her own conscience.

Arms bent, leaning beside her on the stone, Alasdair slanted a look at her. "Pay me the respect o' being truthful, lass. Why did ye turn down my offer o' marriage? Was it because I'm a great brute? Because ye do' no' think it would benefit the clan? Or because ye're in love wi' him?"

Him.

"Farlan MacLeod." As if Alasdair needed to make it clearer.

Moira lowered her head and pressed it to her folded arms. Alasdair had not precisely spat the words *Farlan MacLeod*, but he'd pronounced them with distaste. It did not encourage confidence.

He was right, though. She owed him truthfulness. They were friends, and she valued him beyond measure.

Another silence fell while she hid her face, and he waited with patience rare in him. When she lifted her head from her arms, she had to blink away tears.

"I do love him."

Alasdair remained silent.

"I ha' tried to fight it. But it has hold o' me like—like a fever."

Alasdair grunted.

"One does no' want to ha' those kinds o' feelings for—for an enemy."

"I should think no'." Alasdair's voice sounded hard as the stone of the parapet. No sympathy there. Had she expected any? Nay. To Alasdair, an enemy was an enemy. "He killed yer father, lass. How d'ye get round that?"

"It is no' easy. But the feelings are so strong, even that canna stand before them."

Alasdair grunted another word. "Lust."

That made Moira stare at him. "Eh?"

He slanted her a dark look. "Ye think I do no' understand it? That I do no' fall victim to it? All men do. But ye maun be—be strong enough and canny enough to discipline such impulses."

"Aye." Moira gulped air. She could not possibly be standing here discussing desire with Alasdair. "But it isn't lust." Not just lust, anyway. Farlan sliding the palm of his hand up her leg. Using his mouth to bring her unbearable pleasure. "'Tis the man he is, inside."

"A MacLeod, to the core."

"Ha' ye ever paused to think, Alasdair, that we are all just people beneath the colors o' the tartans we wear? Beneath the skin? At the heart?"

"Nay."

"Well, I have. He is a good man. One wi' a true heart."

"They killed yer brother, lass. And our chief—one o' the best men I ha' ever known."

Another silence fell. This one Moira could not break because her throat was full of tears. He would not understand. Perhaps he could not.

"'Tis as well ye sent him back, considering all that. Even if I am no' convinced of the supposed reason. I ne'er liked the notion anyway o' holding a hostage in order to force Rory to stay his hand."

"Ye thought it made us weak."

"Aye."

She glanced at him. "Ye think me weak."

He shrugged. "As I say, lust can be a powerful force. It can make a man, or a woman, I suppose for all that, do all manner o' foolish things. I merely wanted to know—if that is why ye refused me?"

"Oh."

"For he is gone now. Well out o' your reach. And the rest of us—ye and me—need to go on."

"Aye."

"We face a great deal o' danger because, ye ken, Rory will come. We need to be as strong and as united as we can."

"It is so."

"We would be strongest if ye wed wi' me. I ken because ye've told me fairly ye be in love wi' another. I believe that will fade. I ken I am no pretty lad, like yon MacLeod, and if that is wha' ye want, I canna' help ye. As I've said, I'm an ugly brute."

"Ye are no'."

"But I love ye, Moira, right well. And I've wanted ye since ye were a lass, even before 'twas likely proper."

Stricken, Moira said nothing.

"So gi' me yer answer in the morning, if ye will. And we'll tie the knot early, before we set up our defenses here, together."

Moira could not deny the value of it. She would not have to stand alone, even with Da gone. That aspect was an alluring one. Aye, she'd always known on some level she could count on Alasdair even if he disagreed with many of her decisions. To be able to present a united front to the senior council and to clan MacLeod would be vastly reassuring.

It came at a high price.

Aye, she loved Alasdair as a friend. Her heart was lost to another, and the big man beside her could never claim it. Would such a union be fair to him?

She tried to imagine marriage, and intimacy, with Alasdair. With anyone, besides Farlan. Allowing another into that innermost place she'd offered only him.

She placed her hand on Alasdair's arm, and felt his tension. "Gi' me a wee while, please. A few days to think on it and make up my mind."

"Aye, lass, verra well. But do yer thinking swiftly. I can feel it in me bones, we do no' ha' much time."

Chapter Fifty-One

EVERYWHERE FARLAN WENT within MacLeod's stronghold, he saw the preparations for war. He stumped around daily, ignoring the aches that lingered in his body, even if he could not quite disregard the ache in his heart. The signs were evident. In the forge. On the walls. Most of all, on the drilling field.

Old Bann, Rory's healer, had declared Farlan not yet fit to participate in drills or practices. His ribs, the canny old fellow insisted, were not only battered but cracked.

That accounted for only half of Farlan's pain and frustration. But it made a decent enough excuse, since he no longer wanted to take up a sword against Moira or her folk. Remaining idle, though, lent no remedy. He drifted like a ghost from one place to another, and the very sight of his condition prompted anger among his friends.

To be sure, he was well-liked, and a number of those among the warriors expressed outrage at his treatment at the hands of the MacBeiths. They tended to waylay him in his wanderings, ask for details about Iain MacBeith's death, and what had befallen Farlan as a consequence.

Though he did his best to dampen it, for Moira's sake, his battered condition only served to further enflame them.

The season moved swiftly into summer. Everyone believed this would be the year they achieved their long-awaited goal.

KEEPER OF THE GATE

Clan MacBeith, weakened and devoid of their chief, would be conquered. MacLeod would at last rule Glen Bronach.

When so many hearts and minds threw themselves fervently into the same cause, could it fail?

Rory certainly did not believe so. He too went around the stronghold making his preparations, lit like a flaming torch. He inspired and encouraged. Men picked up his energy and went away with a livelier step. Rory had always been focused. Now his eyes did not waver from the prize.

Indeed, the only person he did not inspire was Farlan. Rory, no fool, picked up on Farlan's continued resistance and avoided him. They were no longer the near-inseparable friends they had been. Another blow to Farlan's heart, that. He'd relied unthinkingly on Rory for most of his life. The breach between them felt like a new wound.

It made Farlan think about all he'd lost in his life. His da. His ma not long after. Ainsley and the wee lad. Camraith. And now, Rory.

Had he lost Moira also? Nay, for he could feel the unwavering connection between them, still anchored deep inside him.

He wished he could get word to her, warn her that Rory prepared to attack. But surely she knew. And she had Alasdair at her side.

She would be all right. Would she not?

Leith, at least, did not go out of his way to avoid Farlan, and in fact took to seeking him out at the end of each day with a flagon of ale in a rather obvious attempt to offer comfort. Ainsley had been Leith's younger sister, and so they were family in a way.

Since Farlan could not ask Rory, he got most of his information from Leith.

"Is Rory ready to move?" he might ask as he and Leith sat over the fire in Farlan's quarters.

The big, fair-haired man would shake his head. "No' quite yet."

"He gives every sign."

At the most recent of such meetings, Leith shared his opinion. "I think he means to hold his hand until the term o' that truce is up, after all."

"Why?"

Leith shrugged. "I believe he does no' want to be accused, after, o' violating it." Leith fixed Farlan with a stare. "He means to crush them, Farlan. Wi'out mercy. He wants it to be complete, and he wants no questions after as to how he went about it."

Farlan swallowed hard, trying to imagine it. MacBeith's stronghold lying in ruins. Fire blackened walls. Blood on the ground. Devastation.

"Does he intend to mak' a siege?"

"If need be. He does no' think 'twill come to that, though. A few fierce battles. Kill their leaders outright and 'twill pluck the heart out o' their resistance."

Kill their leaders. Moira would be fighting in those fierce battles. Farlan knew her, and knew she would be nowhere else save on those walls.

Moira could die.

Aye, he'd known it was so all along, known it since he'd first learned she went out with a sword in her hand. Now he looked at it fairly.

It would be in Rory's best interest for Moira MacBeith to fall, defending those walls. The woman Farlan loved.

He could not stand by while that happened.

Leith, reading his expression without difficulty, clamped a hand down on his arm. "There's naught ye can do, man."

"There maun be. I might try again to reason wi' him."

"If ye think that possible at this stage o' the proceedings, ye be welcome to try."

"Perhaps if he sends me to speak wi' Moira, urge her to accept his terms—"

"Wha' sort o' terms? He has issued none."

"She and her clan might swear fealty to Rory—" Rory may be satisfied with that. And it could be accomplished without bloodshed, or risk to Moira's life.

"Ye think she would?"

Nay. Moira loved her lands even as Rory loved his own. Moreover, she and her people felt they were in the right, having been first in possession of Glen Bronach. Yet they had no true grasp of what was coming, having never faced Rory MacLeod in all his fury.

Farlan had but one choice. He must speak with Rory again, try and reason with him. Call upon the bonds of their lengthy friendship, perhaps. Persuade Rory that a balance of power here in the glen, rather than widespread bloodshed, might be an answer.

For, beyond that, Farlan could see only one course for him, and it was one he did not even want to think about.

HE HUNTED RORY down the very next morning, and eventually ran him to ground in the armory. It was a soft day with mist crowning the hills and drifting down their flanks like ghostly herds of deer. Everything lay drenched with wet. Rory's clothing glittered with it when he turned to face Farlan.

"Morning."

Rory did not look happy to see him. The gladness that used to appear in his eyes at Farlan's arrival was absent, along with any hint of a smile.

"Healing up, are ye?" he asked pleasantly enough.

"All but the accursed ribs."

"Fit to swing a sword?"

"Before long." Farlan drew himself up. "How soon do I need to be ready?"

Rory broke eye contact with him and rubbed at his jaw. He'd failed to shave for the past few days, though as Farlan knew, Rory preferred to go clean-shaven. His fingers rasped on dark stubble.

"Are ye willing, Farlan, to be part o' this fight? The thing is, I thought ye were at odds wi' my intentions."

"Ye've rarely gone into a battle wi'out me at your side." Except when he'd attacked the MacBeith keep in an attempt to win Farlan free.

"True enough. And I want ye there wi' me, if you're fit." His green eyes, looking overly bright in the soft morning light, met Farlan's again. "In body and spirit."

"I've no' fallen mad, ye ken." Just in love. Which might well be the same thing.

"Ha' ye no'? I should say ye've come home wi' your wits scrambled."

"And I would say ye've always been overly stubborn."

"Wha' d'ye mean by that?"

"There's more than one way to accomplish yer goal, ye ken. There be no need to murder half o' clan MacBeith."

"Ye think I ha' no' considered on that?" Now Rory glared at him.

"To be honest, I'm no longer sure what ye ha' in yer mind."

"Nor I yours."

They glowered at one another for twenty heartbeats.

"Look," Rory said then. "I've considered all o' it. I do no' want my men throwing themsel's against MacBeith's walls just to die. No' for the sheer sake o' it." He bared his teeth. "Even though they do seem overly eager to do so."

Farlan puffed out a breath. Perhaps Rory was open to reason after all. He felt dizzy with relief. "Then—"

"I've weighed the benefit to be had in me staying my hand, and marrying the wench."

"The wench?"

"This Moira MacBeith. Iain's eldest daughter. The one ye say has set hersel' up as chief o' her clan. 'Tis a canny solution, if she would accept me. D'ye think she will?"

Aghast, Farlan stared at his friend. *Nay.* Or would she? What would Moira MacBeith refuse to do for the benefit of her clan?

"I might send an emissary, wi' the offer. I might send you."

Och, nay. God, nay!

"I could gi' it a fair shot, and then ye can stop blathering at me about the benefits o' peace. If she refuses me, then I'll ha' naught on my conscience when I slaughter them all."

Farlan, utterly nonplussed, turned away and gazed sightlessly out the door of the armory into the misty morning.

It could save her. It could save all of them. All he had to do was watch the woman he loved pass into the keeping of his best friend.

Chapter Fifty-Two

MOIRA STOOD ON the height overlooking the glen, at the mercy of the buffeting wind. Her eyes rested on the sweet slopes of the green expanse below. She'd come up here, as she so frequently seemed to do these days, in an effort to think. She owed Alasdair an answer, owed him better than dragging her response to his proposal out much longer. Such matters needed to be settled when they moved into war.

She no longer doubted they moved in that direction. From up here, with the glen laid out in all its fair beauty—enough to stir any heart—she could see the signs. MacLeod's stronghold might look small, but men fanned out from it. They drilled, they organized. Attack could come at any time.

Love for this place, pure and strong, swelled in her breast. She'd sworn to keep it safe, promised it to her da as he lay dead. A sacred vow.

Everything that had followed that vow, including her feelings for Farlan, seemed like a dream. Had she truly kissed his lips? Opened herself to him as completely as a woman could? Felt a connection so deep it could never fade? Aye, och aye, for she could feel that connection still rooted within her, as if invisible bonds trailed across the glen, spanned the blue waters of the loch, and anchored in his heart.

And yet life, her life, did not contain beautiful dreams. No real beauty at all except this glen, for which she must fight. Life contained ugliness and blood, struggle and death. She knew that all too well.

How dare she think she was a woman, even if Farlan had made her feel like one for a short time? She was a warrior, after all. A defender. For her, there were no happily-ever-afters. She must live for this place and nothing more.

She needed to stop with dreaming and make up her mind. This very morning, she must go down, find Alasdair, and tell him she would become his wife. It was the best thing to do.

For the clan.

Two tears coursed their way down her cheeks. She told herself they came from the stinging wind, nothing more.

Then her eyes narrowed.

The distance between MacBeith and MacLeod was great, none knew that better than she. She could not possibly espy details with miles of green turf and the loch between. Yet in the clear morning light, she thought she saw—

Perhaps it was instinct rather than her eyes that told her the truth.

They mustered. Clan MacLeod did.

They appeared like dark specks, like an ill tide flung out from the distant keep. Not enough to threaten everything she loved.

But she knew. She knew.

With a strangled cry, she picked up her skirts and ran.

By the time Moira reached the keep, the word was out. Men keeping watch from the tops of the walls had seen the same things she had and given the alarm.

She ran into Alasdair halfway up the stone steps that led to the rampart. Breathless, she laid hold of his arms.

"They come. They come!"

"Aye."

"Are we ready?" Despite the fact that they'd been preparing for days, she had sudden doubt. Was it enough? They'd brought in the clansfolk from the outlying areas, and laid by both stores and weapons. Still—

He made a face and shrugged. Could they ever be ready? "We ha' some time yet. The question be, do we keep to the walls here or march out and meet them?"

March out? Moira could scarcely think of it. "What do ye say, Alasdair?"

He did not hesitate to answer and, indeed, must have been contemplating it for days. "I say march out. And, Moira—"

He paused and seized her forearms in turn with his big hands. All around them chaos raged. Men shouted, relayed orders. Folk called out questions. Moira saw only Alasdair's dark eyes.

"Ye will no' like this, but I am going to ask ye to stay behind."

"What? Nay. If ye march out, I do also. I maun go change into my leathers and gather my weapons."

"Lass, I ask ye to consider—"

"I have always marched out." Raids, skirmishes, battles, pursuits. The fight at the gate.

"I ken that fine, Moira, but things ha' changed. Ye be chief now."

"No matter. Da always went out at the head o' the men."

"And he paid a high price for it, one I would no' see ye pay in turn. List to me. I will lead the men. The MacLeod force is larger than ours, aye. If we fail to defeat them out in the glen, they will come on. Ye will be sore needed to direct the defense here, especially if it comes to a siege."

If that happened, Alasdair would most likely be dead. Moira stared into his eyes while her heart rose in wild protest.

"Ye but seek to protect me."

"It is my place, Moira. And it makes sense. Wha' happens here if both you and I go down out there?"

"Alasdair—"

"I am yer war chief. Let me go to war for ye." *To die for ye.* He did not say that, but she heard it.

She wanted to weep. She wanted to howl and rant and cry.

Instead, she nodded. "As ye will."

"Good lass."

She turned on the narrow, crowded stairs and went back down. On the way to her quarters, she met Saerla, clad already for war.

"Sister!"

Saerla looked at her, eyes full of the mist that denoted a vision.

"Sister, wha' ha' ye seen? A victory?"

"Somewhat comes. Somewhat big comes."

Aye well, Moira knew that already.

Saerla seized hold of her by the arms. "Go to him, or he will die."

Go to him? Farlan. But how?

Saerla did not pause to tell her any more. Armed for war, she pelted off in the direction of the main gates.

In her quarters, Moira hastily donned her leathers and strapped on her weapons, hands trembling so violently she could barely manage the task. Hastily, she bound her wild curls out of the way. An enemy could use flying hair for a handhold while slitting an opponent's throat. All the while, Saerla's words echoed in her head.

Go to him.

Would Farlan be with the attacking company? Had he healed from the effects of the beating he had taken here at MacBeith?

She did not know. But she could think of only one way to go to him.

Back on the walls, she scanned the faces of those swiftly organizing a defense. She saw Calan and Ewan, Orthan and so many others. All dear to her. All family.

She located Saerla in position above the gate. Had Alasdair ordered her to stay back, also? From here she could see the company, with Alasdair at their head, mustering in the forecourt below.

Turning to Saerla, she said, "Ye be in charge here. If it comes to a siege, do no' relent. Hear me? No matter what, do no' give in to Rory MacLeod's demands."

Saerla, most of the dreaming now cleared from her eyes, stared. "Alasdair said you would direct the defense."

"I am going wi' them."

"What?"

"I' am going with Alasdair, and the force marching out."

Saerla seemed to consider on it before she nodded. Her arms came around Moira in a fierce hug. "May God go wi' ye."

Down in the forecourt, Moira quietly joined the company preparing to depart, who jigged and shuffled and rattled in the morning. But Alasdair saw her immediately. He finished bawling orders in his deep voice before marching up to her where she stood, scowling.

"Wha' be ye doing here? I thought we settled it. Ye're to stay."

"I changed my mind."

"Ye fool o' a—"

"I'm marching out, Alasdair. I mean to be there. That's an end to it."

In fury he spat, "I knew ye for a stubborn woman, but—"

"Do no' waste any more words, Alasdair. We will march out and face this together. Side by side."

Chapter Fifty-Three

A BEAUTIFUL MORNING for battle. Farlan could not help thinking as much as he walked out onto the green sward where Rory mustered his men. Golden light flooded over the hills into the glen, and a stiff breeze blew white clouds inland from the sea. Fair weather clouds, these were. But 'twould be no fair deeds done in Glen Bronach this day. The Glen of Sorrow. It had never been truer, at least for him.

He turned his eyes on Rory, who stood clad for war with his dark, nearly black hair shining like the wing of a blackbird in the sun. His friend always reminded Farlan of an arrow, sharp and focused, aimed straight at his desire.

At the moment, he was an arrow cocked. Farlan did not think aught could dissuade him from the course he'd set.

But Farlan meant to try one last time.

He'd spent all the words he had, well into the night, arguing for a permanent treaty—one that did not include marriage between Rory and Moira MacBeith—and an enduring peace. He'd talked at Rory till his friend became right angry with him. Farlan knew better. Rarely did it do any good to badger Rory, especially when his blood ran high.

Never wise, then, to get in his way.

Farlan had one last marker to play. It was an old one, nearly as old as the two of them. And it flew under the banner of friendship.

Accordingly, he walked out into the beautiful morning, into what would either be the quarrel of his life or his greatest victory.

A broad man and a tall one, Rory seemed even bigger in his padded armor and with his shield on his shoulder. He'd tied back his hair, and his green eyes looked hard as flint.

Farlan had seen him just this way more times than he cared to count. Before a raid, before a battle. Before a hunt.

"A word, Rory."

Rory turned and his eyes flickered over Farlan. "Ha' ye decided to come wi' us then?"

"Nay. I wish to ask ye one more time to reconsider this attack. 'Tis no' necessary to spill more blood. For years your da kept from crushing the MacBeiths. Ye might do the same."

Impatience flared in Rory's eyes. "This again? By Christ, Farlan, I scarcely know ye since ye came back from that accursed place. Ye behave like a different man."

"I am a different man. But still your friend, aye? Can aught change that? Rory," Farlan lowered his voice to a low throb, "I call on ye now to honor the bonds o' that friendship. Ye can strike a truce wi' the new chief MacBeith, I know it. Wi'out marriage—"

Rory's green eyes sharpened. "How d'ye ken that?"

"Because I know her." Farlan drew a breath. "I love her, and I ask ye for the sake o' all you and I ha' meant to one another in the past, and by all that's holy to reconsider—"

For an instant, astonishment transformed Rory's expression before his green eyes turned to ice.

"Love?" He spat the word with ineffable disdain. "The opportunity o' a lifetime and ye come to me blathering o' love?"

Several of those closest to them turned their heads. Rory ignored them. His eyes, the color of the ice that rimed the loch in winter, stabbed at Farlan.

"Aye," Farlan told him steadily.

"For the sake o' a woman?" The words came rife with disparagement. "And ye speak to me o' friendship? Wha' o' the loyalty between us, o' yoursel' to your clan? Wha' o' the fealty ye owe to me as your chief? Would you sacrifice that for a *woman?*"

Leith came up beside them, his eyes wide with distress. He shot Farlan a shocked look before he spoke. "Now, Rory—"

"Nay, Leith, I'll no' listen to it. Ha' ye heard this nonsense he spouts to me?"

"Aye, but—"

"Over a woman?"

All around them, the men had gone silent. They listened with disbelieving ears when Rory said, "Ye, Farlan, maun get yer loyalties straight."

"They are straight." Farlan drew himself up. "I canna see ye harm her, Rory. Or wed wi' her either. She is mine."

Rory stared. It took him a moment before he said, "Then ye be no longer my friend, Farlan. Nor, I think, a worthy member o' this clan."

"Rory," Leith began.

"Nay, a man maun choose where his heart lies. It canna' be split between twa' masters."

"Ye're right," Farlan said.

Rory squared his shoulders. "Either ye go and don yer armor and tak' up yer sword and march out wi' me—"

Against her.

"Or ye renounce here and now your birthright as a Mac-Leod."

The silence around them was now so complete it vibrated. No one breathed.

Farlan, facing his friend, thought of all the years between them. Sunlit days and crisp autumn evenings. Getting into trouble and facing Camraith, who was always, always kind. Rory had just struck him a blow to the very soul.

Yet Moira, Moira was his heart.

"Aye then, Rory," he said. "It seems we maun part ways, ye and me."

Rory looked incredulous. He took an abrupt step backward.

Rage flooded his eyes. "Why, ye traitor," he roared. "Ye disloyal, turncoat bastard!"

Farlan said nothing.

Rory raged at him. "Ye'd best go to her! Go to her if she means more to ye than your name. Ye no longer be a member o' clan MacLeod, nor welcome here."

Those around them found their voices then and protested. Leith stepped up to Rory and began to speak, but Farlan could not hear him for the roaring of blood in his ears.

He stood as he'd come from the keep. No belongings. No weapons. He could not go back for them. His chief had just categorically cast him out.

He nodded at his best friend.

"Go now. Go to this MacBeith bitch who has seduced ye. Take up a sword in her defense against us, if ye will."

A long walk across the glen. Farlan was willing to undertake it, to accept the banishment even while the wound of it bit deep, like physical pain.

Yet, at the last moment, when he turned as bidden to walk away, Rory called him back again.

"Nay—ye'll no' go wearing the proud tartan o' your clan. Ye're no longer entitled. Strip it off."

"What?" Numb with humiliation, Farlan stared at his friend. Former friend.

Did Rory think this final insult would make a difference? Keep him from going to the woman he loved?

The focus of an uncounted number of eyes, he shrugged from his plaid. Unwrapped his belt and let the kilt fall from around him. Both he picked up carefully and handed with respect to Leith, who looked appalled.

That tartan meant much to him. Though Rory might not credit it, Moira meant far more.

He turned his back on all he was—all he had been—and nearly naked, walked away to his destiny.

Chapter Fifty-Four

THE MEN ON the walls, with their elevated perspective, spied
him first and sent a runner after Alasdair and his party, who
moved out from the stronghold. A young man fleet of foot called
Ellis, he was, and he reached them breathless when they were still
only halfway to the loch.

"A man, a single man is on his way from MacLeod!" he cried
between gasps. "Ahead o' the main army. They ha' no' moved
out yet."

Moira's heart leaped before she could prevent it. A single
man. There was but one she wanted it to be. But nay, it could not
be.

"A messenger?" she hazarded, looking at Alasdair, who did
not appear happy with this development. "Does MacLeod want
to bargain ahead o' the attack? Announce that the truce is over
and done?"

Alasdair sneered. "Whoever he is, we will slit his throat. Twill
make a fitting answer for whatever message Rory MacLeod sends
us."

Once more, Moira's heart quivered in her chest. Once more,
the word echoed in her mind. *Impossible.*

They marched on, Ellis now following to the rear of the
company. Moira could see the waters of the loch dreaming blue
in the morning light, a deceptively peaceful sight. They would

wait for the advancing MacLeods here, on MacBeith ground. Their own land.

Which would soon run red with blood.

Moira's anxiety grew as she waited, as did that of the men. Even though Alasdair bawled at them to keep still, they could not and shifted on their feet, tense almost beyond enduring.

Moira understood. They faced an unknown future that might contain their deaths.

She peered across the water, trying to catch a glimpse of whoever came ahead of Rory's forces, but the perspective was not good. Who could it be? What might it mean for them?

All at once, someone cried out. Standing on her tiptoes, she could, aye, see the fellow on the other side of the loch, approaching at a steady lope. A single man, as Ellis said. Bare-headed, bare-flanked, very nearly.

She narrowed her eyes against the glare of the morning and strained up still higher. Her heart leaped again, painfully this time.

She knew him. Oh, by Christ's wounds, she did.

"Rory's company," Alasdair muttered. He had been watching MacLeod's fortress while Moira looked for the emissary. "They come."

Aye, so they did. Away in the distance, Moira could see the mob organizing out front of MacLeod's keep. Beginning their approach.

Following the man on the far shore?

But what did it mean?

Her fervent gaze returned to the single man across the loch. The man she loved. He now stood on one side of the water, and she and her company on the other.

I will cross any distance to ye.

Alasdair, his eyes also narrowed, gave a grunt. "It canna be." He shot a look at Moira. "Wha's he doing?"

Farlan glanced back over his shoulder at the MacLeod forces. Without further hesitation, he waded into the water.

KEEPER OF THE GATE

He is coming, coming to me.

The MacBeith defenders had now spread out along the shore of the loch, so all could see. They watched transfixed as Farlan waded out as far as he could, and then began to swim.

It would be a long pull across deep waters, and she could now see little more of him than a wetted head bobbing up and down. Yet, his strokes looked clean and powerful.

Ewan pushed in beside Moira and Alasdair. "Is that him? The bastard who killed Chief Iain?"

"Aye," Alasdair growled in return.

For the first time, incredibly, Moira grasped the true danger of the situation. Farlan placed himself into terrible peril. For her sake.

She turned with her back to the water and faced her own men. "We will hear wha' he has to say before aught else. He may ha' a message or offer o' negotiation from Rory MacLeod. Or a warning. No one is to raise a sword against him till we hear him out."

"Nay, Mistress," Ewan told her with regret. "We will no' heed ye, no' this time." The others of the MacBeith warriors formed a half circle standing against her. "We heeded ye once and let the bastard go. Twill no' happen again."

Desperate, Moira looked to the big man beside her. "Alasdair?"

He glowered, his expression inscrutable. He said nothing.

Moira glanced over her shoulder. She could see that Farlan continued to swim across the gulf that divided them, to his possible death.

Nay. It would not happen. He would not perform this gallant feat only for them to cut him down. She would defend him if she must. One sword against the many.

The young man who had brought the message cried out, "He comes!"

Moira, once more glancing over her shoulder, shifted her position. Farlan—now surely exhausted from his long pull across the loch—would come ashore directly behind her. And aye, she could see him now, wet brown head shining like that of an otter. His pace had slowed, the strokes laborious. She thought of his injured ribs, and all the other hurts inflicted by the same men who now stood among this company.

They had overwhelmed him once. Would they now overwhelm her also in order to beat him to death?

Ewan called out to Alasdair. "Slaughter the bastard as soon as he steps from the water. We will allow ye the honor, since ye were Iain's right-hand man!"

Alasdair drew his sword. Moira searched his face, panic rising hard into her throat. He returned her look, and she saw the emotions burning in his eyes.

Anger. Desire. Regret.

"Alasdair." She lifted the sword already in her hand. She'd never imagined she would draw it against this man, but she could hear Farlan now, splashing through the shallow water behind her, breathing like a man all but winded.

Would blood flow here on the loch side? Could she strike Alasdair a blow, even to defend the man she loved?

Increased splashing turned Moira just as Farlan emerged from the water, and her eyes widened. He drooped with fatigue, and every wound stood out on his nearly naked body. Bruises, most well-faded. Half-healed cuts and abrasions.

His empty hands—for he'd come to her with nothing—hung at his sides. But his gaze met hers steady and level, unwavering as the love that filled her heart.

For an instant, it grew so quiet the gentle lapping of the loch against the bank sounded loud, and Moira could hear Rory's company on the move. Coming for them.

Then mayhem broke out among the MacBeith forces. Men shouted and unsheathed their swords, howling for blood. Farlan's blood.

Moira moved lightly on her feet, shoulders squared and sword up, and imposed herself between Farlan and her own men.

"Silence! Ye'll no' take his life!" It belonged to her, as did he. *Her destiny.*

"Ye'll not hold us, Mistress. We ha' no desire to harm ye—"

"Ye'll need to come through me to lay a blade on him!" Though nearly surrounded by her own men, Moira had rarely felt more alone. She'd always been well-loved by her clansfolk. She'd have sworn all three sisters MacBeith were. But now hate stared at her from familiar eyes.

Even from Alasdair's? Moira looked at him.

He stood close to her and Farlan behind her, closer than the other men. Near enough to reach out and slit Farlan's throat if he chose. Could Moira stop him in time? Could she stop this powerful man at all?

A war went on in Alasdair's eyes, a battle of pain and loyalty and, as Moira could clearly see, the desire for revenge. She had rejected his suit for love of Farlan MacLeod. Here in one stroke, he could repay her for that, and gain justice for the death of his chief.

He could pierce her heart.

He lifted his sword. Light and darkness flickered in his eyes, a message for her in the instant before he moved. Stepped across and took the place on her right.

"And me."

Moira nearly fell down where she stood. Still holding her sword in her right hand, she reached back with her left and grasped hold of Farlan's bare arm, drew him up to stand beside her. Her fingers closed on his flesh, tight.

"Anyone who harms this man will answer to me."

"And me," Alasdair repeated.

What loyalty, Moira thought, dwelt in the heart of the big man who stood beside her. Deep, abiding loyalty and she did not doubt a great measure of love.

Farlan cleared his throat. "Rory MacLeod has stripped me o' my birthright and my place in clan MacLeod. He comes on my heels and ye will ha' a fight, a hard one. He will no longer negotiate or hold his hand. He wants to destroy ye all."

"We stand ready for him," Ewan called. "Let him come. We will slaughter him and all his kin when they come over the water."

"Aye," Farlan agreed. "And if someone will afford me the lend o' a sword, I will stand wi' ye."

Chapter Fifty-Five

I N THE END, Farlan did not fight. Moira did not allow him to. Instead, after a tense, low-voiced discussion with Alasdair, she left the incipient battle and led Farlan away back to the MacBeith stronghold.

Not that it was easy for her. Farlan could see that from her anguished expression, could read it in the number of times she looked over her shoulder, visibly aching to join the battle.

Halfway to the keep, she paused and Farlan thought she meant to do just that. Indeed, she turned toward him.

Her blue eyes, wide with wonder, searched his face. "Ye came to me."

"I told ye I would. Across any distance. I suspect, Moira Mac-Beith, death itsel' would no' be enough to keep me from ye."

"I ha' no wish to find out."

He longed to take her in his arms, to kiss her, but they could easily be seen from the walls of MacBeith's keep, just as he could now see the fleet of dark boats crossing the loch. They would soon land on this side. An unholy battle would ensue.

"I come to ye wi' nothing, Moira MacBeith."

"Did Rory truly strip ye o' your birthright?"

"As ye see. He called me a traitor. I am no longer welcome in the place I was born." For an instant, grief nearly overwhelmed him. Everything he had known, everything he had been, gone.

Moira's expression turned both compassionate and rueful. "I am no' sure ye will be welcome here either."

"I ken."

Tears flooded her eyes. "A dirk in the back may be your reward for returning to me."

"Then I will accept that dirk in the back."

"Och, by God, Farlan! Wha' are we to do?"

"Love each other," he told her with every bit of belief that filled him. "Naught can stand against our love."

NOT UNTIL HOURS later did Moira have a chance to think about it. She'd wanted to return to the battle once she saw Farlan safely into Rhian's care. Her sister had objected to her going back out. As had her love.

Her love.

So she'd taken over the defense of the stronghold from Saerla and stationed herself instead on the wall above the gate with the other warriors, one of whom was Calan. From there, they had watched the battle on the loch shore rage, ready to put up as fierce a battle if it moved to their walls.

It did not. Instead, there on the edge of their lands, the Mac-Beiths fought their battle of vengeance. She and the other defenders could see the tide turn. MacLeods driven back into the water, some of their boats destroyed. A true slaughter.

Her da, so she thought, would have been proud. At least she suspected he would. He had held off, always, from engaging in this kind of wholesale slaughter against his opponent, Camraith MacLeod.

Strange and terrible it was, for from this distance, one could not tell which of the fallen were MacBeith, and which MacLeod. Oh, the MacLeods collected some of their dead when they began to retreat, back over the water. But in the end, dead was dead and no good came of it.

Not until it became clear MacBeith had won this particular contest did Calan come and lean on the wall beside Moira.

"I want ye to know," he said in a low growl, "I will no' accept it. I will no' accept him. Ye bringin' a MacLeod in here, I mean."

Moira's heart sank. She said nothing.

"He's the man, the verra man who killed our chief Iain, and will always be that to me and a whole lot o' others." He slanted a look at her. "How can ye countenance him when he killed your da? Ye should hate him."

"It is no' so much a question o' hate, Calan, but o' love."

"'Tis a question o' loyalties." His glare turned colder. "Let me ask ye this. Wha' d'ye mean to do wi' him?"

Moira straightened in her place beside the wall, understanding the significance of her choice for the first time. "I mean to wed wi' him."

Calan drew himself up also. "Then ye can no longer be our chief."

Aye, but—it was what she was. In many ways, she'd been born for it and had grown into the place since Arran's death.

Yet she'd been born for Farlan also. He'd given up everything for her. Could she not give up her place for him?

She faced Calan. Others around them now listened openly to their conversation. "I understand how ye feel. And I will abide by the wishes of the clan."

"I, for one, will speak up for Alasdair. I believe he should lead us."

"He is a good choice." Moira looked down at the green turf below. Their company had already left the loch side and started back toward the keep, carrying their dead and wounded. Damaged, but victorious.

She could pick out Alasdair, his great height making him unmistakable, at the head of the company. Safe. "He is no' of the chief's house, though."

Calan spat. "It seems plain, does it no'? There are more important things than being a member o' the chief's house?"

What would Da say to that? Had she failed him after all? The very idea put an ache in her heart.

"We will speak of it once our wounds are healed. Hold meetings. Fair ones," she declared, "where everyone's opinion will be heard." She looked around at the men on the wall. "All o' ye will ha' a say."

And let the pieces fall where they might.

For now, she was still chief. She needed to go down and meet their victorious warriors at the gate.

After that, as she must, she would follow her heart.

Epilogue

FARLAN LAY FLAT on his back in Moira MacBeith's bed, the same bed that had once belonged to her father, in the chamber she now claimed for her own.

His entire body throbbed like a bad tooth in time with his heartbeat, and his mind—well, his mind bounded wildly between joy and sorrow.

What had he done? Renounced his birthright. That made him no longer a MacLeod and not a MacBeith either. Considered an intruder here. Mistrusted and despised.

A feather touch flitted over his battered ribs. He'd done some grave harm to them during the swim across the loch. So Moira's sister, Rhian, had told him just before she and he watched the end of the battle from the window of the solar.

Rory would be furious. He'd been so determined to win that fight against what he considered a weakened foe. Was it possible the falling out between them had affected him adversely?

God knew, it had affected Farlan most deeply.

Moira's lips followed the path of her fingers in the gentlest of kisses. Perched on the side of the bed, she raised gleaming blue eyes to his face. "Are ye hurt sore, Farlan?"

"Nay," he lied.

"A fine thing, that." She began to unfasten the front of her tunic. She still wore the clothing in which she'd gone to battle. All woman in a warrior's garb. He promptly forgot about Rory.

Could there be anything more titillating than a removal of men's clothing that revealed a woman's breasts beneath? And Moira's breasts at that—high, pert, and enough to make his heart race double time.

"Moira—"

"Aye?" She turned an innocent expression upon him before stripping off the rest of her clothing. Quicker than he could draw a breath, she shimmied in beside him beneath the counterpane. "We will spend every night this way, will we no'? For the rest o' our lives."

"Will we then?"

"Aye. Och, aye." Her fingers once more soothed across his skin. Her mouth followed.

"Lass," he said with regret. "Lass, I fear I'm no' up to much—"

She kissed him. He decided that maybe, maybe he was up to it after all.

"I want to wed wi' ye, Moira, nothing less," he told her when the sweetness of the kiss ended. "Your folk will ne'er accept that, accept me. I do no' want my presence here to cost ye your place as chief." For folk did not guard their tongues around him, and already he'd heard talk of that. Or, maybe they wanted him to hear. "Wha' are we to do?"

"Wha' are we to do?" she repeated it lightly. "Why, I think we should go ahead and wed."

"Ye do, do ye?" Even if it cost her the place of chief? "How long before ye suppose ye'll become a widow?"

"Och, a long, long, *long* time." She punctuated each repetition of the word with a soft kiss. "They will ha' to accept ye in the end. When they see how inevitable it is."

"Inevitable, eh? I thought 'twas impossible."

"I do no' wish to hear that word on your lips ever again."

She seemed so certain, this strong woman of his.

"They will ha' to accept ye, once ye march out at their sides wi' a sword in your hand." She became suddenly serious and earnest. "Ye will be able to do that, will ye no'? Fight wi' us against clan MacLeod? For I fear there will be many more battles."

Och aye, there would. The rift with Farlan and the battle at the loch side would only stoke Rory's anger.

It would be the ultimate betrayal to Rory's mind, for Farlan to walk out against his fellow warriors with a sword in his hand. What less could he do, though, for this woman he adored?

"I will wed wi' ye, lass," he vowed to her gravely, "just as soon as ye will ha' me. What will come after that, will come. We'll face the joys and the sorrows together," he added just before he kissed her, "for 'tis our destiny." What could a man do but accept his destiny? Especially when that destiny was love.

The End

About the Author

Laura Strickland delights in time traveling to the past and weaving deliciously romantic stories for her readers. Her first love has always been Scottish Historical Romance, and her work has garnered her several awards including a RONE. At home in Western New York, she's been privileged to mother a number of very special rescue dogs. Her lifelong interest in Celtic history, magic, and music, along with her mantra of *Lore, Legend, Love* are all reflected in her writing.

Visit Laura at
www.laurastricklandbooks.com

Milton Keynes UK
Ingram Content Group UK Ltd.
UKHW020956071123
432124UK00017B/681